CATHERINE GILLING

THISTLE
DOWN

He sought adventure, and found
more than he had bargained for

CATHERINE GILLING

THISTLE DOWN

He sought adventure, and found
more than he had bargained for

MEREO
Cirencester

Mereo Books

1A The Wool Market Dyer Street Cirencester Gloucestershire GL7 2PR
An imprint of Memoirs Publishing www.mereobooks.com

Thistledown: 978-1-86151-265-9

First published in Great Britain in 2014
by Mereo Books, an imprint of Memoirs Publishing

The address for Memoirs Publishing Group Limited can be found at
www.memoirspublishing.com

The Memoirs Publishing Group Ltd Reg. No. 7834348

The Memoirs Publishing Group supports both The Forest Stewardship Council® (FSC®) and
the PEFC® leading international forest-certification organisations. Our books carrying both the
FSC label and the PEFC® and are printed on FSC®-certified paper. FSC® is the only
forest-certification scheme supported by the leading environmental organisations including
Greenpeace. Our paper procurement policy can be found at
www.memoirspublishing.com/environment

Typeset in 10.5/15pt Bembo
by Wiltshire Associates Publisher Services Ltd. Printed and bound in Great Britain by
Printondemand-Worldwide, Peterborough PE2 6XD

For Albert Edward
My father. A dear, kind and gentle man.

CHAPTER ONE

"For God's sake, François, are you out of your mind?" Pierre demanded of his friend.

"Pierre, you know I have always wanted to go to Scotland," replied François.

"Roaming around France whenever the mood takes you is one thing. To go there of all places, is – is – stupid!"

François did not even blink at the onslaught that followed. He had already made up his mind, and nothing would change it.

"Go to Scotland? Have you lost your senses?" Eleanor screamed hysterically at her eldest son.

"It is quite safe to travel at the moment" he replied. "It is the perfect time to explore those moors and glens, the wild Highlands and the famous castles Grandma talked of."

"Scotland is a troublesome, lawless and violent place. Your grandmother should never have filled your head with this romantic myth about her homeland. She was only a lowland Scot, what could she know about the rest of that country? What would she remember? She left there when she was young."

"This may be my only chance. Besides, Breny the merchant is willing to pay the sea passage, if I can deliver some letters and documents for him in Edinburgh."

How could she stop him? She had tried everything she could

think of. She had pleaded with him to take his friend Pierre with him or wait until his brother was a little older, anything, just so that he should not to go alone. But, François laughed, Pierre had no desire to travel outside their native land, let alone get into a boat to cross any stretch of water, never mind the sea. And as for his brother, although he was only a few years younger, François had no intention of playing nursemaid to him, listening to his complaints or tolerating his arguments. No, he would not delay, he was happy to go alone; he preferred it. He would please himself.

"Besides, Pierre has his own farm to take care of," he suggested.

"As the eldest, you do have similar responsibilities. When will you be more sensible, wandering off as you do?"

"Now mother, you know I only leave when there is a lull or if I am not needed."

She glared at her infuriating son, with his dark auburn hair, his mischievous hazel eyes and that irritating, charming smile. She put little value on the qualities which others seemed to see in him. His stubborn independence and disregard for any of her wishes made her angry. To her, his self-confidence was simply arrogance. She screamed at him again, her shrill voice now disturbing the tranquil normality of the household. The whole family had suffered the wrath of Eleanor's tongue for their enthusiastic encouragement and envy for his new adventure, but they did not mind. They knew that upon his departure, peace would immediately return to their French farmhouse.

François shrugged off her anger easily, well used to the torrent of harsh words which followed him through the house. He gave them no mind, because the exciting world outside invited his impatient spirit. He smiled to himself. His decision was made; he knew in his heart that he was bound for Scotland. He had a wild, reckless wanderlust which had filled his every fibre and tugged at him from the earliest age. His compulsion had grown until it would not be contained any longer. How could he be satisfied or content until he had exhausted that desire which pulsed through him? Besides, he knew exactly what he was doing.

Like the rest of the family, he was bilingual in the lowland Scots of his grandmother and their native French, so the language would be no problem. Luckily Grandma had always insisted they talk in Scots whenever they visited her, since she loved the sound of her native tongue. Added to which, he was astute enough to realize that the present unusual peace between Scotland, England and France offered him a rare opportunity to cross the notorious North Sea, an opportunity he would not miss. Scotland beckoned him, just as it always had.

In the early hours of the following morning, François slipped out of the house and hitched a lift from one place to another across the countryside until he reached the coast. He had no doubts about his journey, but once the boat he boarded had left the French coast, the sudden change of weather should have warned him that his adventure was not going to be as enjoyable and comfortable as he had first imagined.

Within a very short time, his youthful enjoyment had waned rapidly. A rough crossing turned worse. Confined as he was with the other passengers in the converted hold, where the air was hot and stale because of the hatches being firmly secured against the raging North Sea, he was forced to endure the same wretched misery as they. The perpetual motion of the stormy voyage, the resounding noise of the creaking timbers and the deafening rumble of thunder did nothing to ease his suffering. Enormous waves swamped the decks, while the ship pitched and tossed relentlessly in the turbulent water. Restricted to a small, cramped space,

François lay amidst the other groaning men, not daring to move as sweat glistened upon his now white face. He could only silently pray for relief from this continual swirling sensation. He spent hours clenching his jaw and cheek muscles to prevent the sickness he continually tasted from rising in his throat from his hollow stomach. He felt miserable and wretched as the dreadful crossing prevented any sleep which might have helped him. He should not have taken this ship, at this time, when common sense and reason told him he was no sailor.

At last the ship was safely anchored in the Firth of Forth and the port of Leith stood before him. Still unsteady on his feet, François leaned over the rail, glad to feel the fresh breeze bringing some colour back to his features. Wet and cold, with the saturated rigging dripping about him, he shivered, but he did not mind in the least, because he had reached that shore which still held a spell over him. He could hardly wait to touch the foreign soil.

So this was Scotland! A dull sky and a steady drizzle hung over a grey landscape, dim buildings crowded the harbourside and smoke curled down from the surrounding rooftops, increasing the gloomy impression for the new visitor. But François refused to be put off by the less than enchanting prospect and rapidly joined some of the sour, disgruntled crew who were huddled around a brazier. He would soon be on land.

The crew were keen to ferry the passengers and cargo ashore, and scowled as they hustled them out onto the cold, wet stone wharf. Eager to be free of their burden and to find lodgings and company of their own for the night, they took little notice of the people they had carried across the sea.

Wrapping his cloak around him against the weather, François pushed his way through the press of people and cargo, oblivious to traders, street pedlars, shouting women and pleading urchins and hurried past the dim buildings and sheds which hugged the harbourside. He was anxious to find his first night's lodgings, for like most of the others he was too tired to travel any further.

One of the inns on the cobbled main street provided a room with a solid wooden frame and straw mattress, comfort enough after such a journey. After sleeping well, he woke to gaze around the strange room before remembering where he was. Having dressed and paid for his lodgings he stepped out energetically towards the winding road to Edinburgh, which presented an impressive silhouette, having grown from a single street along the crest of a ridge. The Abbey of Holyrood stood at the foot of the main street, which led to an imposing castle towering above the summit of the rock. The town had long expanded beyond the city wall to the south and there was much for François to take in as he passed along this important thoroughfare into the city. The city itself was full of activity, and there was much to see; traders, merchants, the unusual mixture of cultures and nationalities, narrow lanes and stalls. He was lost in a wonderment of new sights and sounds as he wandered through the streets.

He soon found the appointed merchant's shop Breny had wanted him to contact and after explaining who he was, delivered the letters and documents he had been given. The merchant turned out to be some relation to Breny, and he was so delighted to receive the letters from his far-off relatives after all this time that he insisted on inviting François into the living quarters for a meal as a reward. After the convivial conversation over the hearty dinner, the man felt confident enough about his new acquaintance to offer the young man the loan of a horse for his travels, if he would take similar letters back with him when he returned to Edinburgh and

France. François gratefully accepted, explaining that he had decided to stay for a few days here to acclimatise himself better before starting his journey. His host agreed that this was a wise decision.

That evening, François, finding the local brew rough to his throat and heavy upon his head, decided to seek the cool evening air to cure the effects. He pulled his thick woollen cloak about him and set out to stroll the unfamiliar streets. By instinct he avoided dark alleys, any groups that hung about and even those creatures who lay seemingly dormant in the gutters. He was no fool.

He had not gone far when he became aware of footsteps echoing his own. Cautiously he turned, to find no one in immediate view. He continued and then slowed, listening for the direction of the sound, whilst his eyes searched for any suspicious movement near him.

The footsteps stopped and François waited, alert, fingering his sword hilt. He knew how cities provided a haven for villains and had no intention of becoming a victim so early in his journey.

The street remained empty and uneasily silent. As time passed with no other unusual happenings to bother him, François eventually scolded himself for an over-active imagination and returned to his normal athletic stride.

But a few corners later the footsteps returned, catching his attention again. François was now determined to settle this game. He sought to use the many potentially dangerous shadows to his own advantage and ducked into one of the black recesses, where he swiftly pressed himself flat against the wall. From here he hoped to see who his follower was. He listened as the sound of the other feet plodded on the cobbled road, paused, continued closer and again stopped. François remained still, holding his breath, listening and watching for whoever it was to pass by, but no one did.

The footsteps returned, coming nearer and forcing him to edge further back for safety. His eyes were still fixed on his narrow view of the street. Yet strangely, his follower seemed to have given up. François listened to the steps plodding off until he could no longer hear them, exactly as before. He did not trust this person to have given up so easily after having been so persistent, and he was reluctant to venture back into the open streets quite so soon.

Controlling his thumping heart, alone in the dark, he was alarmed to suddenly feel a sharp tug on his cloak. He spun around immediately, prepared for attack, defensively balanced to counter any blow, but he could see nothing in the pitch darkness before him. He remained still and tense as his eyes struggled to adjust. Before him was the figure of an old woman, holding an unlit lantern in her hand in front of him. As he peered closer to try to make out her features, she shuffled away, beckoning him to follow her. François stood his ground, suspecting a trap. Even when she beckoned him again, he would not follow. He watched her disappear and listened until the occasional creak from the lamp had also died away. He waited to see what would happen next, but she did not return.

The night air made him shiver and slightly apprehensive, and he rapidly returned to the safe shelter of his lodgings. Once settled into the warmth of the inn, he briefly wondered if his imagination had made more of the incident than there really was. Fighting off the tiredness of his exhausting day, he concluded that everything would be back in its proper perspective in the morning and retired to his room. He was thankful to have the shelter of the walls about him and a strong lock on the door.

The next morning François gave the episode no more thought or mind as he set out to make his travel arrangements. Having unexpectedly acquired a horse, he decided to leave on the morrow. The rest of the day passed uneventfully, except for the pestering of a small dirty boy, whom he had had to deal harshly with by swearing furiously in his native language to make him quit.

Thus François left Edinburgh, glad to be on the road at last and happy to be away from the city. There were few people, just the occasional cart and a small group of travellers, all ambling at their own pace. With no one to trouble him, he enjoyed the passing day. He was pleased to be there, pleased to be free and pleased to forget the previous evening.

As he passed the scattered farms and tiny hamlets on his side of the river, he saw Linlithgow Place in the distance. Although his grandmother had once been in the royal household there, he found it impossible to picture her living there, or in this country at all. He rested himself and his horse, relaxed and mildly content, wishing his mother could see how mistaken she had been to worry.

He rode on through the long day until dusk, when, hoping to find a suitable place to rest, he was attracted by firelight ahead in a sheltered clearing. There he found an old woman and a child camped by their small covered cart. The old woman looked up, seemed unalarmed, and nodded her approval for him to join their welcoming fire. After tethering his horse with their pony under the trees, he was offered a share of their evening meal, which tasted delicious; he was ravenous. Refreshed, he leaned back from the cosy fire to stretch his weary limbs. He noticing that the boy had skulked out of the way, and tried to engage the woman in conversation. It proved a thankless task, for like most other natives he had encountered, she seemed reserved and suspicious of the questions his naturally inquisitive mind made him ask.

François received no encouragement; a grunt, a shrug or a nod of the head was all he was granted. Not in the least disheartened by her manner, he studied his host instead, noting her shawl drawn tight about her small thin body, the long wrinkled face and the deep-set eyes that reflected the flames. He had begun to give up hope that she would speak at all when suddenly her husky dry cracking voice surprised him. Her accent at first hard to understand.

"You are a foreigner" she said.

"I have come from France. I thought my tongue was good enough to pass." Being fluent in both the Scots and French tongues, he had assumed his origin would be hard to detect.

"I grant it is adequate."

He was held by the woman's gaze, aware that there was something strange about her which began to disturb his contented repose.

"You carry little luggage. You will need warmer clothing for the Highlands, the mountains and glens are cold even in the summer" she continued.

"What makes you think I am bound for the north?" In fact, he had not decided exactly where he was going or what he would do yet.

"It is in your face. You are bound to go where you should not. Nothing will stop you. I do not understand what you want from Scotland."

"Want? Why should I want anything?" François queried.

"Then why come here? Why come to this miserable country after the sweet warmth of France?"

"I am merely a traveller who aims to explore your country for his own pleasure," he smiled.

"One does not travel aimlessly in Scotland for pleasure, it is not wise."

"Thank you for the warning, but I am no novice traveller," he murmured confidently.

The woman knew more than him. Hadn't she left Edinburgh ahead of him once the small boy had returned alone, just so she could be on the road to meet him? She watched his features for any betraying sign.

"No stranger is an innocent traveller," she scoffed in disbelief.

Unable to comment, he let the subject drop and closed his eyes. He thought the conversation finished, but the woman had other ideas. "Do not waste your time here" she said.

He had not crossed all those miles to be ordered around by some weird pedlar woman in the middle of nowhere. He was annoyed and irritable and in no mood for her advice. A silence fell between them as he prodded the glowing fire with a stick. The flames were hypnotic and soon his eyes became heavy, then very tired as he lay down and drifted into slumber.

When François woke at first light he found the old woman busy reloading her cart. Seeing him move, she turned her attention to him.

"At last the lazy foreigner wakes, with half the morning gone" came her harsh voice, as she pointed to him. "You do not have the look of your French homeland. You are a strange sight, Frenchman."

"How would you be knowing what is or is not common in France?" he retaliated, scowling, his eyes hardened from their normal gaze. It was evident that this ignorant women intended to ruin his day even before it had begun. So much for what she thought she knew about the French! She had it completely wrong. His sister was fair and his brother as dark as could be. They were all different from each other.

"Bah!" she waved him away, implying she could not be bother to argue any more, and turned back to harnessing the pony. She ceased to make fun of him; she read and understood, knowing the quick temper and character of the man. Pensive and agitated, she watched him as he checked his belongings.

"Why not travel with us for a while?" she suddenly asked.

He halted, considering for a moment, wondering if she really wanted his company as protection for herself from other road travellers.

"To endure more of your insults? I think not."

"If you are bound for Stirling, I can recommend good lodgings there."

He had no intention of responding to her furtive enquiry by telling her where he was bound. He looked coldly at her, conveying his disapproval, but her continued compulsive stare awaited an answer. She would not be ignored. Yet François could be as secretive and as stubborn as the best, and confided no more information. He was not stupid.

"I will travel my own route in my own time."

"Brave words. Take care on your journey." There was no real harm in her words, yet he felt unsettled by the meaningful tone in her voice.

The old woman let him go, shaking her head as he disappeared. Only she knew why this one was so important to her. She had been tempted to say more, but left the words inside her head. She could not protect him from himself. She had known he would come, with his manners and charm, those bright questioning eyes and soft merry voice. Her only hope depended upon the fact that his innocence might yet prove the salvation of both of them.

There was little she could do for the moment and she shuffled back to the cart sadly, the dark face frowned and gnarled hands clasped together.

"Shall I follow him?" asked the boy, emerging from the back of the cart.

"No. We shall find him in Stirling. He will be there." She was certain of her words.

François rode on, racing the wind and feeling the exhilaration of speed and the horse beneath him. Once again enthralled as the day progressed, it was only with the quiet of evening as he approached the port of Stirling that his mind pondered the niggling doubts raised by the woman's vague words. He had never worried about his solitary ventures before.

He had headed for Stirling because it was the gateway to the beautiful hills and mountains of his childhood imagination. He had heard much about these wild places and the legends of the Highlands. He had glimpsed the beginning of them for himself, and reality was almost in touching distance. A mistake it might be, but he could not change that now.

It was dark when he found lodgings adjoining the main street and the place was busy and noisy, full of travellers, friendly convivial company and people in small groups chatting over their food and drink. These pleasant surroundings made him feel much better. The evening rushed by, and François began to nod.

The raking of the ashes in the fireplace woke him to join those remaining to make their way to their respective rooms while the host cleared the tables and brushed the crumbs to the floor. His room was up a narrow set of wooden rickety stairs that creaked with every step. No sooner had he stretched out than he slept well and deep.

A dazzling morning sun greeted François as he dressed, and when he peered from the little window overlooking the town, he was pleased with the mood of the day. He gazed at the royal castle pitched high on the rock dominating the town, wondering if he would see any fancy courtiers or finely-dressed ladies from the royal household in the town, as he would have done in Paris. Ah! There was a sight to behold with their dazzling gowns and grand manners, but so out of reach as they displayed their courtly virtues, to the envy of the ordinary people. He realised he had scarcely seen a pretty face here. Maybe they did not have such creatures in this country. The peasant women in their dowdy dress did little to enhance any natural prettiness they might have. It was a shame. How could he forget the teasing, flirting and fun of the French women and especially Colette, the vivacious, tantalizing innkeeper's daughter? There he was, dreaming again! He scolded himself and set out to gather new supplies for the next part of his journey.

Amongst all the normal activity of merchants, peddlers, children and animals being herded to market, François was forced to sidestep a domestic dispute in the street, which caused him to bump into another pedestrian. This man snatched up his dropped packages and turned angrily to vent his displeasure on the clumsy oaf who had made him drop them, but instead he halted to stare uncertainly at François. After a long uncertain look, obviously realising he had mistaken him for someone else, he bowed formally, mumbled something François did not quite hear and hurried on. Bemused, François let him go, unwilling to become involved with long explanations. He lazily strode on through the mingling people to let the rest of the afternoon drift by.

As François slept that night, he had been totally unaware of the shadow which had flitted behind him, following fast and then slow to keep a pace with his wanderings during the day. This man's interest was more than mere curiosity for a foreigner, yet this man was also in turn observed and the boy had hurried back to camp to report to the old woman. Although the woman had guessed the way the situation was developing long before she saw the child coming. It had started, and would soon grow to overtake him.

★ ★ ★

Eleanor gazed from the window, her angry words to François still fresh in her mind. For all her shouting, fussing, ranting and raving, even her absolute forbidding, she had been unable to prevent him going. She blamed her mother for creating this romantic myth about her homeland. She had filled the children's heads with idle fantasies, rather than instilling the benefits of their peaceful, contented home in France.

Her husband Jacques came to put his comforting arm around her, knowing she had been on edge since their eldest had left. This turned her attention to the happy sounds of the farm life outside, mingled with the singing and playing of the children in the barn. Jacques loved all his family and had tried to instil into them all the virtues he valued. His only ambition was that they all grow happy and safe together in this place, where he could support and take care of them.

"He will be back safe and sound, he always is," he said.

"If only he had not gone alone. I cannot help worrying."

"François will be fine."

"He should be here, helping you on the farm."

"He is always here when I need him. He will settle down in his own time. Let him enjoy himself."

"That is all he ever does!" Eleanor complained.

Jacques smiled. He had never had to worry about François. Their eldest had grown into an inquisitive youth. His keen aggression, strength and speed, were tempered with an open honesty and sincerity. His vast capacity for making friends, natural good humour and merry rustic charm often brought enjoyable company to their farmhouse, as he wandered in and out of people's lives.

★ ★ ★

François was happy as he rode northward from Stirling, nearer and nearer to those fascinating hills. Light in heart, he flicked the tree branches as he rode along. A wide grin spread across his face, his eyes were sparkling bright and he glowed with bounding energy. Excitement and immense pleasure filled him as the views stimulated his whole being. He even shook off the memory of the curious glances he had encountered from some of the citizens of Stirling.

Therefore imagine his surprise to find as he rounded the bend a small boy standing in the middle of the road, waiting for him. A boy who seemed familiar; indeed it was the same boy who had been with the old hag who had questioned and insulted him.

"Why has she sent you to find me? Where is she now?" he demanded harshly.

If this was some trick, François could not see it. He motioned the boy to lead him to her.

"How is it that you are now outside Stirling?" he demanded the moment he saw her.

"I have waited for you, to warn you. Your progress has bad omens" she retorted.

"I am sure you mean well and I thank you for your concern, but…"

"I cannot change your mind" she finished for him.

She did not argue or detain him any more. She shrugged and let him go, much to his surprise.

She had not given up on François completely, because although she might not be able to keep up with him any more, she hoped to keep track of the Frenchman. Other pedlars would relate what was happening anywhere in the country.

Relaxed, François rode on far into those hills as the mystic grandeur of the mountains ahead drew him further and further on. Stimulated by them, he listened to no omens other than those which suited him. Continuing to feel content, he wandered aimlessly along through the vast countryside, until he saw a horse and rider standing like a statue above the track. François halted his animal briefly, wary of whom or what the strange figure might be, but the stranger took no notice of François; his attention seemed clearly focused on the landscape behind him. His eyes searched the valley and the track, then, with a sudden urgent swing of the reins and a kick of his heels, he crashed through the thick fern and gorse, to land near François.

François had stopped, startled by the arrival of the other young man so close to him, yet there was no indication of anything but amusement on the other's face.

"Just avoiding unwanted company" the man muttered, bending low over his horse. His appearance was so unusual that François just stared at him. He was of a similar age to himself, and apart from the normal travelling apparel, he was distinguished by his thick fair beard and hair, upon which perched a dark bonnet decorated with a brilliant silver pin, which held a sprig of greenery and a couple of long mottled tail feathers.

"Ssssh!" the man motioned, listening to the sounds. Then he was gone from sight, diving back amongst the mass of cover the greenery provided as other riders came into view along the road behind François.

François let his horse graze as they approached, unsure what to expect from these riders. He did not dare to look in the direction in which the stranger had gone, in case he unwittingly betrayed anything to these men, but they scarcely gave him a second glance as they rode by, their attention fully concentrated on the road ahead. François waited apprehensively until they had gone from sight, half expecting to see the fair head pop up again from somewhere, but it did not. There was no sight of him. François looked all around, slowly studying the trees and hillside, and found nothing. Everything was the same as it was when he had first ridden along the road. How could the man have completely vanished?

François felt disappointed, he had quite liked the look of this interesting character and had hoped he would provide company along the way. Instead, it seemed he must continue alone along the track.

Entering the next village later, François noticed two men arguing on the wayside. The object of the dispute was lost to him, since he could not understand their broad Highland accent. As he dismounted at the tavern, the argument between the two men had developed into a brawl behind him. Although no one else seemed to take much interest, François's natural curiosity had him wander in their direction.

Advancing slowly, he saw an arm stretch out from a stack of wood, blocking his way.

"Do not get drawn in" came the soft dialect. A figure stepped forward to complete the barrier.

"You again!" François exclaimed.

It was the man he had encountered earlier, the man who had disappeared like a ghost. François was surprised by his intervention.

"We are both strangers here. This could so easily be a trick" the young man continued as he ushered François away from the scene. François pulled back, uncertain if this man was also part of a trick, but the young man answered his doubts with a merry laugh and a forgiving sigh.

"These people are none of my kin. Being much too far from my home, I am extra careful that I return there safely," he said.

He introduced himself as Lachlan, the son of a minor Highland family, whose ancestral chieftain and kin were occasionally called to arms to defend their own lands. Lands, cattle and men were all important in their struggle to survive, he explained. François was so intrigued by his new acquaintance that he abandoned his original idea of heading east to Perth, preferring to accompany his new friend on his route instead.

As they headed out, Lachlan interrupted their conversation to indicate the scene on the road below, where the earlier victim and protagonist walked together in close harmony.

"You see the man walks with his enemy. I suspect they hoped I would fall into their hands" said Lachlan.

"Why would they want you?" asked François, a little concerned for himself.

"Revenge, I expect. I have been known to sell their cattle at market, pretending they were mine" he admitted in mock regret. "If they think I am in the area, they will be keen to find me." The two men steadily put a safe distance between themselves and the other pair.

François enjoyed his jovial company along the way and time passed swiftly, despite his companion's sometimes odd behaviour. Lachlan was never still. He kept darting about, his odd antics making François' head spin as he tried to keep track of him. They would be talking away when François would suddenly find himself talking to himself and feeling foolish, as Lachlan would ride off the track to check the surroundings from another vantage point. It was obvious that Lachlan would take few risks after his recent activities, but since they had not encountered any other travellers since they had left the village, François was curious.

"What are you looking for?" he asked.

Lachlan would only smile enigmatically. "Friends."

"And are they near?"

"Not yet" Lachlan replied thoughtfully, as if he expected this to change.

By the end of the day they had practically exchanged their complete life stories with each other, both of them enjoying each other's adventures. François was struck by the stark contrast of their different lifestyles as he described his warm, beautiful home in the rolling green hills, his brother Jean-Paul, his sister Suzanne, his best friend Pierre and his latest conquest, Colette. He even confided the previous events concerning the old woman who had plagued his early travels. Lachlan laughed at the stories in France, but made little fun about the ramblings of the old woman.

"One does not ignore those with second sight" Lachlan advised. François did not believe he actually meant it.

"That does nothing for my self-confidence. Are you saying she is a mystic, or a witch?"

"I did not see her. That is for you to decide. There are those who know the very souls of men. They are feared and respected, since they can cure or curse animal or human alike. As for myself, I will be glad to reach the ground I know best."

François was puzzled. Then the sudden serious tone disappeared and Lachlan went on to explain some of the more unusual customs of the Highlands and distracted him further by pointing out the various rough-haired cattle, goats and small brown sheep as they came into view.

Meanwhile Lord Lyle sat in his ancestral home, not too many miles distant, cursing his men for not delivering the daring prise he had so impatiently waited for. Lachlan would have been a useful pawn. It was not often that this Highland buck roamed so far from his home, and these fools had just let him ride away. God! He was astonished at their stupidity. He really could not believe his simple plan had failed. Here had been the perfect opportunity, and they had let the company of another man put them off. What was the matter with them?

"We expected him to be alone" said one of his men.

"So why didn't you take both of them? If we couldn't make use of the other one, we could have disposed of him!" Lyle bellowed.

Thurn had just returned from Stirling with news for his master from their informant there. The report concerned an unknown traveller who might be of interest to them, but Lord Lyle was in no mood to listen to anything which interfered with the present business. Refusing to let this delay become a severe setback, he swiftly sent his men back after the pair of them, this time with the reluctant Thurn to lead them.

Enjoyable as it was, François and Lachlan's journey together was brief, for late the next day they were intercepted by a fiery, bearded character who galloped up the hillside towards them from the cover of some woodland. François had been about to draw his sword when Lachlan indicated there was no need; this was no attack, he knew the man. The rider breathlessly threw himself forward as Lachlan dismounted at equal speed to meet him. The message was urgent, judging by the change which came over his companion. Lachlan's expression hardened as he straightened, and his eyes were cold as he gazed to the mountains.

He returned to François with a regretful gesture while the other man waited.

"I am sorry I must leave you to the mercy of these hills, my friend. I cannot guide you any further. I must be home immediately. My brother is dead and my uncle cries murder. If he is right then more blood must be spilt."

"I could be of use."

"No, Frenchman. This is not your fight, our weapons are different to yours and our way of fighting. I would not risk your life. These are matters of family, clan loyalties, we have no law or justice in the Highlands except for our own strength, and we expect no favours from any other than our own men."

He slapped François on the arm, apologising for this unforeseen event.

"It is not advisable you continue northwards on your own, you must either turn back or join up with the group of drovers who will be in the next valley tomorrow, for your own safety," he reassured François.

Then, with a wild, piercing yell, Lachlan was gone down the precarious slope, scattering the loose stones and branches about him, his companion preceding him in the race.

The sound died away around François, leaving him alone on the quiet hillside. He felt a strange emptiness in the loss of his cheerful acquaintance. He did not want to turn back after having come so far, and his own determination to continue made him dismiss all natural caution. If the drovers would have him, he would join them.

The quiet of the evening found François still riding, crossing the ridge into the next valley, the mist having settled into the gullies of the undulating land ahead, creating an eerie illusion as the treetops merged into the blue of the mountain tops. The solitude brought back those niggling doubts caused by the old woman; not the words in detail, just the strangeness of it.

Led by Thurn, the men were disappointed to find only the solitary figure of the stranger on the track before them, but surrounding him, they demanded answers.

"Where is your companion?"

François calmly soothed his mount after their hustling and jostling arrival, and remembering the lawless nature of these parts, was cautious in his choice of words and reactions. For although he did not show it, he recognised two of them from the incident at Crieff and realised the potential danger in this confrontation.

"Which companion?"

"You were with Lachlan a while ago" said one of them.

François had proved in the past that he could walk away from trouble without a word or gesture out of place, and he hoped he could achieve the same now.

"That fellow. He is long gone. He offered to be my guide, I even paid him, then he disappeared as soon as we were out of sight of the town," François complained.

Thurn, who had remained apart from his men to observe every detail of the stranger, called to them.

"We have wasted enough time here. This one deliberately delays us. We must move on."

The horses were turned from their melee as instructed and one of them threw him a parting warning.

"Had you still been with him, your blood would have been split with his."

François, his hand already on his sword, would not have made it easy for them. He glared after them, thankful that Lachlan, however dangerous a liability he might have been, was safely well on his way north.

Thurn returned alone to his master, where there developed a long and heated debate, for Lord Lyle was far from pleased at having to abandon his hopes of catching Lachlan. Thurn repeated his arguments that the Frenchman who had been travelling with Lachlan was worth a deal more attention.

"He is the man our agent saw in Stirling. From his description, it could be no one else. There is no mistake. You only have to see him to know."

"To know what?"

"That he is more than he seems. His presence in the Highlands makes me uneasy."

The overcast sky heralded rain, and François rode more slowly in the driving rain, until gratefully he found the drovers' camp for the night, in the ruins of some small dwelling. The smoke drifted and swirled about and the wind whipped through the gaps in the stone wall, allowing little comfort, despite the fact that they lay around the fire wrapped in blankets. François slept fitfully on and off until early light, occasionally stirring to watch the mass of spiders' webs which defied the laws of nature to swing above him.

Come the morning, the roads were deep with mud and the going was difficult and slow. Mud-splashed, damp and his beard itching, François paused for a good scratch and yawned. He was pleased that he had decided to let the stubble on his face grow, since beards were more common in the Highlands, and he hoped that he would not stand out so much. He found himself grinning to himself at the thought of the reaction it would have caused at home. From his shocked and aghast mother, his baffled father, his aggravating brother, his sweet kind sister to his friends and locals, would make fun of it, taunt him and even attempt to tug at it. What comments he would get there! Yet why was he thinking of the people at home already? So he might miss them at times, but he still had to satisfy his obsession with Scotland, be it good or bad. It was something he had to do.

Looking at the vast landscape, he was glad he had the company of these drovers to protect him from further unwanted meetings where he was outnumbered. But later, when they made a stop for watering the livestock and another lone traveller asked to join them, François became suspicious. The coincidence was too soon after his recent encounter. His suspicions were proved justified, as the man carefully worked his way through the other men, chatting with them briefly until he approached François and tried to engage him in conversation.

The man had begun casually enough, but François played the guileless wanderer, over-eager, interested and inquisitive, openly and innocently curious of everything around him and of the man himself. He deliberately threw question after question at him, allowing the man little time to ask his own, which caused the man to become flustered.

"Wait, wait. Enough!" the man raised his voice.

François looked surprised as they came to another rest spot and stopped.

"I thought you were keen on conversation."

François sighed unconcerned, then bent to scrape the now-dried mud from his horse's hooves, his brain working fast and watching the man as he did so. The man seemed unsure what to do, anxiously watching the rest of the camp after attracting too much attention after François's loud conversation.

"If you hope to ensnare any poor simple travellers by befriending them, then you have made a mistake this time!" François hissed. "And you can tell that to your friends."

"What friends?" the man uttered.

"Those you work for!" François snapped.

Turning his back on the man, François returned to mingle with the drovers as they began gathering their cattle again for the move. From the safety of their company he observed the man gradually falling behind and then disappearing through the trees, and as time passed he was glad to find there was no sign of him at all. The stranger had obviously abandoned his journey with them to return to those men who had sent him.

Would there be other attempts to intercept him and question him about Lachlan? Unfortunately these men knew where he was, the company he was with and the course they took. The journey, being slow by necessity, would give them plenty of time to plan any abduction if they wished. His grin was gone. He had always strolled through life so easily before, now instinct made him tense and alert, as he frequently checked the track behind him. How long could he rely on the safety of remaining with this party?

François left the company of drovers. He could not afford to be here when the man nor his friends returned. Alone, he would have the advantage of speed and the ability to hide more easily. He would take his chance. Yet despite his objective reasoning, he spent time evading imaginary shadows until he was relieved to see signs of civilisation across the valley.

A small abbey stood prominent against the dark trees, its light-coloured stonework and outbuildings a stark contrast to the peasants' shabby dwellings around it. Nevertheless François preferred the safety of any poor religious lodgings rather than spend the night out here alone.

The unusual lack of any sound worried François as he carefully walked into the blackness. Suddenly the squealing hiss of some animal startled him enough to stop. Then, before he could react, he was taken, swiftly and neatly by experts of their trade, leaving the place to its same eerie quietness except for the occasional chime of the bell from the distant abbey.

CHAPTER TWO

When his vision focused, all François could see was a lantern against the blackness and the only sounds were some voices from somewhere behind him. His body felt numb. When he tried to turn his head, a sharp pain shot around his skull to prevent him. He could only close his eyes again and lie still.

A hand grabbed his hair and yanked his face upwards, causing him to groan aloud. He could see nothing except swimming faces.

"What do you think? Look at him!" said someone.

Two of the men hauled him unsteadily to his feet and held him between them, while someone else enjoyed dealing out a barrage of blows that left him limp and semi-conscious. He had never suffered such treatment and never known such sickening pain before. He was unable to understand why his body was so powerless to support him and why his brain refused to work properly.

"We have no time for games. You will answer our questions," they demanded of him.

The questions came, each with a spitting, venomous hate from different voices in the darkness, wanting to know everything about him. Who was he, his name, where was he from? Who had sent him, where was he going and who was he to contact?

Again and again the same questions pounded in his ears, accompanied by more blows as they received no satisfactory reply.

François could only close his eyes to shut out the bloodied fist which repeatedly hurled itself towards him. His head felt giddy and his brain scrambled. He did not hear half the words. The pain made him sick and weak. He longed to scream at them to stop, but he could not find the breath to try. His lungs hurt as he fought to retain the air he snatched in between the blows. The voices boomed inside his head, which jerked and jarred under their aggression. François longed for the safe comfort of unconsciousness to blot out his torture. He could see nothing and the whirling sensation in his ears grew until he collapsed into a senseless heap.

They had already searched him for letters and his money lay scattered unimportantly on the ground, the empty leather pouch flung aside with the coins. Likewise his boots had been removed in case they hid anything, and flung into the corner. The pause in the proceedings allowed them to divide the spoils. Then, disgusted at the poor pickings, they returned to their victim, reviving him by throwing water over him before continuing their interrogation.

As they wrenched his arms even harder behind him, François could not help but cry aloud, which pleased them. He had tried to answer them, though it was difficult with a swollen and cut mouth; not that it mattered, because they did not believe anything he said. It was useless. Dazed, he reverted to his native tongue, mumbling incoherently. He did not know what they were on about or what they meant. He pleaded with them to believe him. What else could he do? There was no way out, no end to this.

"Do not act the innocent with us. There is no escape for you" said one of the men.

François tried to concentrate, but it was hard. One of them held his sword, feeling its lightness. He flicked the fine blade from side to side, deliberately swinging it just under his throat.

"Are you murderers as well?" said François brashly, though he already knew the answer. He should not have spoken, for the man lowered the sharp steel to trace it across his already bruised chest, making François wince and pale. He had tempted his luck too far. It was obvious these ruthless men meant to kill him.

"What have I done? What do you want of me?" was all he could ask.

"Evidence. A confession."

"Admit why you are here, my friend. Who are you an agent for?"

"Seemingly a clever agent, at that."

François was stunned by the accusations. His mind whirled. How could he prove they had made a mistake? He had already told them everything they wanted.

"I am no agent. Who are you? Where are we? Am I under arrest? By whose authority do you hold me?"

The voices laughed at his stupidity.

"You are here to answer questions, not to ask questions. This is no legal court, no trial. We want information and so far, my fine fellow, you have told us nothing. It seems we must persuade you a little more."

"If we have to we will start breaking bones, think on that. One finger at a time to begin with, then your toes, your legs and arms. I do not think you will survive any further."

"We can easily make use of you dead, or alive," another voice threatened.

Francois' eyes were dim, matching his fading hopes as his heart thumped with fear. The renewed beatings gained them nothing except the same slurred French sounds as before, which they were unable to understand. Eventually they tired of even trying to revive his senses and left him to the cold darkness.

François lay exhausted on the cold stone floor, unable to move, devoid of emotion and traumatised by the events which had overtaken him. He ached all over, he was cut, bruised and bloody, his mouth swollen, stiff and sore. His jacket was gone, his shirt torn to shreds. He could not believe the horrifying nightmare, yet the sharp pain in his ribs every time he breathed told him otherwise. His whole body trembled and a cold sweat shone on his face.

Then panic seized his racing brain. He was terrified of the prospect of death, terrified of what they had in store for him. He had never experienced such fear before, and it shocked him. He swallowed hard. He could not accept the finality of not being. He shuddered uncontrollably, his heart was beating so fast. It would not be easy to die in the manner these men intended. Who were they? Not that it would have made any difference if he knew. He could not even lie or guess enough to tell them anything which might delay the end. There was nothing which would let him live.

The men had not finished with François this night, deciding upon another method. The strong hands took him to another area of the darkness. Here they held him firmly and shoved his face into water, their hands about his neck and shoulders, forcing him deeper and deeper. His struggling and thrashing were useless against them. He could hold his breath no longer, and he choked violently as the water rushed into his nose and mouth, his head bursting as he tried to push upwards for air. Everything was distorted as they lifted him out, only to thrust him back again after a short gasp, this time for longer. He had thought he could endure no more and last no longer. All he could do was take in the foul water, his lungs struggling with the mixture, his brain exploding and his eyes bulging. He heard nothing of their words or fresh demands; he had stopped struggling. Almost drowned, they hauled him out, dumping him on the floor, where they left him for fate to decide his chances.

François, his eyes red and sore, lay shaking violently as he expelled the water, the contorted irregular spasms making him sick and aware of his own wretchedness. The whole of his strength had gone, its total resources spent in the struggle for survival. He did not even realise that the men had left him. He only knew that he was dazed, stunned, cold and wet. There was no relief from the shivering and twitching of his limbs and he lay there a long time, the promised punishment ahead vivid and haunting his mind. How could he endure it? What had he done wrong? Why had this happened?

Not even the old woman, for all her wisdom, could tell when or where it would happen, only that it would. She sat enduring the same pain as François, his choking, his struggle, her eyes becoming his, seeing what he saw. In her undefined state she twisted and turned, shouting out incoherently and so frightening her young companion that he stood frozen in the shadows. She was many things. He had witnessed the terrifying trances when she was not herself, where strange voices came from her in gasps and moans. No one would believe him even if he had told of the things he had seen. She collapsed exhausted after the effort, then opened her eyes to the present surrounding and continued to sit silently for a while.

She had tried to warn the Frenchman, but he had been stubborn and refused to listen and had not believed the danger he was in. The lodgings she intended for him in Stirling would have prevented the encounter with that other man. If only she could have turned him back, stopped him from going north, then he would not have been noticed by the wrong people. He would be safe, and so would she. Even now she knew the depth of his despair. She had to reach his mind, but again he was stubborn, he would not listen. His senses were not receptive, and she was physically drained by her efforts to help him. She rocked herself from side to side, murmuring and wailing softly, reluctant to call upon those other dire and dormant powers which lay within her grasp.

François pulled his torn shirt around him and managed to sit up by propping his back against the wall. Slowly he took in the details of his prison with the aid of the little light filtering through the floorboards above. It was a bare stone room with no windows and one solid door. He watched the dirt fall from the rafters as his captors moved about above him, and wondered how long it would be before they returned. He sat huddled facing the door and listening to their movements above, and for the footsteps which would inevitably sound on the stairs. Voices argued and died away. The men ceased to move and François could do nothing except wait in this dim, lonely hole. He wanted to sleep, but feared he would never wake again, doubting the length of time they would wait until they killed him.

He could not shake off the fear of death, nor regain any of the composure he needed during the lengthy hours. He could see no future. His mind was lost and blank, and all hope had vanished with the acceptance that he would cease to be. The blackness would be unending, and he would never wake, never see, never feel, never experience anything. He would never see home, family or friends again. There was no one to help him, no help of any kind. No one knew he was here. God, he did not want to die in this foreign place.

Thurn was a professional. He knew men, their weaknesses, their fears and their instincts. He did not understand or believe this François, his name or his origin. He had given nothing away and admitted nothing during his beating. What was his mission? Why would they send a Frenchman to travel so openly? No wonder their agent in the royal court had been alarmed by the appearance of this stranger in Stirling. Had the subsequent meeting with Lachlan been purely accidental? That young rogue, as far as they knew, was involved in nothing more serious than the feuding between some minor Highland families. Had it been a distraction to deliberately put them off guard? How clever was he? How well trained? Yet they had taken him easily once he had parted company with Lachlan and was travelling alone. No one had seen them take him, no one knew where he had gone, but as yet no one had missed him, nor was anyone looking for him. How important was this man? With all these questions still bothering him, Thurn still could not fathom any of the answers.

The man François had bumped into in Stirling had been the same man who had kept a careful watch at the lodgings later that night, because he had to make sure of him before taking further action. He had met with Thurn soon after to assure him again and again of what he had seen. He had now made the journey to Lord Lyle's home, to convince him of the seriousness of the matter, concerned to find out exactly who this Frenchman was. He explained that there could be no mistaking the man. His features were quite distinctive and yet precisely because of that, it made no immediate sense to have put him so close to the royal court. Whoever was behind this would have been more careful. Unless they meant to sacrifice him, to draw others out, to see the interest aroused by his appearance here. The long debate continued between them.

It had been a hard ride back to Lord Lyle, and Thurn knew the news he carried would not be well received. His master, always a quick-tempered man, kicked the stool across the room and pummelled his hand repeatedly on the table. He was angry at having learnt nothing. But if by some chance he really was innocent, then he was a gift they could hardly waste. He must be kept somewhere really safe until they could make use of him.

There was no one to help him, but himself. François realised that, as his sapping body recovered from its state of shock and his mind finally shook off the depths of self-pity and despair. The longer they left him alone, the better were his chances to recover some of his former strength. This faint glimmer of hope had returned to his dull eyes and to his sagging spirits. He dragged himself across the floor to retrieve his boots, which once on made him feel a whole lot better. Just the sensation of them covering his cold feet made such a difference to him. For a moment he luxuriated in their comfort before turning his attention back to his situation.

As evening came, the jailers still made no attempt to return to their prisoner. They were even reluctant to leave their sheltered room to attend to the nervous horses as the force of the wind and noise increased to a sudden gale. Only when the animals broke loose and scattered in the torrential rain did the men stir grudgingly out into the night. There was grumbling and cursing as they squelched through the mud and thickets, sliding and crashing about, shouting at each other for directions.

The remaining man moved nearer to the fire, mumbling to himself, stamping his feet impatiently and causing a shower of hot embers to fall onto the floor. Then, before he could stamp them out, a sudden fierce gust of wind swept down through the chimney to flatten and fan the fire outwards towards him. Without time to react, the dust, ash and smoke spilled out as a second gust burst through the badly-latched door, flinging it open and causing a whirlwind effect to swirl the smoke around the room, forcing the man to flee.

Below the room, François saw the smoke drifting down towards him. He was trapped in this underground cell. He beat against the door with a frantic and useless pounding, desperate for anyone to hear him. Meanwhile, coughing, choking and eyes watering, the solitary guard stood in the heavy rain outside, waiting for the smoke to clear. To his annoyance, it grew worse instead, and it became clear that he would have to rescue their prisoner. It was more than his own life was worth to let the Frenchman perish now. Begrudgingly he stumbled down the steps, unbolted the heavy door and dragged the surprised François out, both of them scrambling on their knees until together they fell out into the clear damp air.

The wet ground was like new life to François and he took his only chance. Springing to his feet, he dealt the man the best blow he could manage and, without waiting to see the result, turned and ran. He ran as hard and as fast as he could, driving himself on and away from the shouts behind him. On and on he ran, desperate to get as far away as possible; it did not matter where, just as long as he escaped. Stumbling and slipping, blindly he continued, his legs aching and heavy, his breathing painfully laboured as he gasped for oxygen to ease his starved lungs. Every moment was precious in putting distance between him and his enemies. How close or far behind they might be he could not tell, nor did he want to find out. Trees, ferns and bushes contrived to block his way as he dodged and brushed past them, wet stones and rocks slowed his tiring feet, while overhead the clouds were still dark, thunderous and threatening in the heavy rain. Although soon drenched, François scarcely noticed, for the pain in his side had become so excruciating that he had to stop.

He was lost and it did not bother him, for he was free, free to run and hide. He might have nothing to defend himself with, but they had to catch him first. A grin flickered briefly across his face. It would not be so easy for them the next time, he promised himself.

He did not dare rest long, even though he could not hear his pursuers, but he began to pace himself better. There were no tracks or paths to guide him. The light was bad and there were only the dark hills on every side, yet he had to push on while he had the advantage, for come daylight he would certainly have to hide. These men would know the area and would know where to search, so he would have to outwit them.

Pausing for another forced rest, he heard horses thundering towards him in the downpour and barely managed to throw himself out of the way of the splashing mud and hooves, before the horses crashed by – riderless. Relief and exhilaration pushed him on, kept him going. The rain, his panting breath and his pounding heart were the only sounds he could hear. He was safe in the knowledge that his enemies were still on foot and these animals were obliterating any sign he might have left.

François woke to a flickering light which hurt his eyes so much he had to turn away. He did not remember sleeping, for it seemed hardly moments before that he had risked stopping for another dangerous rest.

He sat up cautiously, searching the surroundings for any movement. Scattered trees sheltered him on the large grass slope, which fell away to a shallow river bed, where the sun reflected the dazzling gold ripples through the early morning mist hanging above the damp ground. There were no other sounds except for the water and leaves stirring in the light breeze, as he listened for a long time before moving from his cover. Damp and stiff, he got to his feet, every muscle complaining as he moved his battered frame towards the water. He was scratched, sore and further bruised by the mad course he had run through the night. His dark auburn hair was wet and clung flat to his head, while his clothes hung uncomfortable to his skin.

He took a long drink of fresh water, which was icy cold to his stomach, and he doubted he had done the right thing. The long grass and trees showered him with dew as he brushed his way back to the safely of his hollow, before making the most of the mist to help him reach a higher vantage point. Steadily he moved up the hill, through the bracken, rocks, gorse, trees and gullies and keeping to the thickest of the scrub, hoping he had not left too much of a trail for his pursuers to follow. Constantly alert for the signs of danger, he kept turning and checking his route until he reached the crevices of rock at the top of the rise. He had hoped to see the abbey he remembered before his capture to work out his bearings, but there was nothing except endless hills merging into the distant mountains. He was bewildered and confused. How could he be sure his next step would not lead him straight back into their eager clutches?

The men had been surprised and angry by his sudden escape. They had not believed it possible after the treatment he had endured, and abandoning their fruitless search for the horses, they were soon in pursuit on foot. They fumbled and bumped about for hours before accepting that they had lost their captive completely, and decided they would have to wait until dawn for any chance to find a trail.

Expecting that he would have headed for the abbey for safety, if he could have found it in the storm, they visited it the next morning. They knew a little gold to the priest would have allowed them to abolish any claims for sanctuary the youth may have sought there. Unfortunately there was no such prize awaiting them, and the disappointed churchman looked very upset to have missed out on a reward as they rode away.

Thurn was furious to learn on his return that they had lost their prisoner. He had been safely and securely locked away. How could they have let it happen? After two further frustrating days without a glimpse of their quarry, he spread his search out to new ground with freshly-hired men. It had now become vital that they bring this matter swiftly to a close, fearing that rumours about this Frenchman would reach the king. The worst problem of all was the effect it might have if this youth or his corpse fell into the wrong hands. Lord Lyle and the other pro-English supporters wanted no incident which would drive the old alliance of Scotland and France together against England. They would lose too much.

Ayles was an insignificant pedlar who had travelled the whole of Scotland for too many years to count. His worn and tired old bones had seen many changes and his weathered face had experienced all the seasons without complaint. He sat lazily, his feet dangling over the front of his cart, taking his journey more slowly than usual for the sake of his poor one-speed horse, spending his time thinking ahead and checking the details of the passing countryside.

He had worked for various people and was fully aware of the political unrest that troubled the nobility. He knew their agents and their aims, who to avoid and who to trust, when to speak and when to be silent. He was a prudent man, over-cautious and very careful with the important papers he secretly carried for one man, since these smuggled messages had kept him and others employed for many years. So when he heard a group of men galloping down the track behind him, Ayles swung his cart aside to let them pass quickly by.

He was alarmed as they pulled to a halt around him and several rough-looking men began to poke and turn over his humble goods in the cart, forcing him to scramble about to save his wares falling into the dirt. He had never come this close to trouble before, and although remaining blank faced, he feared they would search his person next.

"Can I sell you something? What are you looking for?" he asked them.

"A man."

Ayles looked at them and shook his head, before suddenly seeing a profit in this.

"What does he look like? Is there a reward?"

They ignored his questions and rode off, gathering speed once more to continue their hunt and leaving him puzzled by this activity. He knew of no trouble that could account for their behaviour.

To begin with François had not felt too bad, easily warding off the pangs of hunger by his preoccupation with the landscape and any odd movement in it. Although not fit enough, he pushed himself on relentlessly, stopping by any trickle of a stream to drink and splash it over himself before striding forward again. Despite the cuts and scratches on his hands, he scrambled and clawed his way over the rough terrain, keeping in amongst the trees, in an effort to avoid and out-think his enemies.

He had nothing to guide him, and he had no understanding of the character of the place, since much of it looked the same. He had no idea where he was. Forests stretched the length of the undulating valley, with patches of clearings scattered haphazardly up through the treeline to the harsh rocky outcrops above. How could he tell if any of these dips in the valley was just another gully ending nowhere, or would turn eventually into a pass leading him where he wanted? He could not waste precious time exploring every gap in the hills or trust any of the narrow meandering paths he saw occasionally.

Gone were his illusions of the Highlands. It became obvious that he would have to find a quicker and easier route to follow if he was to remain ahead of them, although sticking close to the main open trackways would make his journey more dangerous.

He had been relieved to see a wagon crawl into view, thankful that the area was not totally abandoned of life. He had started to creep forward when the sight of the riders made him duck down, slipping as he did so, to end up lying face down in a weed-covered ditch.

Ayles shrewdly surveyed the youth as he drove by. Whoever this stranger was, he was none of his business. He could be anything, a murderer, a thief, or possibly not even the one they were looking for. Complete ignorance seemed the best ploy, as he did not want his face remembered. The letters the old man carried were too important to risk him becoming involved in this matter. He flicked the reins and the cart jolted forward over the stones, leaving the man to his fate.

His head hurting, François sat up, his first worry being the memory of those riders, as he had little doubt who they were. Still, they had gone for the moment and he allowed himself the brief indulgence of considering if he should dare to find the man's camp later and beg some food. At one time he thought he could smell stew being cooked, and it was heaven to his senses. He could taste it in his mouth and his stomach complained. Yet as he reached the sight of the small fire, he stopped and turned, dejectedly dragging himself away. He could not trust it. Any camp, however inviting, could so easily be a trap. He could not trust anyone, not yet.

He sighed and shook his head, having realised his mistake. He had been wrong to take the easier ground. Now he would have to turn back to the harshness of the harder terrain, where they were unlikely to follow.

The old woman had given him all her strength to help him escape, using her powers to create the whirlwind to hamper his pursuers.

She knew François was free and lost, but he was still resisting her attempts to enter his head. She now had no choice except to try to find him and guide him, although he was far away. She had seen through his eyes the faces of his enemies, so she recognised them when she met them on the road a few days later as she made her way northwards. They had wanted to search her cart, but their leader was in no mood for more delays and impatient to move on.

"You are wasting your time. He is too clever to be caught here. He has taken to the hills" he said. He shuffled his horse past the vehicle and rode on, forcing his companions to rush to catch up with him. The woman knew they would soon find out about her asking after the Frenchman in the villages she had passed through, so they would soon return for her, convinced she was also part of the mystery. This was her fate, and there was no delaying its progress.

Depositing her small friend from the cart, she bade him hide and stay safely hidden until after she was gone. The boy was still of use. She had important instructions for him, which he would not like, which he would not follow, but it was necessary that he remembered them for others. She knew he would not obey her once she was not there to control him, and because of that she had been reluctant to teach him the herbal remedies, fearing he would use them for the wrong purpose and unwisely. He had a vengeful streak hidden by childhood, and she foresaw the hand which would pay back all his hurts. But she could not change that either, just as she could not change François or his looks.

Thurn was quick to learn of the old woman's own search for the Frenchman, and their accusations of her being a witch allowed them to arrest her and take her away. This old hag would compensate his master for the loss of the youth, and she would be easier to question. His men were well practised in prolonging her life as they tortured her, reviving her each time she slipped near to the edge of oblivion. She might not be strong, her frail body might give out sooner than they expected, but they were skilful in their art. They would find out her part in this.

The irons rested in the crackling heat of the brazier; hot irons which would inflict the pain of torture and the suffering she would not endure. She stirred in her huddled position and looked deeply into the red, burning coals. Although she was a prisoner in a lonely dungeon, they were not aware that her mind was not with them. Her presence was beyond the limits of these walls. She still struggled to reach the Frenchman's mind, to make him hear her words to take her final advice, but there was no controlling his head. She could do nothing to help the young man, whose arrival had been predicted as heralding trouble and her own painful death. Her visions had been clear, and nothing could change them. Her fingers picked at her cuff in agitation, the stitches pulled to reach the remedy she carried. She thought no more about the Frenchman, the boy or herself as she emptied her mind completely and swallowed the tiny seeds.

The boy had disobeyed her instructions. His loyalty and devotion belonged to the old woman, and her safety was more important than finding some Frenchman. He owed her everything; she fed, clothed, sheltered him and protected him. He had watched her arrest, and it was dusk by the time he had followed them to the poor woman's prison, an old fortress with its broken-down outer walls and a few outbuildings adjoining the keep to form a courtyard. The boy crouched low as the guards passed and then dived into the makeshift stable block, where the snuffling and snorting of the horses became his only company during his vigil.

The quiet of the night was suddenly pierced by a scream which paralysed the boy where he stood. Its prolonged, sheer agony echoed in his brain, yet the sound which had disturbed the world quickly faded. He clung to the wall, his little fingers screwed tightly into the crevices between the stones, to stop himself from sobbing. He could not curb the anguish he felt for the woman he could not help. He could not blot out that solitary cry, its haunting sound burned forever in his memory. The morning found him still staring at the building, fearing to move. He knew she was dead.

Eventually he returned to tend to the pony and cart, and was leading it towards the last village they had encountered when he saw a procession on the road, the like of which he had never seen before. He stared at the escort of uniformed soldiers, the line of chanting monks and the dominating religious figure, who was bestowing blessings on all who came to him along the way. A deep aura of reverence and love flowed from the people to this priest, as his sincerity and goodness reached out to them in return. The boy knew what he had to do. He had to tell him what they had done to the old lady. He darted forward and clung determinedly to the leader's robe, ignoring the outstretched hands that made to drag him away.

The man brushed these others aside, bidding their silence as he bent down to talk to the child. Their kind, benevolent reverend father had changed his manner to furious anger by the time the boy had finished babbling out his story.

Not long afterwards, the demanding command of the Abbot rang through the ruined keep, his retinue of royal soldiers and monks in close attendance. The Abbot strode into the dungeon, ready to deal with any cowardly men there, but they had already fled, warned of his arrival. Kneeling by the poor dead soul, he was moved by the pitiful sight he found. He had no forgiveness for men who committed such crimes. The boy pushed forward from behind to put his arms around her and wept, his little frame shaking so much it made him speechless.

As the Abbot made the sign of the cross on her head and murmured the Latin prayer, her eyes opened to look directly at him, startling him into silence. She uttered two words, then her breath ceased, her life was no more and the tired old face took on a serene peaceful expression.

The Abbot was mystified, wondering briefly if he had imagined the whole thing. It did not seem possible. The Abbot did not like these signs of the supernatural world, and he questioned the boy in length as to what kind of creature the woman was. The boy confessed that she had strange mystic powers, and was known to heal and treat illness. As for her last words, they were connected to the stranger they had encountered. The Abbot nodded, he was duty bound to report this event and this terrible act of injustice and brutality to James personally. For the Abbot was the King's man, a loyal man who had the King's ear. His own travels about the country to check on the distant, remote churches and the accountability of the priests also allowed him to keep an account of what else was happening in the kingdom for James.

The Abbot ruffled the boy's unkempt hair and hugged him close. At least this little one would be protected from witnessing further suffering such as the woman had endured. He would take him back with him. He would see him schooled and educated for a better life.

François was starving and found it hard to judge how far he had travelled each day. The few berries he tried to eat made him sick and the lack of nourishment was taking its toll. Without food he knew he would become ever weaker and more defenceless.

Gone was the inspiring awe for this country which had

hypnotised him at the beginning of his travels. Pierre. his friend, had been right. It had been madness to come, and his own obsession for adventure had delivered him into this dreadful predicament.

Ahead, the circling of some crows drew his attention, as they squawked and swooped down to land in a patch of grass. Had they found what he could not? He ran at them, waving his arms to chase them away. It was a dead hare, the meat torn and already half-skinned by their efficient claws and sharp beaks.

Thank goodness! He tore at the skin, desperate for food. At the nearest stream he found rocks to mash the animal to pulp, disposing of its head, unwanted bones and other parts. Washing the meat he then continued to pound it between two stones until he had managed to tear it all into the minutest of strips. When needs must, he thought, forcing himself to chew the first slither of raw, bloodied meat, glad of its meagre nourishment. Then, gathering the rest of the pieces, he sacrificed one of his tattered shirt sleeves, knotted top and bottom, to carry the remains of his precious supply with him.

It sustained him for a couple of days, but he was soon hungry again. There were no more crows fighting over scraps of dead animals, nothing but the quiet of an empty landscape. It was devoid of people, shelter and even more importantly, crops or vegetables. Nothing. He had no weapon to hunt and no means to light a fire; not that he could risk that luxury.

He stared at the daunting, endless wilderness of mountains, trees and lochs, their vastness too much to take in. There seemed little difference between any of these hills; they were all depressing, dark and forbidding. Where was the way through this?

He shuddered, wondering how he was going to survive. This landscape was nothing like any he had ever seen. Where were the gentle meandering tracks and farmland he had been used to in France? It was madness to go on. He might have been driven here by circumstance, but now he had to stop. He had come too far north. He had to make a decision. He would follow the next track, left or right.

The next track took him through a narrow gully and higher up the hillside, but luckily near the top it seemed to turn back towards the south. South – to civilization and salvation. South to face his enemies and yet avoid them, for even they would not expect him to heading in that direction.

Still he hobbled, limped and staggered on. Although his head hurt and his eyes ached from the constant strain of watching the landscape, the instinct of fear dominated his actions. The dread of stopping anywhere too long pounded his brain. To him his enemy waited in every shadow, an enemy he did not know or understand, an enemy who would not let him rest.

At times the air was heavy and oppressive, and it was hard to breath. His mouth and throat were dry, his body lethargic, and he realised he would soon fail. There were moments when he felt so weary he could not concentrate; drained of every ounce of strength, he struggled to stay awake. He could not allow himself to sleep in the daytime. Not that he could sleep properly at night either; the nights were cold, too cold sometimes, despite the bracken he packed around him for warmth. His mind wandered and images changed before his eyes, and then a jerk of the head would wake him up again with a start, the remains of a sound nagging his nerves. Was it was only the wind howling through the crags or someone calling out?

He was hot, sticky and parts of him were blotched by insect bites. Stomach cramps occasionally gripped him, curling him into a huddle. He knew he was ill, but he ceased to care any more.

Why had he come? Why had he ignored every plea his mother had uttered? Why had he been so stubborn? Because he had always been so self-willed, so selfish; he could see that now. He had gone through life without a care in the world, because his adventures had always been harmless. Nothing in France had ever been like this. France, home, the memories! What hope did he have of ever seeing those he missed again? Never to hear his mother scold him, to see his father's kind face, to spoil his sweet shy sister, to be repaid by her beaming smile, never to tease his moody jealous brother, who had grown too handsome of late, never to rescue him from a fall, or cover up his mistakes or sport with him on the farm. Never to know this or to find his friends at the inn with Colette. He could not bear to think of having no future at all, and tears stung his eyes.

At last he saw a faint wisp of smoke ahead – habitation, and hope. He slid down the rocky slope, scattering the stones noisily, weaker than ever, knowing he could not make it back up the hill even if he changed his mind. He needed help. With his eyes squinting in the failing light, François focused on his goal, determined to reach the source before the smoke vanished.

He stared at the small building the smoke had been coming from. There were no tired horses heralding his enemies' presence here, only the sound of the wind and a creaking gate in the yard ahead. Making another great effort, he swayed unsteadily to the door. He had made it, yet he stood rooted to the spot, unable to lift his hand to knock the door.

The householder peered out at this strange lone figure. Then, to scare the dishevelled dirty beggar away, he swung back the heavy door, glared and shouted at him. François did not hear him. The light and the warmth had spilt out to engulf him, almost making him reel. His eyes pleaded as he struggled with the thickness in his throat to try to speak. He stumbled forward, longing for the comfort within, and fell into a crumpled heap before the man, who made no attempt to catch his body.

"Bring the poor soul in, Angus, he is too ill to stay there" said a woman's voice.

"No, woman. I will not have such in our home. We want no sickness here" he argued, and shut the door on François. François pushed himself up to his knees and sat on the step, burying his head in his hands. He wanted to cry, but he could not even manage that. Self-pity swept through him. He could not go on, he could not.

The man opened the door behind him again, ordering him to get away from his home, shouting at him to remove himself. Then, because of his slowness to obey, he started beating him with a broad stick. The blows drove François to the ground. He had no strength to protect himself and could barely crawl away from the man as he was driven back across the yard.

The man did not persist chasing him any further than the broken fencing, and left him to lie beside the trackway, at the mercy of the elements and any other creature that came by. François had no inclination to move. He had given up. He was tired of fighting, tired of trying. He was defeated.

He no longer thought of home, his family or France, because he could never imagine seeing any of that longed-for place again. It only hurt to think of them. They were out of reach. Survival was unimportant now. At least his body would be found.

He closed his eyes, knowing he could let go of all feeling and of all senses. He felt no compulsion to help himself, because he saw no reason to recover.

He lay there all night and well into the next day without stirring, before he felt a hand shake him. Suddenly it registered; the hand was real, and so was the bread being thrust towards him. But he could not move to take it. The woman had to physically wrap François' hands around it, urging him to eat.

It took an age to bite, chew and swallow that first mouthful. He could not taste it. It made no impact, but he persisted in the slow process, while she watched him. When he had finished, she helped him up, assisting him to a three-sided stone shelter in a field where the hay for the animals was stored. There she made a hollow hidden behind the front bales and covered him with an old blanket. François had no words for her, no thanks he could utter, but she seemed to understand, smiling benevolently at him as she left.

There François remained hidden to rest and recover, the woman tending to him only when her husband went to check his fields. She never stayed long in case of his sudden return, and she only brought food when she knew Angus would not miss it. François had never been so grateful for someone's kindness, nor for the food he swiftly devoured, having rediscovered his appetite.

This simple sanctuary was all he wanted, but even cocooned here he could not shut off his mind to its natural workings. His recent vivid experiences overwhelmed his brain and woke him from his sleep, making him shout out.

Had anyone heard? He glanced from the shelter to find nothing had stirred, then lay back, trying to shut out the fear and waiting for sleep to come again.

The woman had become nervous of the odd looks she and the shed received from her husband, although he never made any reference to it or attempted to approach the store of hay. If he suspected the presence of an unwanted guest, he gave no indication to his wife. It was only when this man of exact routine set off to ride to the nearest village a day earlier in the month than normal that instinct warned her she could not trust his actions.

She did not argue or dissuade him, knowing it was safer to let him go. But once she was sure of his departure, she rushed to gather up provisions for François, along with an old shirt to warm him, a blanket as a cloak and some food hastily tied in a cloth. Explaining her fears, she urged him to flee. François was not recovered, but he knew it was time to go. He tried to be calm, but even now he felt he might have left it too late.

His skin turned to gooseflesh and his knees weakened temporarily as he looked forlornly once more to the skyline. Out there somewhere men still waited to kill him. Out there was a different proposition. So it would begin again.

The woman pressed his hand, but he scarcely felt the touch. He had hoped the isolation of this place would have been a benefit; he should have known better.

Into the daylight he strode, first gently, carefully testing his strength, this time with the advantage of a knife the woman had added to his bundle. It was not much of a weapon, but it could make a difference between survival and death next time. He swung the blade about him, holding it at arm's length to judge its distance and suitability. Although he was not satisfied with this rough-looking implement, he was glad of it, and planted it firmly in his grip.

He had cleared the valley, had eaten and had satisfied himself with the distance he had made when the sound of wild yells exploded in his ears. François froze as a host of wild men leapt from the gorse and heather and charged at him. Whether they were his previous adversaries or bandits it made no difference, since he was outnumbered and cornered, and there was nowhere to run.

He knew he was beaten before they swung their first blow. His knife was no use against their heavy wide-bladed swords. He was struck by a searing pain as a blade tore deep into his side, staggering him, followed by a second and third. As if in slow motion, he saw the offending sword withdrawn covered with his blood, as the man took a step back and waited. He saw his own hand drop the knife; it fell gracefully to the ground, where it bounced and lay still. He did not know if the agony made him scream out as he crumpled, his world fading into shades of grey and then nothing. Limp, he tilted and then tumbled precariously down the small incline, tearing the loose ground with him, and then slipped over the edge of the small ravine, smashing against the jutting edges on his passage into the swirling water far below.

Their attempt to prevent the loss of their prize brought several of the men close to following François' descent, but they managed to save themselves and scrambled back up the slope, sending the scree, stones and boulders into the waters below, splashing and hitting the body as it drifted away from them. Their difficult detour to the water's edge to attempt to retrieve their prey bought them no satisfaction, because the churning water had carried François out of sight and far out of their reach.

Unconscious, François was swept crashing through rapids, waterfalls and hollows, mercilessly onwards until a fallen tree snagged his arm and swung him into a calmer shallow pool. For a moment he felt the shingle under his face and his hand clawed into the soft shore, hoping it would hold. He could taste his own blood in his throat. His head was split open and his other arm had been broken during the initial fall. He could not move. He lay there helpless, there for anyone to find, his life's precious source ebbing away across the wet shingle and sand.

Ayles had completed his journey north. He had delivered his letters safely and was now returning south to meet with the Abbot, as was his routine. He had not seen or heard anything of the fight. He knew nothing of the preceding events. He had not been looking for anyone when he saw the body near to the water. He was therefore mystified that the robbers should have left the body, still recognisable and clothed, as evidence of their crime. Cautiously he scanned the scenery, wondering if they were about to return to claim their spoils, for the remoteness of the spot was to their advantage.

Should he risk investigating or not? Somehow he found himself bending over the man and found to his surprise that he was still alive. The wounds were bad, the sword damage deep and messy, the limbs battered, the flesh torn and the gash on his head had matted his hair together. He could not turn his back on the youth. He had to drag him up the bank and use his basic skills to stop the flow of blood. He was no physician, but he plugged the wounds with rags and bound them tight with torn strips of cloth before tending to the other injuries. He bathed the caked sand from François' face and forehead, pushing his hair out of the way. The short beard had been flattened to his skin, making it easier to study the features of the injured man.

Ayles stopped, his eyes checking every detail of the face as something nervously registered in his brain. Then he shivered. He needed nothing else to tell him that this was the man being searched for, and why it had been so important for them to find him.

He swore under his breath, realising the danger they were now both in. For while François was simply in danger of dying from his wounds, Ayles was in danger of attracting the unnecessary attention he could not afford in his work, by taking him to safety. Anxiously he lifted him into the cart and carefully covered him. He was angry because of the additional burden on his shoulders; he did not want the responsibility, yet he could not do otherwise. His duty lay in serving Scotland and the King, and sadly this person concerned both.

There was only one place to take him, and only one man honest enough to protect him.

CHAPTER THREE

Quick to follow the information he had paid good coin for, Thurn had nearly throttled the hill farmer Angus on finding his quarry gone. Was he ever going to recapture this Frenchman? This was twice he had slipped his clutches, twice he had lost him, just as he had lost out with the old woman. She had defeated them too, cheated them of information by taking her own life. She had swallowed some poisonous berry, her dying scream ending his chances.

He was further grieved to discover that François had become another victim to the local bandits. Thurn had to teach these locals a lesson. He took reprisals, and they paid the price of their interference with their lives. Not that it helped him find the body.

Meanwhile Lord Lyle had quizzed his agent thoroughly once more before leaving to meet with Lord Hume, demanding that he be absolutely sure he had identified the man's features correctly.

"I am positive. I have been in the court long enough. This is no mere coincidence. He was sent here for a purpose" the man insisted.

"Who says it was not well planned, if he was deliberately kept in France until now?" admitted Lyle.

Lord Lyle deliberated, for to show any hand openly in this matter was a great mistake.

In his unconscious, limp state, François knew nothing of the problems he had caused to others or the extent of the injuries he suffered. In his troubled mind he was still falling, tumbling, whirling around and around, spinning ever downwards in a circle that would not stop. He screamed silently with every ounce of breath in his lungs, but the churning sensation continued and no one heard.

Ayles had put his wagon inside the large barn adjoining the abbey as normal. No one took any notice of his arrival nor of the contents of his cart, for they were well used to his coming and going. Yet the Abbot was shocked at the package Ayles delivered to him for safe keeping. He had been expecting his good friend to deliver a special order of wine, not the Frenchman so recently mentioned. Now he understood the last few words on the woman's lips, and why she had been so insistent that this Frenchman be found.

"Is he anything to do with the King?" Ayles asked.

"I doubt it."

They had much to tell each other, but not until they had done all they could to save his life. Without hesitation, François was taken into the Abbot's private rooms to be protected from prying eyes. Once there, the formidable elderly man personally took over full control, for it would take all of his medical skills to perform the miracle they hoped for. François' broken arm was set in binding and light ash splints, his head tended, then the deep wounds on his body were cleaned and stitched twice over to keep them closed, until at last they were done. François quivered and shook, a soft gasp escaping when spasms tensed his body, and then relapsed into a limp form, while the Abbot tried to reassure him softly in his own tongue. François had lost too much blood to survive and the Abbot at first doubted he would live, because he breathed too shallowly and was too weak.

The only way to improve his chances was a rarely-used formula the Abbot kept, if only they could get the unconscious François to take it. Ayles supported his head while the Abbot tried to trickle the liquid into his mouth, but he could not swallow naturally or unaided and it was difficult to persuade the throat muscles to swallow the vital tonic. It was a slow process and one they repeated hourly through the first night, in between watching him closely, the candles burning through the long dark hours.

Later the Abbot prayed for guidance, for tomorrow he had an appointment at the castle; tomorrow he must speak to the king.

François knew nothing of the man's touch. He did not wake, and he gave no flicker of reaction to the kind nursing he received. His head pounded with a burning pain and a tight band heavily compressed his head. He wanted to push it away, but the struggle in his dark world registered no outward signs. His eye sockets were dark and hollow, his eyes aching with the irritation behind them and beneath the lids they moved continuously as the images relentlessly changed, droning and echoing in his head. He struggled against an overwhelming sensation of some other deeper darkness trying to drag his whole being somewhere sinister beyond reach, yet from somewhere he found the ability to fight against it, refusing to let it win. Whatever this malevolent spirit was, it would not take him yet.

François was weak. He felt the pain in his chest, a pain so severe it shot through every nerve in his body, making him rigid at any moment beyond the shallowest of breaths. He wanted to open his eyes, but they would not obey his wishes as the strange sounds came and went around him. At times he was aware of a taste in his mouth; sharp and sour, it spread slowly through every part of him. He was unable to resist or fight the now warming liquid, poison or not, but it brought a welcome restful comfort, allowing him to relax into a proper sleep.

The Great Hall was busy with invited barons, prelates and important burghers, as the Abbot waited patiently for a few words with the King. James IV was a vigorous, intelligent man, fluent in many languages, generous, courageous, a humane prince with few faults, an honest king whose deed was as good as his word, a just, fair man with the ability to temper mercy with his immense power. The combination of all these virtues made him well loved by his people.

James took the Abbot's hand, pleased to see him there today, and jokingly enquired if the church continued to do well these days, hinting at the tradition of the dues he could expect from the church and its lands. The Abbot smiled and slowly guided him away from the ears of the rest of the court to walk out into the walled garden.

"So, who has misbehaved now? Which priest has misused his authority? Or am I the one to be reprimanded by one of your eloquent sermons this time?" James asked good humouredly.

"It is a most confidential matter" insisted the Abbot.

James was immediately interested by this curious comment, for it was most unlike the Abbot to begin his report so strangely.

"Who is endangering my kingdom and authority this time?"

He listened with expectation for something more serious than a brief tale concerning an old woman, the arrival of a foreigner, her concern for his plight, her terrible demise and his present confinement at the abbey.

"The courts will deal with the injustice both he and the old woman suffered. They are the correct authorities for such matters" James replied coldly.

His mood had changed, as it did whenever he felt he was being instructed by others on how to govern his country. This priest, although his eyes and ears, was also renowned for speaking his mind as in the case of the reprimand he suffered for giving his first son Alexander Stuart the title of the Archbishop of St Andrews.

"Not in this case, your majesty. Although some of the men have been arrested concerning the crime against the old woman, the problem about how to deal with their masters is more difficult. And it all depends upon how you perceive the importance of this Frenchman, as to what should be done or not done."

"What do you suggest?" James asked calmly.

"That you come to the abbey quietly without too much ceremony. It is important for you to see him for yourself, then you will understand the problem."

It was not like the Abbot to bother him unnecessarily and James was compelled to agree. He would stop at the abbey tomorrow when he was out hunting and visit this secretly-hidden foreigner.

Meanwhile Alexander and his younger half-brother James Earl of Moray, both at the present court by the King's benevolence, both watched the meeting from the terrace above, without taking much notice of the exchange of expressions. Alexander could not help teasing his half-brother by suggesting that the latter's jealous sulky behaviour had to be the object of the discussion, causing the youngster to stomp off without answering. James, who longed to be the favourite, was determined that tomorrow would give him another chance to impress his father and win the King's favour during the royal hunt.

Ayles had already departed, having moved on in his casual unobtrusive manner to complete his other assignments, amidst his idle roaming. Thus he was long gone before the tired hunting party arrived at the abbey. While the attendants rested in the abbey forecourt before their return to Stirling Castle, the King escaped his companions and went to find the Abbot, who awaited him in the cool of the cloisters. He walked purposefully behind the Abbot as he was led to and then ushered into the simple interior of the quiet inner most room, where the Abbot gently closing the door behind him, leaving James alone in the inner chamber.

James approached the bed in the corner and stood surveying the state of the battered body, which did not stir amid the crumpled covers. The blood from his wounds still dampened the bandages. Such wounds were more than those earned in victorious battle, here indeed was evidence of intended murder. After all his tireless efforts to bring law and order into this kingdom, this did not please the King, and his sympathetic hand reached out to this latest victim. It touched his heart to see anyone so badly treated, but he still could not understand the reason for the Abbot's insistence for his visit.

He came closer to the ruffled hair, close to the damp face so unexpectedly before his own. He stared at François, studying him, unable to believe his eyes, to find it hurt and affected him deeply. He gently ran his hand over the contours of François' face. How could such a thing possibly be? Yet there was no mistake; here were the same features and the same distinctive colouring. What accident, coincidence or fluke of nature could create every detail of his own living image in this stranger? No wonder he had aroused suspicion and danger since he had arrived. Emotionally James turned away. God, what was he to do now?

The King gazed silently into space, trying to be objective and consider all the aspects of this dilemma. His day had been ruined. Was he to be tormented again? He was sceptical about this, for past history had provided many hard lessons and bad experiences. He would have suspected a trick, if it had not been for the Abbot's involvement. He was angry with this complication, angry with himself and most of all angry with François, however innocent, for coming to Scotland.

The Abbot had waited patiently outside the thick panelled door, until after a long time the King emerged. The Abbot noted the flicker of desperation appear on his face, one he had not seen for many years. It was clear that the King was shaken.

"I do not like what I found" James commented in a husky whisper.

The Abbot poured James a drink, which the King absently sipped.

"Will he live?" the King asked the Abbot.

"I am not sure. I have done all I can."

"I shall need to know everything about him."

"He cannot tell us much yet. I believe he is completely ignorant of his problem. Why else would he have ridden about so openly?"

"How can you know?" James scoffed, his active brain sending out the defensive signals that the past years had driven home, for his trust was no longer lightly given.

The King was in no mood for the intrusion caused indirectly by the young Earl of Moray, who had sent the monks on behalf of the impatient company outside to enquire as to the hour of their departure. The King sent back a stinging retort, that they need not delay on his behalf, and commanded them to return without him immediately. Only the few attendants of his personal bodyguard would naturally remain as escort.

The young Earl, thus having conveyed the King's orders to the others, decided to wait and ride back with the his father, hoping that would please him, but as the length of time increased, he began to doubt his decision. For the indications of the meeting within the abbey were that James was not in a friendly mood and that maybe he should have gone with the others. He now feared that his actions would be misinterpreted, and was about to ride off when he heard the King coming. Instinctively he hid to avoid a confrontation, thus remaining quiet and unnoticed, but he could not help but overhear the end of the conversation.

"Thank you, my friend. There is much to consider."

Glad to be alone, the King felt uneasy over the matter and in a pensive mood failed to notice the rider who followed him on his return journey, keeping out of sight. His mind was in a turmoil over this François, whoever he was, A Frenchman with no connections here. If he was French! He shook his head to clear it for the evening's festivities, because he must betray no suspicious signs to any of the assembled company, let alone to his wife, the Queen.

He had had a busy day after the hunt, there had been matters of state to attend to, ambassadors and emissaries to employ his attention and discussions to exhaust his interest as he played diplomat to their demands. The King looked wearily from the papers in front of him to his wife, who sat across the room by the fire, with her ladies.

If only she had been the other Margaret, the one who remained closest to his heart, dearest darling Margaret Drummond, whom he had loved so deeply, the lovely Margaret whom he had planned to marry despite all his ministers arguments. Only her sudden death had made him settle for the political advantage of a foreign marriage alliance with this Tudor princess.

Here sat Margaret, his Queen. Unhappy Margaret, so jealous of his love, unable to accept his illegitimate children or the knowledge of his earlier mistresses; Margaret Drummond who had given him young Lady Margaret, Marian Boyde, Catherine and Alexander's mother or Janet Kennedy, the young Earl of Moray, James's mother. He loved all his children and despite Margaret's dislike and furious protest of the continual show of affection to them, he enjoyed having them at court, seeing them grow and taking care of their upbringing and education.

The hurried footsteps announced Alexander's arrival, giving the

King an excuse to stop, and he arose, arms outstretched, to clasp his son warmly about the shoulders, but the delight at seeing his eldest son was soon overshadowed by the reported behaviour of his half-brother. The boy had apparently returned late after the hunt and even after the King, and had then retired unusually to his bed. The King stiffened, worried by the nagging prospect that he would have to watch the youngster and be extra careful not to arouse too much interest in the abbey.

At last François flickered his eyes open briefly, struggling for some degree of consciousness, as a faint glow wandered in and out of the blackness. Alone in his nightmare, shapes loomed towards him and then vanished again as he squeezed his eyes to shut out he distorted interruptions. There seemed to be a heavy weight pressing down on his limbs; even if he had wanted to move, he seemed powerless to do so. He could not understand the restrictions, the aches, the pain and the frustration of his confused brain.

Much to the relief of the Abbot, the sign of improvement had begun after weeks of little change to the body lying before him. He had almost despaired of his patient, fearing he would easily slip away, his breathing hardly detectable, and there were times when the Abbot had thought him gone. He had prayed that he would survive, although he failed to see how any good could come of his recovery.

Baffled by the sounds about him, François was still vague and confused. His attempt to move his head resulted in failure and he closed his eyes again, but the voice was real, different, soothing and in his own language, tempting him to try again. Gradually he managed to recognise the man and his kindness and accept his word on the safety of these surroundings.

François had watched the Abbot come and go so many times

that he wondered at the nature of the man who had done so much for him. Not for him the indifference of some infirmary or the care of novice monks; he was in a room of his own, with a window that let in the sun. Truly here was a man to be trusted. He might be the only person in the whole of Scotland he could risk talking to.

"What did I do wrong?" he asked the Abbot some time later.

The Abbot did not have an answer.

"Nothing that I know of."

"Then why did these men take me prisoner and question me?"

"I do not know" the Abbot lied protectively.

"Who were they?"

Again the Abbot could not help.

"Were they the King's men?"

"No, certainly not. That is not the King's way."

"I thought I had broken some law or that it was because I had been with Lachlan, but they were not interested in him at all, once I was in their grasp."

François needed to talk, to ease his own mind, until the Abbot insisted he should stop tiring himself out.

They talked on and off in the following days. The strain of the long conversations made François' head ache fiercely and he felt too exhausted to argue; in any case, there were never answers to satisfy him. By confiding all, he hoped that this wise man could suggest an explanation, but the Abbot had no answers.

"Suspicion and fear cause ruthless men to do stupid things" he said. It was not his place to enlighten François as to the truth of his predicament, that was yet for the King to decide, for it was the King's problem most of all.

"Not everything in life can be explained. We do not control our destiny."

The Abbot might have been speaking spiritually, but François was thinking on a lower plain.

"Some men do."

The Abbot looked questioningly at him.

"Some powerful men do exactly as they please with ordinary people, without punishment."

How could the Abbot tell him, to explain the mystery and justification for his plight. It was natural that François needed to know if he was still in danger or if it would happen again and that he would have no peace of mind until he knew.

All François wanted was to regain his strength and get back to the sanity of France, but to do that meant rest and sleep, sleep which was far from restful, as the nightmare still haunted his slumber. He had nightmares in which he doubted his senses, where he woke hot and sweating until he realised where he was and felt relief to see the same room, safe from the rest of the world.

It was weeks before François began to recover fully, and the King could only wait for news from the Abbot. He was not certain of his own intention on this matter yet. He could hardly expect the man to die after all the Abbot's skill, despite the fact that it would have been more convenient all round if he had. A simple burial would have solved the problem altogether. As it was, he lived, and there would be the consequences to deal with.

What of this Frenchman? So innocent, so ignorant and so wounded. He had wanted nothing, claimed nothing except answers, but James did not trust easily. He frowned, considering just what he was to do with him. He could not be allowed to wander free once he had recovered, and he could not stay hidden in the abbey forever. The problem niggled him and side-tracked his thoughts until he had to ride out to the abbey again for himself.

And what of these men who captured the Frenchman, those who had tortured the woman? Those men who had issued the orders? Thurn was known, plus his master. Did he, the King, make a great show of tracking them down and risk even more attention? If they believed the Frenchman had died after his attack by bandits, then surely it was best left. That way these men would less trouble.

François had one aim, to get home. In whatever condition, whatever it took, he meant to get there. He wished his wounds would heal faster, and the slowness of improvement made him impatient. No longer satisfied to relax in the comfortable bed, he gingerly stretched his listless body into some exercise. Although the bandages bound his wounds tight to prevent movement of the tender flesh, he found he could lessen the pain by holding that part of his body with his good arm as he moved. Wincing and taking a deep breath to counter the twinges, he slowly and carefully managed to push himself upwards to sit upright. Having accomplished that without too much discomfort, he kicked the remaining covers clear to put his feet on the ground.

The stone floor was cold beneath his feet and he was shocked to find his legs would not support him as he gingerly shifted his weight from the edge of the bed. Dizzy, he collapsed back onto the mattress, and the movement sent a fresh, searing pain through him, forcing him to lie there panting until he felt better.

Surprised at his own inadequacy, it was some time before he could summon the energy to try again. Today was not a day for defeat, he told himself, and he persevered until at last he stood, clutching the furniture. Then, with the walls for support, he managed a few stumbling steps from the foot of the bed to the window, where clutching the window ledge for a rest, he felt a wonderful soft breeze on his face. He had been in the darkness and shadows too long and he felt exhilarated by his small success. Then, distracted by a sound in the adjoining room, he instinctively turned, lost his balance and fell.

François lay winded and in some pain, totally unaware of anything else for some moments until he looked up to observe first a fine pair of boots and then the bulk of a man towering in the doorway. Startled, he tried to pick himself up and found he did not have the strength to do so. He nervously waited, knowing the utter vulnerability of his position.

Whoever this man was who gazed so astutely at him, he seemed unsurprised to find François here. This made François hope he was a friend of the Abbot, since there was nothing threatening in his manner. The man, who remained calmly where he stood, held an air of importance, dignity and power, as if he was well used to respect and obedience. Instantly recognisable as a nobleman by his clothing and stature, he betrayed an expression of kindness.

François returned his smile weakly, wondering if the man had been among the illusions recently floating in and out of his semi-conscious mind, yet he did not feel he had the right to speak. There was something about him, an aura, which held François's attention. With so much to take in, he had scarcely noticed the iron belt which hung heavily about the man's waist. It was a belt well-known by anyone who frequented the royal circle, and it would have identified the man instantly. François was curious as to his silence. He felt awkward and unsure as this eminent personage offered no conversation to ease his disadvantage.

"Good day, my lord" François attempted.

The King had had no intention of seeing the Frenchman when he had returned to the Abbot's study; he had come to tell the Abbot about his decisions and seek reassurance. The Abbot had not been there, but as one of the monks went to find him, the unfortunate crash in the inner room had brought the two of them face to face.

"Good day to you, young man" replied the King, giving nothing away.

"Forgive my ignorance, sir. Should I know who you are?"

James relaxed, his hand resting upon the comfort of the cold metal belt, content that his identity remained a secret. Without further hesitation, he swept forward to help François up and lifted him back onto the bed, pulling the covers back over him. James paused to study the Frenchman, conscious of the fact that it was a luxury he could not afford to indulge in as he finally shook himself free, knowing he had stayed too long.

"I have business elsewhere" he said.

James closed the adjoining door to the study behind him, having caught sight of the returning figure in the outer room.

"We cannot let him go back to France in ignorance. He deserves to be told" said the Abbot.

"I do not agree. That he came for adventure and found more than he bargained for, is not my fault."

"Your judgement seems harsh. It would help him understand."

"Abbot, I am no fool. I know the complications. Do not oppose me!"

The King spoke coldly, determined to avoid any pressure, however well meant, before sweeping past the Abbot.

The young Earl of Moray had been puzzled by the prolonged visit to the abbey this day, unable to believe there could be so much interest in just wine and conversation. He witnessed the useless polite conversation at court, and hated it, just as he hated his lessons. He had struggled hard with them to please his father, yet the relentless studying had never reaped one word of praise, approval or the extra affection he had craved for. He wanted to be the favourite, wanted the respect of others. If only he had been the eldest, or the heir of Scotland! That would have been best of all. He had no friends to trust or confide in, so he set out for the abbey to attempt to please the King. If he could ride home with him, he hoped he could provide sufficient entertaining conversation to impress his father.

The small personal royal escort of soldiers waited outside in the courtyard, while beyond the closed doors, the abbey continued its normal religious devotions. With the escort and the monks refusing him entry, the young Earl sulked and refused to leave.

"What are you doing here?" came the angry voice from behind him.

"I came to accompany your return. Although I doubt my intellect is fine enough now, after the hours you spend in these hallowed walls" he sneered at his father.

"You insolent young whelp!" the King roared, his short reply followed instantly by a blow which sent his son flying across the ground. The Earl knew he was on dangerous ground. The ferocity of the King was evident as the man towered over him. He was truly frightened of his father and he had every justification to be after provoking him unnecessarily.

The Abbot had left the nave having heard the voices, to witness the boy scrambling to his feet and rushing to obey the order to return to the castle, where he would learn the punishment for causing the King's displeasure.

"Do we need to worry about him?" the Abbot enquired, once the boy had left.

"Not when I have finished with him" came the King's assurance. Although in truth, James was concerned by the fact that he had been followed out here for no real reason. Then, calling for his escort, James left abruptly to set out after his hothead son.

Thankful he had escaped so lightly for the moment, the young Earl had spurred his horse in an effort to reach the safety of his own apartments before the King caught up with him, without success. The King and his men were at his side before he had covered half the distance to the castle and a grim silence completed the journey. Marching inside the castle, they were met by Alexander attempting to join them, but he was quickly dismissed. Then, alone with the King, his courage deserted him. There was nowhere to hide. God, what had he done?

"How dare you interfere in the King's business! How dare you follow where you are not invited!" The King's voice trembled with rage. "Well, speak, if you have the nerve to."

The boy stood in terrified silence while the King paced up and down, waiting, daring the boy to speak. The longer James left the quietness unbroken, the worse it became, until the Earl knew he had to answer, had to say something. But panic guided his words and he spoke hysterically.

"Why did you spend so long at the abbey?" he asked his father.

"You would question me?"

The boy was a nuisance. James knew he must put a stop to his inquisitiveness immediately and find a way to cure the youth's impetuousness. James knew it was not easy to gain entrance to the Abbot's private quarters, but he must make sure he did not return to the abbey until the Frenchman had safely gone.

"The most important thing I have in the abbey is the council of a loyal and very wise churchman" he said. "He is a man whose opinion I value above other experienced statesmen, nobles and generals. And depend upon it, whenever I choose to consult him, at whatever hour I please. I shall not be explaining my actions to you or anyone else. Do you understand?"

The youth nodded and hung his head. He was not stupid enough to challenge the King's patience further. He cowered away, his face pale and frightened, eager to be left alone.

The King's next words surprised him.

"Since I find such a benefit and learning in this churchman, I think it would benefit your education to be tutored by such clergy. I shall arrange to send you to study with the monks at Dunkeld, where hopefully you might also gain some humility."

The look of horror on his son's face convinced James that his suggestion had been effective.

"You will confine yourself to your rooms, until the arrangement have been made."

The King prayed he had terrified him enough. For the moment the Frenchman was safe, and likewise his own dilemma.

The King nearly knocked Alexander over outside. He was in no mood to talk, let alone explain anything to his eldest son. He sent him away with orders not to speak to his brother, the King's voice ringing through the whole castle for all to hear.

"He is to be left alone to mend his ways" he ordered. "He is confined until further notice and allowed no company."

François had questioned the Abbot about the nobleman's identity, only to be told he did not need to know. It would be to no one's advantage to complicate the situation. And despite all his determined persistence, the Abbot refused to tell him anything about the man.

"I have never thanked you properly for saving my life. If you had not found me."

"Someone else found you, not I. It is thanks to him that you were brought here. I did not know of your existence until the old woman, who against the laws of nature, mentioned you, after she died."

Indeed the Abbot still did not like thinking about that moment. He had trouble forgetting the phenomenon, but it had happened, he had seen it.

"After she died, the old woman? What do you mean?"

The Abbot slowly related the manner of the old woman's death, the details of which were hard to accept. The poor woman was dead because of him and her sacrifice naturally weighed heavily on François. He felt even worse than before, for now guilt rested heavy on his heart. It was too much for his taxed brain and depression once more took hold of his soul.

"If I had listened to her, she would be alive now. Why didn't she avoid capture if she could see the future? No one chooses to die!" he declared with conviction.

"You are not responsible for another man's crime" the Abbot reminded him.

"And the boy?"

"Is safe and being cared for in Dunfermline. Well away from trouble."

James had been constantly preoccupied by the unfortunate complication of François. James bowed his head in thought. There was no way François could remain here for long; it was too easy for others to find him again and use his image to cause unrest. Fingering his belt, he remembered being helpless himself in the hand of powerful nobles when he was younger. At the age of fifteen, rebels had forced him to fight with them in battle against his father at the horror of Sauchieburn. The resulting murder of his father had led him to be crowned King and the iron chain belt he wore was a self-imposed penance for the continual sense of guilt, a guilt no one could absolve him from. No, he would not let François be used.

"Oh Thistledown, why did you have to come?" he sighed softly.

He could have had the Frenchman disposed of, but after the care the Abbot had already been to to save his life, it did not seem right. This man had a family and home somewhere, with people who no doubt wanted him back in one piece. To let him go free meant he would be doomed to live with this terrible shadow hanging over him for the rest of his life. But was it safe to let him go? James knew he could not protect him once he left. If he was made to realise his own danger, then surely he would never come back to Scotland. No one in their right senses would.

James had made his decision and acted quickly upon it. François must be sent back to France immediately.

François was stronger now, having slowly achieved another step towards recovery. Although his muscles often trembled with the exertion, he was on his feet and walking between the two rooms with ease. He had forced himself to use his bad arm in order to strengthen it, raising it as high as he could and lowering it until the pain became too much. He might not be completely recovered and fit enough, but if he could walk, he could sit on a horse and ride. He was eager to depart soon. All he wanted was home, peace of mind. It seemed such a simple expectation, and he pleaded with the Abbot to make the travel arrangements, but the Abbot was reluctant to let him set foot outside these rooms.

"Surely I am still safe. Your monks are no threat" said François.

The Abbot smiled sceptically.

"Only a few men know you are here. We will be advised when it is safe for you to leave."

François was puzzled by the ambiguous words. What was he implying?

"I await instructions" said the Abbot.

"From whom? I thought you were master here."

"Here – yes. For the rest of Scotland – no. It is not my position to make such preparations."

The other man, the nobleman – who was he? He had asked the

Abbot many times and always the Abbot kept very silent about his identity.

Then amidst his silent pondering, they were interrupted by the very man François had been thinking about. Waving away any greeting, King James closed the door firmly behind him and leaned back on it, surveying the scene. He had not expected François to be in the study with the Abbot, and had been intending only a few words of instruction with the priest. He was now forced to reconsider his approach. He bought himself thinking time by walking around them to pour himself some wine from the cupboard, carefully avoiding the Abbot's masterful stare, which he knew followed his every move.

"I believe you are keen to leave us, Frenchman" came the cold tone, as James turned his attention to François, his expression unreadable.

"Indeed sir" François agreed rapidly, glancing at the Abbot for some guidance.

"Your wounds have taken a long time to heal. I had hoped you would be gone sooner. Never mind. You will leave Scotland by the end of the week. An escort will provide for your safety to the coast and your passage is arranged on a ship to take you back to France."

François was delighted by the news. He was going home at last. Then he remembered the loss of the merchant's horse and the letters he was supposed to take back with him for Breny. The merchant would have despaired of ever seeing his animal again and likewise Breny, back at home, would have almost given up on François returning at all after so long.

"I cannot leave the merchant with such a loss to his pocket" said François.

"All will be dealt with. He will be given a replacement animal and the letters will be given to you in Leith."

François smiled broadly at the quiet Abbot and then back to the nobleman, eager for more information. If this man, whoever he was, was important enough to have the authority to arrange this, then he man would know more than the humble Abbot and could maybe give him the answers to his other questions.

"Can you tell me what I did wrong?" he asked.

"Nothing that I know of."

"Then why was I taken prisoner, accused and then hunted?"

"They made a mistake. It was because they thought you were more then you were."

Francis did not understand. Was this to be the only explanation he would get? More than he was? What did he mean? Had he been mistaken for anyone in particular, a messenger or an agent of some kind? He had certainly been questioned along those lines when he had been captured. Or was it his mistake to be in the wrong place, when they were expecting someone else?

There was a long delay while the look between the Abbot and the nobleman developed into a strange silence. It left François with no choice except to sit quietly, leaving them to their own private confrontation, until one of them decided to continue.

"The reason for the interest in you is that your face is cursed with unusual features. It bears too much of a resemblance to one of the noble families of Scotland" James explained.

François still looked mystified, bewildered that this news made any difference. If the reason had been so simple and acceptable, why had not the Abbot told him? In fact he realised that the Abbot had said very little since the man's arrival. He had not addressed him by name or referred to him by title, yet this was obviously an important man. The Abbot respected him. François became aware that there was something else, something special about him. What was so frightening about this man's rank and position? Who was this man who held such power?

"Who are you?" François asked.

The King smiled. This interest would soon be curbed by other considerations. Now he had spoken, James knew François would have to carry the burden of this knowledge for the rest of his life. Was he mature enough to handle the responsibility the truth involved? How could he tell?

"It is unimportant. But it is important that you listen carefully to my next words" James told him sternly, keen to have his absolute attention. "The reason for the interest in you, is because of your likeness to the house of Stuart, the royal house of Stuart."

The King waited briefly to allow this to register, before completing his announcement.

"It is unfortunate for you that you resemble the King of Scotland. You have his face, his colouring, amongst all of those in Scotland including his own children, by some fluke of nature, only you are his image."

François gulped. He did not believe he had heard correctly, and continued to look at him uncertainly. No, no this was ridiculous. Why was he being told such lies?

"It is true" the Abbot confirmed softly at his side.

François sat down open mouthed. This could not be right, it was another mistake. How could he look like the King? It was impossible. This had been the whole cause of his trouble here. He trembled uncontrollably, then leaned forward to rest his face in his hands whilst other words became incoherent to him as the enormity of the statement sank in.

"Do you understand now?"

François nodded. He understood very well. He understood why those men had hunted him so keenly; he understood the danger he had put the old woman in. He also understood that he was frightened at the danger he was still in.

"This is hard to accept at the moment, but you must come to terms with it before you leave here" the King went on. "Innocent as you are, your face is dangerous here, for yourself, for the King and the security of Scotland. Although the common man may never recognise the members of the royal house, there are plenty who would. Plenty who would use you to discredit and harm his majesty, thus interfering with the statesmanship of this realm. You are the greatest danger to Scotland I have known in a long time. I must have your promise that you will never show your face in Scotland again."

François did not refuse, it was all he could do to speak. He was too stunned.

"The biggest danger to you is yourself" the King went on.

François stared into space, seeing nothing. This was an illusion, it was not real.

"There are conditions to your departure. We must not tempt fate any further. Your beard and wild hair at least act as some disguise. They must remain until you are home. But most importantly for your preservation, as well as ours, I must have your word that this secret remains a secret. You will not breath a word of it to anyone, not to your closest friend, not to your family. Do I have that promise, Thistledown?"

François promised. As if he could possibly refuse.

"Remember your promises" James told him.

The King looked François in the eyes for the last time, without further demands or recriminations and was gone; gone with a heavy heart and some relief, to try to forget the Frenchman. He made for the royal nursery at Stirling Castle, where David Lindsay watched over the prince with the utmost care. Here James would take time to play with his healthy, strong young son, for this life was important to Scotland, more important than anything or anyone else.

Grateful to be alone to think, François lay restless, tossing and turning on the bed, his thoughts distorted and churning in the darkness, his brain too active to sleep with such a pile of words bouncing about in his head. He wanted to be rid of this burden. He was no longer free to be himself. He wanted the simple life he had had before, with few responsibilities. Instead he had to learn to live with this awful secret.

François was angry at the King, angry at the Abbot and angry at the old woman.

"Why didn't she tell me the reason I was in danger?" he asked the Abbot.

"I don't imagine she really knew. She merely sensed you would come one day, that your face would have consequences and that men would seek you out and herself. She simply saw you in her strange visions. How could she or the common man realise you bore a resemblance to the King, when they had never seen the King, a statue or a painting of his likeness?"

He turned on the Abbot, demanding to know when he had known of this likeness.

"As soon as I saw you, even with the beard, but it was not my place to tell you, nor my decision. It was for the King himself to speak to you, no one else."

"That – was – the King?" François whispered, almost not daring to say it aloud.

The Abbot nodded, and François fell silent. He could not help shivering at the significance of that meeting. He had been face to face with the King of Scotland! A face which had been his, a face which gave nothing away. A man who must have cursed him for the threat he posed and the trouble he had already caused. Yet this powerful man had uttered no word of blame, and simply dealt with the matter as he saw fit.

The Abbot had tried to distil some reason and sense back into François, but the youth's reproachful expression stopped him from saying anything else. François had his own mental battle to fight and he did not need more words to confuse him.

It was hard to believe that the King had been generous and compassionate enough to let him live, since he could easily have instructed the opposite, because his very existence was a threat. That he had personally arranged for his clandestine departure had surprised him more, although only the King could have made this possible. François could only imagine the high degree of secrecy it required and he wished he could have thanked him.

It was best he was gone, best for himself as well as for those who had done so much to protect him so far. With so much to remember and so much to forget, he wanted to pretend it had never happened. He had been desperate to reach home, to feel the soil in his hands as he worked the land alongside his father, the rough and tumble of teasing his brother, to laugh, drink and fool with his friends, to flirt with the girls in the village, to hold them in his arms and feel their warmth against his skin. He wanted all these so much, to be as he was.

That night he left the abbey and rode silently behind his companion on the dreadfully slow journey to the coast. The high collars of their plain cloaks would hide their faces from any curious looks, not that they expected many. Yet François found the open spaces bothered him; he felt vulnerable and uneasy and the thick woollen cloak was clumsy and restrictive over his own clothes. Despite the promise of his safety François was not convinced by the single bodyguard entrusted to protect him; he could only pray that there might be more somewhere as an extra precaution, not that he saw any. The man answered no questions, made no conversation and only spoke to direct them on their route.

As they gave the shadow of Linlithgow Place a wide berth, François could not help give it one long withering glance, the strong walls a far from welcome sight. No wonder his grandmother, one of the household of the Princess Isabella, had accompanied her to France when she married the Duke of Brittany. Who in their right mind would want to stay in this country?

The journey required several changes of horses, all of which seemed perfectly planned, although he was especially glad when they reached Leith without being intercepted. There he slipped from the saddle to swing the cloak tighter around himself and follow the next man who met them to the dock side. Here he was handed his travel documents, given his instructions upon landing and the letters to take home from the merchant, leaving François to wonder how it was all so easily done.

Safe on board, the receding shoreline gave him no comfort. He could not relax, preferring to keep his own company, and he settled down well away from the other passengers and their conversations, to concentrate his thoughts on France and his family. Home! How he had longed for it over these past weeks. It was hard to believe even now that he had survived and that he was really going home, thanks to the most important man in Scotland. A man he now admired, a man he would have liked to have known better. A man he would never see again.

CHAPTER FOUR

François was happy to feel the French soil beneath him again and happy to have his haunting memories fade as he travelled inland from the coast. The horse he had purchased made the journey easy and a good deal quicker than expected.

His first port of call on the way home was to visit Breny, deliver the overdue the letters and make his deep apologies for the delay of his return. Breny was more concerned about his acquaintance's health, apparent by his loss of weight and less than fit condition.

"I had almost given up on you" he said. "I admit I was impatient for the letters. But looking at the toll this request has taken on you, I would not dare to expect you to repeat that favour. I would not want to be held responsible for the deterioration in you. You have been ill."

"Indeed. And to be honest I would not wish to go back there" François admitted, without going into detail.

"Quite so" the man acknowledged. "I would not ask it."

They parted amicably. The first hurdle was over. The next was to shave and trim his hair, and hope that his family would not be as observant about his fitness.

With the warm autumn afternoon sun lazily casting patterned shadows across the road in front of him, François automatically turned off to pass through the familiar back lanes and tracks he and his friends always used. Ahead in the mellow light, a lumbering cart pulled by a fat horse came towards him, the owner peacefully dozing on the seat, letting the horse find its own way. Suddenly the sleepy fellow found himself tipped off into the dirt. Shaken, he looked as François laughingly swung his horse about to face the sprawling figure.

"You are back!" Pierre exclaimed.

"This very day" François confirmed.

Pierre jumped up and they threw themselves at each other, just as they had always done. François, relieved that nothing had changed between them during their time apart, relaxed and listened to his friend as he gushed on about the escapades and scrapes he had missed, and they walked on until Pierre turned off for the village.

François had reached his home and he paused nervously. His longing for home had seemed a hopeless dream during the past months and now he had safely arrived he almost wept for the reality of it, the house and the people there. Although longing for the comfort of it, he had to compose himself before facing their exuberant welcome. He had to appear normal and unchanged to face them all, to laugh and amuse, to regale stories they would believe. After months of fear and illness it would be difficult, but home, with all its emotional strain, had to be a thousand times better than the experiences he had recently endured.

With a surge of pleasure, he leapt back on to his horse, impatient to make sure everything was the same as he had left it. There was joy in his heart as he spurred the horse faster and faster across the fields he knew so well, aware of the power of the horse beneath him. At last he felt the tingling energy of exhilaration return. His natural enjoyment had been dormant too long, and that high fence at the top of the meadow just had to be jumped again. He turned off through the trees for the most exciting approach, in and out of the saplings, twisting and turning to duck below the branches and then the short clearing before the rails. He cleared the fence at a gallop and let out a loud whoop of glee, the wind rushing past his face as he raced down the slope on the other side, oblivious to the other animals which disdainfully turned their heads as he few past. A few more fences and he would be there.

His mother Eleanor was the first to see him, although she never understood what made her look out of the window at that precise moment. She needed no second glance to recognise the horseman, even at that distance. A sixth sense told her, and her heart missed a beat. She had been terrified that he would not return at all. She should never have let him go, but there had been nothing she could have done to stop him. She had tried, God knows how she had tried, but her words had been of no importance to him.

The eagerness of his approach gave her no indication of how his foreign experiences had fared. Now he was in the yard and she ran through the house noisily and clumsily, to be the first to greet him. She had to touch him, hold him to make sure he was real. She reached the front door, ran down the steps without hesitation and stood there, her arms outstretched, calling his name.

François had hardly dismounted when, before he had time to say anything, he found himself caught in his mother's arms. She clung to him crying, unable to say anything except his name, over and over again.

"I take it you are glad to see me" he joked.

Then her brief moment alone with him was gone, for the others who had been startled into life were rushing across the farmyard to join them, yelling their delight. He had to disentangle himself from one to the other as they hugged him repeatedly. The fuss overwhelmed him. There were noises of all kinds as they crowded around him, everyone talking at once, and he was lost in the din of excitement as his father also grabbed his hand and drew him into a long, welcoming embrace.

Slowly sanity was restored and the servants bustled off to prepare a meal for the dirty, dusty tired traveller, as François was finally led towards the house.

Later he lay at last in his own bed, in his own room, safe at home. His hand followed the edge of the bed, stretching out to touch the rough surface of the wall, remembering it all. Nothing had ever felt as good. Here he could relax and lie there, just listening to the familiar sounds of the family and farm beyond. How long he had waited for this moment?

The discomfort of the day passed; his sore and aching ribs had withstood the attention and were now allowed some relief. Thus François fell asleep, a deep, well-deserved sleep where there were no nightmares to disturb him for once.

He woke with a smile, completely content. Home! There was no place like it, it was everything he wanted. He slept late every morning for days and was left to make his own adjustment. Soon the utter tiredness was gone, his heart had stopped racing and his head ceased to ache. Here at home he could feel the sun on his back, the wind on his face and the sweet fresh air to fill his lungs. Here he could eat, sleep, ride, work and make love. What other pleasures were there in life? What else did he need?

The next few days had been a repeat of his arrival, his brother and sister pestering him for tales of his adventures, hanging onto every word. The house became busy with the rush and clamour as friends and neighbours, upon hearing of his return, also came expecting exciting stories to satisfy their curiosity, all of which he managed to deliver successfully using all his powers of exaggeration, until eventually and thankfully they soon tired, eager to relate their own stories instead.

Suzanne and Jean-Paul had been to Paris to visit their grandmother with their uncle and aunt during his absence, and there, together with other families, they had seen the royal entertainments, floats on the river, musical displays and a carnival. Suzanne had returned excited by all she had seen and was bursting to divulge every detail to him, as if it was yesterday. She would not stop until she had. In addition she had discovered a host of young men to talk, ride and dance with, all of them paying attention to her. It was wonderful. François smiled. It seemed his sister had grown up, and she was clearly smitten by one young man in particular. His sweet sister had discovered the most unpredictable emotion, love.

Love, real love, he sighed, was an unknown quantity. He doubted he was capable of anything which required such commitment, for he was content to be the master of the light insignificant dalliance or flirtation. His restless pursuit of freedom prevented anyone coming close enough to capture his wild spirit, although, he smiled, the anticipation of renewing his reunion with Colette was something he was eager for.

Pierre arrived at the farm, urging his friend to join him riding for a while, and François did not refuse. They rode over the local hills and tracks, with few words between them; there was little need for words, as they knew each other so well. Although Pierre noticed his friend's stiffness and remarked on it, guessing there was more to it.

"I was attacked by bandits. I am nearly healed" was all François would say, making light of the matter.

"What was Scotland really like?"

"It is a cold, hostile, barbaric place. I never want to see it again" François declared.

"Well, that is an honest answer."

François grinned. He was trying hard to get back into his old ways. Pierre smiled.

"You have too much time on your hands. We must put that right."

François was glad of his patience and undemanding companionship. They were here to enjoy the day and Pierre never complained. Feeling guilty about his selfishness, he suggested they went to the tavern. There Colette, the innkeeper's daughter, welcomed him, her hand trailing around his shoulder as she went to serve the other customers or touching the back of his neck as she stood beside him, her whisper to his ear, her breath on his cheek, her mass of long dark curly hair brushing his face as she turned out of reach. Her eyes flashed with expectation. She longed for his favour, his undivided attention, and to be in his arms once more.

"You have a rival. Your brother has been making eyes at Colette during your absence" Pierre informed him.

"I doubt he is the only one. Who wouldn't be interested in Colette?" François sighed appreciatively.

Colette was a vivacious, pretty creature with fire in her soul, who easily caught the eye. She was never short of admirers and never at a loss for company. She delighted in teasing the young men who enjoyed her flirtations, never taking any of them seriously, not even François, although he was dearer than most and for whom she would abandon the others immediately he appeared.

Later she ran the short distance along the river bank to join him where he lay under a willow tree staring up at the sky. There beside him, she turned her head to his, nibbling playfully at his ear and nuzzling his neck. Then her hand gently stretched out to touch his face. It only needed her fingers to trace tantalisingly down his skin, to stir the senses afresh, to embrace that warm, inviting frame. He kissed her brow, her pretty nose, her long dark lashes, her shoulder, her throat and finally her soft lips. She could make a man forget everything. She was the best diversion to any problem and the best therapy he could want.

Jacques, who knew his son, had at first been satisfied that François seemed to have come through his adventure unscathed and had survived the long months away with little difference in him. Yet as the days passed, he was not quite so sure. On the surface it seemed the same François who laughed, teased and played with his family and friends, filling his days with pleasure and hard work. His outward characteristics seemed the same, although Jacques sensed there was something he could not place.

His father was already hot and had stripped to his shirt, busily shifting bales in the barn, when François joined him. The work on the farm went on regardless and François loved it.

"Where is Jean-Paul? He knows there is work to be done" said Jacques.

"I have no idea" answered François, setting to work beside him.

Jacques grumbled mildly, dismissing his other son, for here was his chance to tackle François without interruption.

"Have your adventures in Scotland quelled your wanderlust for a while?" he asked.

"For quite a while" François replied, pulling a face, shrugging and then carried on working. As the weeks had passed he had slowly healed, both in his mind and body. He had gradually been getting fitter, although he was thoughtful in his actions, since the occasional twinge still caught him unprepared.

"Would you go again?"

François shook his head. His father stopped to look at him, unable to understand why, after his obsession for Scotland had driven them crazy for years, he now made so little of it.

"For as long as I can remember you have thought of nothing else but Scotland and now you are home, it was as if your stay there never happened" he said.

"It was nothing like I expected. The people are sombre, their lives pitiful, their homes poor."

Jacques nodded satisfied with his explanation, relieved that nothing too terrible had taken place. He gave him an affectionate clip around the shoulder and returned to his labour.

"I am glad to have you back. I missed you."

"I missed you too" came the old flippant reply, to hide the embarrassment of the compliment.

They worked hard together with little need for conversation, each knowing the tasks out of habit, his father glancing up occasionally and luckily missing the winces which shot across his son's face or the deep breaths he took to control them. Those healing muscles beneath the scars which he had kept so carefully hidden were playing him up today, and the hours of non-stop continual physical exertion had begun to make his muscles ache so much he had to stop for a rest.

"You are out of condition, François" his father joked.

François agreed and sat down, waiting to regain his energy, when a careless movement by Jacques caused one of the bales to fall, hitting François fully on the shoulder and knocking him sideways into some of the wooden slats of the stall. He groaned and instinctively clutched his side before turning away to hide his discomfort. Then he staggered back to his feet as quickly as he could, hoping the moment had not been noticed, but the observant

Jacques looked shrewdly at him.

"What is wrong? You look…"

"It is nothing. It just winded me" came the reply, a little too hurriedly as he made to recover from the spasm of pain.

Jacques was not fooled for one second and approaching his son, he had his thoughts confirmed as François backed away from him. Jacques stopped and they stared at each other.

"I will ask you again. What is wrong?"

"Nothing" François insisted, unable to stop the smarting muscles from throbbing.

"I don't believe you. Undo your shirt" was the stern command.

François would not, and as his father came closer he was forced to back away further, this time bumping into a pile of stacked bales and more stall planking. Then, trapped, he was forced to grab his father's hand and push it away as it came towards his shirt. Jacques glared angrily at him. He could not fend him off. The older man took a firm grip on his son's wrists and simply by using his superior strength, he pulled François's arms away from his body, holding him still, before he swiftly let go and pulled the shirt away.

There was a brief silence as his father absorbed the scarring. He looked into his son's eyes and let him tuck his shirt in again to cover them from sight.

"What happened in Scotland? How came you by these wounds?" Jacques demanded.

François refused to speak.

"You will not move from here until you have told me" his father promised, although he knew threats were not enough to force the truth from his son. "Since when did you become secretive and deceitful? These wounds are not accidental, they are serious. I will know the reason for them."

François did not want to remember, did not want to relive any part of it. He feared his voice would betray him if he was forced into some quick response, but he realised he could not keep all his secrets for long, however he tried.

He began to confess that he had been attacked by some lawless Highland bandits, sticking to the same story he had told Pierre, thus telling very little of the truth. He related his escape from these violent men by falling into a river and finally told of the Abbot who had nursed him and kept him safe. He could not have said the rest, the capture, the torture, the meeting with James; such were not for these ears. He must deceive his father, there was no other way.

Jacques had listened quietly and patiently to the horrifying tale, and was frightened for his son. He could so easily have lost him. He clasped him to his arms briefly before pushing him away to hide his own emotion.

"Everything is all right" François whispered, his voice dried to a soft low sound.

"Are you sure?"

"Yes" he lied, while the voice in his head wished it was true.

They returned to work, and François felt some relief that this discovery was over and forgotten, with no need to alarm anyone.

François found himself amusingly diverted by his sister, who pestered him, demanding his full attention. She had been invited to return to visit her grandmother near Paris again before Christmas and she pleaded with him to escort her this time, preferring his company to that of her other brother.

François was flattered, but he was unwilling to play chaperon to her when it was obvious that these plans to visit her grandmother were only an excuse to see the young man she had met there before.

"Jean-Paul has volunteered already, he will be reluctant to relinquish his duty to me" he pointed out.

"I do not want Jean. He is more interested in being with Raoul's sister Marie."

"I would have thought that would have been to your advantage" he teased.

Dear Suzanne had fallen in love, her first love. She could talk about no one else, and it was no surprise to learn that the young man had confessed to her; he felt the same.

"You must come and meet him" she insisted.

"You do not need me."

François continued to decline. He had other interests of his own and would not be persuaded. Instead he resumed his habit of joining his friends at the village inn, where Colette looked forward to their visits. She lingered at their table, resting too long at his side hoping for a squeeze of his arm about her waist. François, unlike the others she tormented, refused to respond to all her attempts to make him jealous, preferring to sit quietly relaxed and taking no notice of her. Maddened, she deliberately knocked him with the tray as she passed, then with a jug the next time; the third time he ducked. She tried ignoring him, making a great show of her scorn, but she could never keep it up. It wavered and eventually softened as he sat there watching.

"Don't you like me any more?" she whispered, laying her hands around his neck.

"Well enough, when you don't spill the wine" he teased.

She had turned away in a fresh rage, her head tossed high to hide her disappointment, when he caught her arm and hauled her back and into his lap. Then he tilted her chin and kissed her, at which she instantly forgave him anything. Not surprisingly, many evenings were spent here in such pleasant and congenial company as the months sped by.

So the year passed on, and with the end of the year 1512 François found the haunting memories of Scotland were far behind him. In the winter and spring months, he and his friends Pierre and Gaston wasted away their hours, revelling in the comfortable freedom of their old ways. François was his old self again, fully recovered and wallowing in the pleasure that life was once more for living, his spirits soaring with excitement and joy, with the result that the small farmhouse was continually busy with laughter and people again.

The charming François had no favourites in his vast capacity for attracting, sometimes unwittingly, the favours of the young ladies in the area, which resulted in complaints from his friends and more especially his brother Jean-Paul, who had grown too handsome for his own good. Jean had pursued Gaston's younger sister since his return from Paris, with no result, because she had eyes only for François, a situation in which Jean's ego demanded satisfaction. In a sudden fit of rage he turned on François after being scorned by Natalie again.

"I wish you had stayed away!" he snapped.

Unaware of the cause of the bewildering outburst, François looked at the others for some guidance, yet they were equally as ignorant.

"Natalie ignores me, when you are around. She worships you."

Had he forgotten Raoul's sister so quickly? He was tempted to make some mention, but decided against it. There was no keeping up with his brother's infatuation.

"Don't be so idiotic. She is only a child."

"She hangs on your every word."

François raised his eyebrows, his eyes twinkled merrily and a bemused grin spread across his charming face, much to his brother's annoyance.

"And I had not noticed! Well well, to find such good taste in one so young. Never mind, don't be so impatient brother, she will get around to you eventually." He could not help teasing.

François ducked as Jean-Paul lashed out, then backed away as his brother continued to come after him. He did not want to fight him despite it being clear that Jean was intent on hurting him. François could not take him seriously, and even when he tripped over his own feet to lie on the ground at Jean-Paul's feet he could not keep a straight face. His brother stood threateningly over him, his young face hot and red.

"Tell me she means nothing to you!" he hissed.

"I promise Natalie means nothing to me" he managed to stutter, his hand on his heart to prove he was serious, whilst smothering a laugh.

Unfortunately Natalie had appeared at that moment and burst into tears, making them both turn around. François frowned. He had not meant to upset the girl and kicked his brother, pushing him after her.

"Go on, go and comfort her. Here is your chance."

His brother did not wait, but rushed off to let François return to his friends. There was no doubt his brother was a fine handsome youth, with the ability to flatter and tease, but he was too young, serious and tense to enjoy the subtleties of his experienced elders. It was just as well Jean was going off to Paris again with his sister, thus giving him some peace.

Returning from the horse sales at Epple, where he had gone with Gaston and Pierre, François noticed the unattended carriages and horses left in the yard. His siblings were home and had clearly brought other visitors with them to the house. Not in the mood for socialising, he avoided the unknown voices and the noise within the house to head for the kitchen, where he anticipated sitting alone and relaxing after his dusty ride. Instead he was met by a flurry of activity and an abundance of food being prepared, and he was swiftly sent packing as he attempted to help himself from the table.

Outside he saw his father strolling with strangers, allowing François the opportunity to wander to the cupboard for some wine, without being drawn into the growing squeals of delight and laughter from the next room. Cup in hand, he made for his escape, considering the barn the safest place, when the other door opened and Suzanne immediately threw herself at him. He tried not to spill the drink he was carrying. She beamed at him, her eyes bright and her face flushed.

"Oh François, I am so happy."

"Goodness, I am pleased to hear it" he offered, trying to deposit his cup safely on the side table so he could take both hands to hold her still for a moment. "Now tell me what you are talking about."

Already pink from the exertion of dancing about, she blushed deeper and became shy, embarrassed because she found it hard to confide her private innermost secrets to her dearest brother.

"Oh, I never thought we could be together. There were so many things in the way. He is from an influential family and we are not even minor landed gentry."

"Suzanne, we have title to our lands, not many have that! We are not rural, uneducated peasants."

"I know."

"Does he love you?"

"Oh yes."

"Then I am sure something can be worked out" he whispered encouragingly.

"That is the point. Raoul has no intention of letting convention stand in his way. He won't have any nonsense about a dowry or other unimportant traditions stop us from marrying. He will brook no opposition, not that there has been any. I still cannot believe it."

A dowry? Surely the idea of dowries were for the higher society of aristocrats and royal houses, François had nearly said.

"All he wants is to have me at his side and make me happy" she whispered softly.

And why not, he thought. It was natural that his sweet sister would attract admirers, and to find one prepared to care for her this much was truly wonderful.

There seemed little doubt that his grandmother had had a hand in this match. It should not have been such a surprise that on her visits she would have mixed with those other families of former fellow court attendants and second-generation Scottish migrant families. But he was prepared to forgive her meddling, because Suzanne was so very much in love and Raoul had proved himself equally devoted.

"So Raoul Martel has asked for your hand and you have accepted." He swung her full in the air, as he had done when they were younger, and then held her away from him to look at her again.

"So my sister thinks she has grown up. You have made your decision so soon, when there are so many more hearts you could have broken" he teased. He hugged her again, kissed her affectionately on the cheek and, bending down low to her ear, was about to whisper something else when he caught sight of the other girl standing in the doorway.

"I forget my manners – we have visitors" he apologised, straightening up and brushing some of the dust from his clothes.

Suzanne rushed to pull her new friend forward to be introduced.

"This is Marie, Raoul's sister. Father is showing everyone else around the farm. Marie, this is my other brother François."

They exchanged the normal polite acknowledgement of each other, and while Suzanne gabbled on at both of them, the girl stood shyly in front of him, her eyes lowered. So this was Marie, he mused, the girl his brother had been so in raptures over last year. He smiled to himself, wondering how Jean-Paul would explain this to Natalie once she knew of this visit. A smile which confused their guest, until François indicated they should fetch the others since the servants were nearly ready with the food collation in the kitchen.

Raoul and his family had accompanied Suzanne and her relations back here, in order to be introduced to Suzanne's immediate family. François attended the formal introductions, was on his best behaviour and decided he liked Raoul. He had a firm handshake and an honest face, and from everything he had learnt he knew his sister would be happy.

Escaping to the loft of the barn as soon as he could, François smiled that soft smile to himself, thinking of Colette and how much he preferred her lively temperament to this quiet girl he had just met. He lay back in the hay, relaxing his supple body, dreaming to himself. He had just decided to go to the village when his brother arrived.

"Their grandfather owns the Belmonde Estates" he told him.

"Good" François mumbled. He was in too mellow a mood to think about the advantages of his sister's match. If she was happy and in love, what else mattered? He did not want to debate it. To stop his brother from bothering him further, he deliberately asked him if he was going to see Natalie soon. Jean-Paul scoffed loudly, informing him he did not have time for children any more, which made François grin widely. Obviously poor Natalie had been replaced in his affection. Marie now had his full attention once again.

François had no need to say anything else. The moment the two girls appeared in the yard, he was out there, offering to accompany them wherever they wanted to go. François could not believe it as he watched his brother's mooning affection as he followed them everywhere they turned, hoping to impress or please Marie. It was a devotion which showed a different side to his character, but in watching him François could not help notice the girl also. Although he thought her quite pretty, with dark shining hair and long lashes around her brown eyes, flattering her small oval face and the becoming glimpse of a smile, he found her demure and much too meek natured for his taste.

François had given little attention to their guest until their departure. Jean-Paul was still close to her side, but to his brother's annoyance, it was François who caught Marie when she slipped on the smooth pebbles. He simply stepped forward to catch her arm to steady her, at which she mumbled her thanks and blushed at his touch. Deliberately slow to release her, as was his way with any female, he tried to look into those eyes, hidden by her lowered head. She was such a timid thing that she refused to look at him and he let her go without comment as she hastily hurried to the coach. He shrugged off the lack of interest and promptly forgot all about her once she was out of sight, unlike Jean-Paul, who sulked at his brother's act of gallantry and bemoaned his lost opportunity.

François was indifferent to his brother's complaints and to the news that Suzanne had invited her to return for a longer stay, since her presence here was unlikely to involve him too much. Indeed the prospect made no difference to him at all, although he knew Jean-Paul would be delighted beyond reason.

Within weeks Marie had returned, and as expected she became a welcome sister for Suzanne to confide in and the target for his brother's constant attention. Jean-Paul sought them out wherever they went. No task was too much for him and no problem too difficult where Marie was involved. He was her servant, her slave and his reward was simply paid by a smile.

Continually finding them under his feet wherever he went, François paid little concern to this development, with a half-smile on his face as he leaned back to merely observe. Marie gave Jean-Paul no encouragement and at times she permitted herself a glance in his own direction, as if silently indicating she wanted rescuing from the ever-persistent Jean-Paul. François tried not to interfere, but felt his brother needed some gentle guidance to prevent his foolish behaviour becoming an awkward embarrassment for their guest. He understood his brother's feelings and frustration, yet whatever words he used to explain, they were deliberately misinterpreted. There was no way emotional young love would suffer advice or listen to a potential rival. So, aware he was doing more harm than good, he let the matter drop, leaving it to Suzanne to continually shout at him for being a pest. Eventually she had to ask their father had to step in.

"Marie will be staying with us for a while, she will be excellent company for your sister" said Jacques. "While she is a guest in our house, I want you both to behave properly."

Jean-Paul did not even understand what his father was trying to say.

"You, Jean-Paul, will treat her with respect and stop pestering the girl" his father finished.

"At least I am more suitable company than François, considering some of the people he mixes with" Jean-Paul protested.

François feigned a look of shock and laughed. "Why? I really have no idea what you mean."

On the first really hot day in May the family decided to indulge themselves with a picnic in the bottom meadow. Jacques and

Eleanor were sitting in the shade of the trees whilst the others played by the stream, the boys jumping from one stone to another, splashing each other, and the girls shouting their encouragement. A pleasant peaceful picture, which summed up how their parents saw the rest of their lives.

The game of tag between the youngsters gradually developed into a wild scramble, with squeals and shrieks, amid running, pushing and side stepping, which left them breathless and panting in their enjoyment. To avoid Jean-Paul's mad grasp, Marie had been forced to twist sideways and duck out of reach, a movement which caused her to accidentally bump into François, so that he overbalanced, sending him into the stream with a loud splash.

There was a brief silence, followed by laughter as his brother and sister ran away, leaving Marie standing nervously on the bank to face him, unable to move. She insisted it was an accident, that she had not meant to push him in. At first he sat there, then slowly he stood up and shook himself, trying to wring out his shirt as he advanced from the shallow water. A mischievous grin lit his face and the telltale twinkle of devilment appeared in his eyes, making Jean-Paul yell a warning to Marie, but it was too late. François was out of the stream, the wet spray following his steps as he easily caught hold of her and swept her off her feet to carry her struggling vainly against him, back into the stream.

"You are making me wet. You will damage my dress!" she complained, trying to push away from him.

"If you struggle too much. I will drop you" he teased, striding further out into deeper water.

She instantly changed her mind and clung to him, her arms about his neck, as François, full of fun, made to let her fall and then caught her up again.

With the sunlight dancing on the water, the warmth of the sun on his back and Marie in his arms, he did not realise his expression had changed. For that brief instant he was aware of no other experience except the two of them, the sensation of holding her tight against him, her soft skin brushing his and her hair tangled on his wet face as he stood there. The water dripping from his own hair into his eyes, he looked at her properly for the first time, stared curiously at her soft features, and was tempted to kiss her. He hesitated, and then the spell was broken by Suzanne yelling from the bank to him.

"François! Don't you dare!"

There was anger in her voice, and a touch of desperation, because she saw the danger of this impetuous act before François knew himself.

"Don't you dare drop her in the stream!" she called again, diverting him completely. Then the stern voice of their father interrupted them all, as he came to bring order to the situation.

"That is enough foolery! This rough house is out of hand. François, come out of there immediately and put Marie down. She is a guest here and not used to your wild behaviour. Apologise!"

François obeyed, setting the girl safely on the bank and asking forgiveness, explaining that he had forgotten for a moment that it was not his sister or brother whom he was teasing, for they were used to such bad manners. Suzanne rushed her away to sit with Eleanor and Jacques followed them back to the shade of the trees. Deflated and still dripping wet, he could only gaze after them, his fun gone. Then, determined to have some revenge, he dived for his brother so that they rolled and tumbled together until they lay exhausted in the sun.

François tried to dismiss the memory of that moment when he held Marie in the stream, but he could not. He had held her too long. In the middle of the confusion there had been a change in him, and although he could not identify it, he meant to avoid any such complication. Marie was not for him. She was too gentle a soul to understand or handle his normal rough and meaningless flirtations. As it was, he had almost done something really stupid, out of habit. He could not hurt her in that way. To prevent her becoming a victim of his customary irresponsible ways with females, he concluded it would be better to keep his distance.

The idea was fine, except that when he made to walk straight past Suzanne and Marie, his sister rebuked him for his rudeness and indicated that he should join them for a while.

"Marie is to go to Scotland to be married. She is betrothed" she said.

François smiled politely, wondering if Suzanne was gently warning him to forget any ideas he might have had. It was a shame the same fact had not changed Jean-Paul's infatuation.

"Suzanne tells me you have visited Scotland" Marie gushed eagerly.

François nodded, hoping she was not going to ask him any awkward questions or to elaborate on his opinion of the country. As luck would have it, he was saved by his brother's interruption as he suddenly burst into sight and dashed to join the little group. He had been anxious because he could not find Marie, and having discovered François in her company he was not best pleased. He glared at his brother and glared even more when Pierre and Gaston arrived. They had been looking for François but were quite willing to stay around adding to the party and regaling Marie with tales of their own escapades, gently making fun of each other for her amusement by disclosing the failures in each other's character.

"François is always in trouble, it follows him wherever he goes" laughed Pierre.

"Even in Paris" Jean-Paul mocked.

Glad of any opportunity to put his brother in a bad light, he gloated as he told Marie how his brother had been sent home in disgrace for his behaviour from the school and then tried to impress her by boasting how he had taken his place there. He fancied himself better than François for having completed his education.

"So what, I had the more fun" François declared, cuffing his brother playfully.

Paris! François smiled to himself remembering. Paris, where his tutors had despaired of the rough country youth who disrupted the lessons. His casual attitude had exasperated the scholars who tried to change him. The swordmaster screamed at him, calling him clumsy, oafish, lacking in style – yes, he had been everything they said, deliberately. For all their wisdom and education, François had been the more cunning. He had no regrets; they had been wrong to imagine he had had learnt nothing there. His skill with the sword was too dangerous and he knew he had to find other diversions by experiencing the city.

He had escaped to learn and observe the real people in the streets. He had seen the elegance and beauty of the royal buildings, the court ladies, the fawning false nobility with their exaggerated manners, the flattery and pretence. François knew his own mind. Paris was not the life he wanted.

Jean-Paul wished they would all go away, as he wanted to be alone with Marie, but there was no hope of that when she seemed so enthusiastically interested in every word and anything that was connected to François. He was passionately jealous of their acquaintance and sulked, hating his older brother. How was he to compete for her attention?

François was forced to admit to himself how recently he had begun to find himself listening for Marie's voice and waiting for a glimpse of her, stealing a look at the details of her features which he had scarcely taken notice of before.

This was no good. He needed to put everything back into perspective, to visit the village inn where he could relax with Colette. Colette, who he could hold on his knee, who was warm to the touch and who would let him put his arms about her waist and nibble her ear, whilst she giggled and responded to his every move. She was always capable of making him forget, and he wanted to forget.

Jean-Paul had been in the village on an errand and upon seeing them together, he came over to interrupt his brothers enjoyment.

"Go away, Jean-Paul." François instructed, without looking up from the embrace he was buried in. There was no way his brother would obey. He stood there until Colette, in a mischievous mood, raised her head and pulled away from François.

"You are a fine young gentleman, maybe you would be more congenial company than this fickle rogue" she teased.

"Whatever suits you, my sweet" François responded, letting her go. He faked a yawn, stretched his limbs and made to move, only to have her relent, throw herself into his arms again and hug him tightly, pleading that she did not mean it.

Jean-Paul pulled a face as the two of them returned to their fondling. It made him squirm, to see their physical contact demonstrated so openly, when he wished he could interest Marie enough for a similar reaction.

"Even Marie prefers your company to mine" he said bitterly. Damn his brother for reminding him! He felt Colette stiffen in his arms and knew he was in for trouble from that quarter as well now.

"That is not surprising when you act the way you do" François sighed.

François grinned, trying to make light of it in front of Colette, but she was not easily fooled and she pushed herself from his lap, glaring at him, and then gave him a resounding slap across the face.

"Well thank you, Jean-Paul" François snapped. It was no good wasting his day here. With a last glance in the direction in which Colette had disappeared, François also left.

Marie was fed up with Jean-Paul and disturbed by François, although they had barely spoken or exchanged pleasantries since that trivial incident in the stream. Except it was not trivial, because the experience of that close contact with this man had shocked her. He had made her feel so nervous, so strange, perplexed, flustered and self-conscious, and always thereafter she had been aware of his glance in her direction. She struggled hard to regain her composure, but try as she might she could not shake off this feeling. She had never been this edgy before, and she scolded herself for giving him any mind at all.

As Suzanne chatted on about her hopes, so Marie thought of her own future. Hers was an arranged marriage, a family matter. Raoul would inherit the family property and all its wealth, so he could please himself. She had no choice, but she could not help wondering what her husband would be like. Would he be handsome and kind, would he be like... François? She stamped her foot at the unwelcome thought. Not to be put off, Marie was determined to find out more about her future country, excited to gain any information which would concentrate her mind. She approached Eleanor, hoping that she could give her some sense of the place to her. Eleanor, however, had other ideas, insisting that her information was only hearsay from her mother and that François should be consulted, as he had better and more recent knowledge of the country. Marie sighed. How could she protest?

François shook his head. How could he refuse his mother's instructions to tell her all about Scotland? Scotland – why did they plague him with the place? Marie asked him what it was like there. He did not want to answer, as his experiences would not allow him to give any objective impressions. They could only dampen her hopes, ruin her dreams and frighten her. He had no right to do that, yet to think of her there in that harsh country did not please him. There was little he could tell her and tried to end the conversation swiftly.

"The country is so vast and different in every area" he said. "I only saw Edinburgh and Stirling, briefly. I have no doubt your husband will make you so happy and you will love being there."

Marie blushed at her own thoughts, while François sat impatient to escape. He felt the tremble of her hand come to rest on his as she thanked him, and wished for all the world she had not touched him. Without knowing why, François found himself searching her face, held by her eyes and her smile. In the stillness between them, they read each other's expressions and were both alarmed by the situation. Marie snatched her hand back quickly and stared at the floor, as he, tight-lipped, strode abruptly away, desperate that others in the room did not see the tell-tale signs.

This was ridiculous. Madness! He had no right even to think of her when she was betrothed to some Scottish nobleman. He busied himself in others' company and hoped his mellow smile and false laughter would not be noticed or remarked upon. He was not that lucky. Suzanne's keen intelligence soon recognised the problem, first in Marie and then in her brother, both of them doing their best to deny they were attracted to each other. Wishing she had been wrong, she confided her suspicions to her mother, who blamed herself for encouraging Marie to ask François about Scotland. Eleanor shook her head and sighed, praying François had the sense to continue to keep his distance from her.

"At the moment they are not talking" she said. "But how they can they continue to ignore each other, when Marie is staying here?"

"We shall arrange a visit for you and Marie, back with your uncle and aunt."

In her heart Suzanne did not believe this temporary separation would solve anything. For all her youth, she had more perception when it came to François, because she knew him better than her mother.

Suzanne was not the only one to notice the strain between them. It was a state of affairs which delighted Jean-Paul. With a gleam in his eye and a vicious nature, he taunted his brother, enquiring what had happened, but François tried his best to remain controlled and unprovoked.

"Why have you and Marie fallen out?" he jeered.

Jean-Paul instantly regretted his words, finding himself grabbed by the shirt to be pinned to the wall, so quickly he nearly had the breath knocked out of him. He had never seen this expression on his brother's face before. The merry hazel eyes were dark and dangerously still, and the coldness of his warning burned into Jean's head. Not a muscle moved or twitched in the face which stared at him, making him shudder. It was not his brother who stood there, it was a stranger.

"Let me go!" swallowed the youngster.

"Only when you promise not to cause trouble."

"Why should I take any notice of you?" spat Jean-Paul foolishly.

"Because it would be better for you" François growled.

François released him abruptly, giving Jean the chance to take a swing at his brother, a move which caused François to step sharply out of the way and let his adversary crash to the ground. The youngster leapt to his feet and edged backwards ready to defend himself, expecting some punishment, but none came.

Their father's arrival on the scene prevented any further trouble, as he complained that they were making too much noise and disruption in the house. He reprimanded them for forgetting that they had a guest in the house who was not used to such horseplay and suggested they go outside if they were going to continue.

Jacques detained François for a private word.

"Is there any difficulty I need to worry about?" he asked. "There is no ridiculous fondness or attraction on your part for Marie?"

François was startled by the direct question, but shook his head and reluctantly admitted they were not even friends.

"I know better than to ruin matters for Suzanne and Raoul by being foolish."

"That is just as well. The only attention I expect from you would be her protection while she is under our roof, nothing more."

A week later his sister and Marie had gone to visit other relations, and the temptation was thankfully out of reach.

CHAPTER FIVE

That midsummer, François' lingering memory was jolted by Marie's arrival back at their farmhouse. Here in his dirty dishevelled attire he stood momentarily dumbstruck before straightening up, a brightness in his eyes and a smile creeping onto his face. No one had warned him; not that it mattered, not that he cared. She was here, and he needed only a glance to know how things stood between them.

The awkwardness had vanished; the confusion of denial had magically been mellowed by their brief separation. That recognition of awareness had been controlled and put behind them.

He worked in the fields, happily remembering Marie's face and waiting to hear her voice on his return to the farmhouse. It was a pleasant interlude. It made him smile to see her around the place, giggling with his sister and enjoying the sunshine. Often he would find she smiled in his direction.

In the days that followed they found their casual friendship blossomed naturally. There was a softness to the looks they exchanged; a silent smile confirmed the danger was over. They would never allow themselves to become involved. They could be friends, exchange a smile, talk a little and walk together briefly. As long as he did not touch or hold her, he felt he was safe from his previous folly.

Content with that, François had not deliberately sought her out; instead fate put him to the test. Chasing after Suzanne in the garden, Marie had rushed along the path, to be met by a large puddle across her way. She looked at her elegant satin slippers, which would be ruined by the water, and stretched out one foot several times to see if she could possibly manage to cross it with one big step, but it was impossible. Finally she gave a deep sigh of disappointment, before being startled to find someone else so close. Not far away, François had watched bemused and silent behind her, preferring to study her antics. François resisted teasing her; he simply took a step forward to lift her into his arms. She was a light as a feather. He took two paces forward, and without a word he gently set her down on the other side of the offending puddle.

Marie thanked him for his gallant action and let him walk beside her for a while.

"You always seem so content. It is a pleasure to be in your company" he complimented her.

"Thank you."

"May I continue? You make no favourites in your acquaintances. I notice you do not flirt, even a little. I thought it was second nature for a woman, to tease, to pretend indifference, to interest and attract the male admirer."

"Where is the need? I have no wish to attract admirers. We either like or dislike people. That is common nature. Why pretend otherwise?"

"I cannot believe you do not secretly enjoy knowing when men are attracted to you."

"You are the expert on what ladies like, so I will not argue with you" Marie conceded, in such a manner as to indicate that she meant the opposite. He pulled a rueful face and gave her a quizzical look; she had never been brave enough to tease him in this manner previously. Her eyes sparkled as he concluded that there was much more to this creature than he had first imagined. Then they smiled and parted, with nothing else said.

His actions had been automatic. He had not even thought about what he was doing. It pleased him to have assisted her even for that moment. He had promised himself not to get that close, and now he had held her in his arms once more.

Without any planning, their exchange of a few words became more frequent, as François walked where he knew he would find her and rode where he knew she would pass. Each time their conversation was carefree, their laughter light and refreshing, and before he knew what was happening they found themselves looking forward to these private moments they had together. They were blissfully content with each other's company. They made no demands on each other and it became a habit to find each other, when the bustling house hold paid no attention as to where they were.

Marie sat making daisy chains and singing to herself until his shadow crossed the grass beside her. He threw himself down to join her as she smiled at her friend.

"Do you like it here?" François asked casually, chewing the end of a piece of grass and then rolling over to tickle her with it.

"Of course. You have a lovely home" came her giggling reply as she tried to dodge the wavering blade of grass which brushed her face and neck. Quickly she snatched at it and retaliated at François, who did everything he could to ignore its irritating presence, as she persisted in trying to make him squirm.

"I hate to think of you living in a cold isolated castle, in a foreign land."

Marie took no notice of his remark and went back to continue with her daisy chain.

"I mean it." He spoke so sadly that it startled her. She did not like his serious manner and shivered suddenly. She hung her head. Maybe she knew what was already in his mind, but she did not want confirmation.

"Don't say any more, don't spoil it" she pleaded.

François took her hand and felt it tremble before she snatched it away from his grasp. He had no choice but to let the matter drop rather than have Marie leave his side. With no further attempts to continue with this topic, she relaxed again and the pair of them lapsed back into their private dreams, content to sit together silently enjoying the sun.

The sight of a girl in the meadow with a figure sprawling at her side was nothing unusual, nothing to worry about. Except that they had sat there too long. François had sat with his back against the tree, as she lay with her eyes closed close to him, her wide skirts spread about her. François was in his own heaven, there with Marie beside him. He heard the footsteps approaching, but was reluctant to disturb this warm creature or ruin this perfect moment. Besides, he no longer cared who knew about their friendship, for it was only friendship.

Jean-Paul was shocked at his discovery. Even as he stood before them, he felt his blood boil. When François made no attempt to move or offer any explanation, he became more angry. Finally he tore off, until, wide-eyed and damp with perspiration, he stopped to catch his breath. He would make François suffer, that he promised himself.

Marie had woken at the sound of his departure and saw him disappear.

"Will he tell?" she asked worriedly.

"Will it matter if he does?" François asked softly, looking into her eyes. "What is there to tell?"

"Oh François — you know he will make more of it than there is. Anything could happen."

François sighed regretfully and climbed to his feet to go after his brother. If only it had not been Jean-Paul. Pulling Marie to her feet, he brushed the top of her head with his lips. How was he to prevent that devil creating a scene at home with this revelation?

Jean-Paul pulled away from his brother's grip, turning spitefully on him. He had been horrified at what he had discovered. François with Marie! His damned brother! He seethed with jealousy. He had worshipped her from the first time he had seen her, longed to be alone with her, longed to be the one who could take her in his arms and hold her. He cursed his brother and he cursed himself for his own stupidity. He had mistakenly believed that they were barely on speaking terms, as there had been no sign of anything between them since her return. How clever they had been, and how François had deceived them all, especially after them both being deliberately warned not to compromise her stay here.

"I will tell. I will tell everyone!" he screamed at his brother.

"Tell them what exactly? That we were sitting together in the meadow? What's wrong with that?"

"You were alone with her. She was almost lying in your arms."

"Almost is not a crime. She was resting, nothing more. It was completely innocent."

"Innocent!"

"You will only hurt Marie by taking this tale home, certainly not me."

François stood before his brother, his eyes distant and unseeing, with the truth in his head.

"She is bound for Scotland, unless your kindly interference may create enough scandal to ruin her prospects of this arranged marriage."

"Oh, no. You will not win her with my help" his brother snarled.

François should have known Jean-Paul would not keep his mouth shut too long and could only wonder how much he had blabbed when his father sent for him.

"How far has this relationship with Marie gone?" Jacques demanded.

"What do you mean?" François returned so innocently. "There is no relationship."

"I want an honest answer. Do you mean to pretend there is nothing between you?"

François was firm in his reply, leaving no doubt as to his exact meaning either.

"We talk and enjoy each other's company. That is all. I wish it were more. How I wish it were more."

"Enough! Alone and unchaperoned. You know better than to compromise her position here. You will cease these secret meetings."

"They are not secret. We do not hide away, guilty of our association. Our friendship is nothing to be ashamed of and it is only other people who make more of it than it is, with suspicious gossip."

"You will end these meetings, François!"

Jacques knew that his free-spirited son was not one to be controlled by threats. He expected that the respect François held for him would be enough to keep him in line. The conversation was at an end. Jacques expected him to obey without having to extract a promise from his son, and he did not doubt this assumption would be proved right. There had been no fuss, no great commotion, recriminations or accusations, in fact very little had been said, although François had expected a lot more.

His father's words had little effect on him; in truth there were no words in the whole world which would have changed François's intentions. He saw no reason to end his meetings with Marie when they hurt no one, and bound by their strict conventional upbringing and sense of propriety, there was no risk of their relationship developing any further. For the present, to be together was enough.

Days later, when the chance presented itself, François led Marie down to the stream and she let him take her hand.

"I wish things were different" came his husky voice.

"Hush!" she whispered, stretching her hand to his mouth.

There was an air of sadness between them as he removed her hand from his face and kept it wrapped in his as they walked on. There was so much he wanted to say, yet he could not find the right words because he knew they would change everything; it would cause them both pain. Instead they continued strolling in perfect harmony along the water's edge.

Until now he had been quite content with the moments they shared together, but the fear of losing her after Suzanne's wedding, when she would return to Belmonde, made him unhappy.

"I wish you were free. I do not want you to go to Scotland" he said. How ironic that he had made a mistake by going there and now she was about to make the same mistake.

He gently drew her into his careful embrace, where she automatically nestled her head into his shoulder, unafraid of his affection. His arm stretched lazily about her waist.

"I love you" was all he said.

Marie did not need telling, because she already knew both his heart and her own. Yet she dreaded the consequences of actually saying the same fatal words. She did not dare admit her own feelings for the charming François, especially at this moment. She felt the beating of his heart, knew his immense strength and tenderness, saw those soft hazel eyes in his familiar fond face, those handsome features which delighted her whole being.

"How can you be this close and deny the truth?" he asked.

"Don't break my heart, I do not want to know!" she cried before turning from him.

François's heart was already broken; he had never felt like this before. How had he learned to care so much about her? She was unlike any other female he knew. There was something magical about her quietness and composure. The girl had no experience, no way to defend herself. He wanted to protect her, care for her, hold her and desperately love her. He had promised himself not to let this happen, but there had been no stopping it.

"Marie, I care so much it hurts" he said. "You are all that matters to me."

Marie knew he meant every word. His words were honest and alarming, now that he had honoured her with the complete truth. And as a result they made her wretched because of the answers she was compelled to give. She knew the importance of her need to stay resolute and certain of her intentions. Despite her own wishes, she really did have no choice; she was trapped by family honour. The problem was how to convince François when she could not convince herself. How, after falling in love with François, could she ever be happy with anyone else?

"François, you have known from the beginning that I must go to Scotland" she said. "My marriage is arranged, there is no other course. I will not dishonour or disgrace my family by failing in my commitment."

"What about happiness?"

"However much we torture each other, however much as we care for each other, I will go to Scotland to be married."

She was cursed to be in love with the wrong man. In Scotland a husband waited for her, and her only salvation against this miserable situation was the hope that he might be even more charming and handsome than her dear François, and like him, completely attentive to her.

"No one can love you as much as I do" he said.

Marie turned on him, angry and hurt, and scornfully challenged him. "He might put your comprehension of love into the shade by comparison" she said.

François did not believe anything she said, because those soft, wet eyes were unable to look into his. It was his fault she was hurt, he had pushed the matter too hard. He remained calm and patiently waited until he could pull her back into his arms.

Eventually she leaned against him again, her hand lightly on his chest, absently fingering his shirt. She felt his torment, his dejection and his longing.

"Oh, François, what are we doing?" Marie asked sadly.

"Only hurting ourselves, no one else" François admitted.

His arms enfolded her, his face bent to rest on her hair, his lips brushing the shining darkness, while his eyes closed to wipe out everything else. She slipped her arms around his back as he hugged her and buried her face into his shoulder. She was warm, gentle and loving in his arms as they stood wrapped together for what he wished would be an eternity.

"We pretend we are not too fond of each other, we keep our affection held in check. We both know it is an impossible situation, yet we continue to be together. The most I do is hold you, take your hand, smile and look at you. I try to be content, just being with you. For I dare do nothing else. Inside –

"I know" she said sadly.

Her ribs and arms ached where they had held each other so

long, but she would not end this silent moment between them. She felt every movement of his body, every beat of his heart, the sighing of his lungs, the long rhythmic breath he took and the tension in his muscles. She heard him sigh and knew the extent of his self-denial. There were no words left to say. She shivered at the mistake she was making. Only when she was alone would she allow herself to cry, too easily and too frequently, for what she could not have. Then it was safe to think of François and forget all about Scotland.

"Who is this man she is marrying?" François demanded of his sister.

"It is none of your concern" she pointed out defiantly.

"It is if I intend to change her mind."

"Oh, François, you are hopeless!" His sister laughed. Enough was enough. She could not believe he was serious.

"It is an arranged marriage. Their grandfather wanted to preserve his link with the old country."

"So she is to be sacrificed to please his ridiculous sense of loyalty to the past?"

"Sssh, Raoul will hear you."

"Scotland is not a suitable place for her. It is too harsh, she will hate it."

"It is not for you to interfere. You will just have to accept it."

It was not that easy. Why should he accept it? It had not happened yet.

He stomped off to see Pierre, to find a sympathetic ear. Pierre had admired Marie, just like most of the rest of their friends, but unlike François he had always accepted that the most they could do was settle for admiring her from afar. They were pleased enough if they received a smile from her.

"She will soon be gone. There is no point in hurting yourself more." Pierre advised.

François had never meant to fall in love, and he did not know the extent of its real power. He had never experienced the uncompromising, overwhelming effect as it dragged him from the deepest of lows to the highest euphoria. Their time apart did not exist. Whatever else he did was obliterated from his memory. He had never wanted anything or anyone as much as he wanted Marie now. His mind was full of wild ideas of how to keep her here, but none were practical. All he wanted was Marie, nothing else, just a simple life with her at his side.

They could do nothing except repeat their earlier scenes with the same emotions, arguments and useless persuasions.

"Please François, do not make it worse for me than it already is."

"Are you so determined to go to Scotland?" he asked.

"Yes I am" came her quiet reply, every time.

When François realised he was only making her miserable, he decided to fill these days with happiness. His whole purpose was to keep her content and pretend there was no tomorrow. Let each day be another day to be together. Except, nothing was that easy; and things were about to get a lot worse for him.

Jacques had seen them together more than once since his last orders to François on the matter, and he meant to correct this deliberate disobedience as he waited for his son's solitary return to the house. Dragging the startled François from the path, Jacques hurled him to the ground, delivering a severe blow as he landed which caused a dazed François to stagger up, his hand clutching his jaw.

"What was that for?"

Jacques had never been so angry, and he bellowed at him for all the world to hear.

"You know damned well what that is for! For ignoring my instructions. I made it clear these assignations with Marie were to cease. I trusted you. I thought I had your promise."

François straightened up to his full stature, undeterred by the blow, although it had made his face sting. The normal influence this older man held over him, that dutiful parental respect, refused to register.

"I actually made no such promise" François declared defiantly.

"I thought your brother was stupid enough, from you I expected better."

"We are not harming anyone. What is wrong with a few moments shared together?"

Jacques looked at him shrewdly for a moment, before hitting him again across the face. His son offered no resistance and merely smiled in return, his eyes registering only the slightest twitch of defiance. Jacques knew this would not be enough to stop him.

"What is wrong? Marie is my responsibility while she is in my house. The consequences of your actions could ruin her future. I don't want any scandal or gossip ruining her marriage prospects."

"You intend to stop me being with her?"

"You only hurt each other by this nonsense, however innocent it may be. I will have an end to this. For once you will do as you are told. I cannot physically make you behave, therefore there is only one way to prevent you from this folly and that is by your absence. You will remove yourself from the house and grounds instantly. You will not step foot on these premises until the morning of your sister's wedding. I am going to keep an eye on you."

"Banished from my own home?" François mocked.

"Yes. I will see Pierre this very hour and have you stay with him. You need not even collect your belongings, I will have them sent over."

"All this fuss will surely cause speculation" François pointed out.

"I shall tell them the truth. You are an irresponsible influence and better out of the way!" his father stormed at him.

François shrugged, letting him depart, not the least bothered by this new inconvenience. It would make no difference to his plans.

At their next meeting, Marie saw the bruising on his face and automatically went to touch it, only to have François flinch away.

"Does it hurt?" she asked, put out by his rejection of her concern.

"No. It is not that which hurts" came his dispassionate reply.

Marie knew what he referred to, but she refused to pursue that line of conversation because as with many times before, it led nowhere except to sadness.

"Was it Jean-Paul?"

"Do you think I would let him mark me like this?" he scoffed.

"Then who?"

"It does not matter. I am banished to the safe distance of Pierre's residence. Pierre, of all people!" He could not contain his laughter.

"Because of me?"

"No. It was my own fault. I have been truculent and difficult. There is nothing for you to worry your sweet head over. It makes no difference to us."

Pierre was delighted to have his friend share his empty house for whatever reason, expecting a resumption of their old times together, but he was disappointed to find François was not interested in their previous fun. Instead there was little enthusiasm to journey anywhere, and even less conversation from him. François came and went exactly as he pleased without explanation, not that Pierre asked for any. For despite his own suspicions, he knew better than to tackle François. His friend was too smart at changing the subject whenever it suited him, which seemed to be all the time these days.

Somehow their meetings were not curtailed by this latest development. Marie and François snatched every chance to see each other, their fleeting steps dashing to the path by the stream, where their feet slowed to lingering steps as they grasped each other's hand, excited at their accomplishment in being together despite the difficulty. They said very little, simply content to be together, to be close, to lean against each other and hold hands. To feel the comfort and warmth of the other's touch, they blended together, instinctively recognising the other's mood and responding accordingly. They had stopped trying to persuade each other, because it only caused them pain. They put it out of their minds, pretending her departure would never happen.

She cried with joy to be there and would collapse into his arms, while he would wipe away her tears as they trickled down her cheek, tracing her features and caressing her soft skin. He would stroke her dark satin hair, running his fingers through it and twisting the strands as he did so. It was such beautiful hair, belonging to a beautiful prize. François was quite happy just to look at her, because she was his every breath, his every thought. The sight of her gave him life, filled him beyond imagination and gave him an inner glow to his very soul. It satisfied his senses, relaxed the desperate need and gave him a gentle reassurance.

But pretend as they might, they both knew their meetings could not continue forever with the approaching wedding day. Naturally Marie was drawn away by Suzanne to become more and more involved with the arrangements, helpless to refuse and longer and longer apart from François.

With time running out, François was now desperate to see her, desperate enough to risk returning to his home, to watch the house and wait for his chance. The opportunity seemed impossible, and with darkness he left the outcrop of trees to creep slowly forward to the inviting lights. The sound of feminine steps crossing the yard gave him hope, and as the figure entered the buttery he swiftly followed, but as the lamp swung around at his entry François was startled to find it was the wrong person. It was Suzanne who stared at him.

"What are you doing here?" she whispered urgently, frightened in case their father should find him.

"You must go. You will be in terrible trouble!" she insisted, trying to push him on his way.

"Suzanne, please!" he pleaded, grabbing her hand.

She would not listen. Her concern for his departure was her only thought, until he slipped the catch behind him and blocked her own exit, to gain her full attention.

"I must see her. Tell her I am here. Fetch her, please."

How could she? It was not possible. There was no way Marie could slip out unnoticed. She tried to explain, tried to stress the difficulties, all to no avail. He stood unmoved and silent, until she could not stand his pained expression any longer. She could not bear to see the brother she loved most dearly so sad. Although it was madness and wrong, she promised to try. Then she squeezed his arm and was gone.

Marie ran to him and he swept her into his arms, wanting to keep her there forever. They clung desperately together, each unwilling to release the other, savouring the final moments they were able to touch, feel and belong to each other. Their kisses were tender, gentle and lingering.

Too soon she was gone again and François was on his own, alone in the darkness and full of regret. He had said none of the things he had meant to say, and there was so much on his mind which needed to be talked out. Left with mere memories to carry him through the dark hours, he began his walk back to the lodgings he shared. How could he live on memories once she was gone? Such were his thoughts as he trod the track, and so deep was his mood that he scarcely noticed the rain which soaked him or the mud-splashed ground which marked his boots.

His father's horse by the house brought François out of his trance. Damn, he thought, had he been caught out? There was no way of knowing how long his father's horse had been there. Saturated, his very appearance was an instant give away; it would be obvious where he had been. François could think of no convincing or convenient lie, and rather than risk his father's anger with a bluff, he decided to avoid the confrontation altogether. He could not face him in this low state. Retreating into the barn, he shook his wet jacket before throwing it up into the corner of the hay loft and then clambering up after it, relying upon his friend's ingenuity to find some excuse for him until his father had safely gone.

He settled down to wait and was startled when he heard Pierre lead his father into the barn.

"Hey! François. Have you fallen asleep up there? Didn't you hear your father arrive at the house?" he shouted cheerfully.

François sighed thankfully. It was clear his friend had seen his return and in a few words had also indicated his father had not been there long enough to guess the truth.

François yawned loudly and mumbled before making a great show of lazily poking his head through the opening to gaze at them both. Sending down flakes of straw he had ruffled from his hair, he peered sleepily at Jacques and then looked from one to the other, curious of their interruption.

"What — yes! Hello father. Did you want me?" he yawned again.

Jacques looked at the idle horses in the stalls and was satisfied.

"No. Not particularly. I just wanted to know where you were."

"Where else would I be but where you bid me stay?" François mocked.

His father eyed him suspiciously, having been unable to check on him until this late stage in the day because of other commitments. He knew he could not accept his son's word even if he asked it. François could lie convincingly when it suited him, and now, as he looked him straight in the eye, there was not a flicker in his expression to betray any guilt. Although Jacques had not caught François out, there was enough doubt in the back of his mind to worry about this hardened attitude which his son had presented so easily and so often of late. But without evidence, he could not say anything. Nodding his reluctant acceptance of the situation, he left with a few words of parting wisdom.

"You had better stay inside tonight, the weather has turned foul" he grunted.

François threw himself away from the opening and back into the hay, while Pierre anxiously watched Jacques ride off before managing a sigh of relief. As the horse and rider disappeared, François swung down to join his friend and clasped him affectionately around the shoulder.

"You were lucky that time" commented Pierre, giving him a playful clip. Then, picking at the wet clinging shirt on François, he remarked that the hay loft must have been very hot to make him so damp. They both grinned and simultaneously burst into laughter, then made their way to the house.

Despite the brief periods of normality when he allowed himself the luxury of his old humour, François found little enjoyment in the following days, as he was completely deprived of seeing Marie, even at a distance. He tried to fill his hours, to find some diverse amusement, but none could hold his interest or keep his mind occupied. He knew time was running out, and it was already too late to change things. That moment had passed.

Resigned, he sat alone, for he was best left alone in these moods, until his peace was shattered by the unwanted arrival of his brother, heralding even more company in the shape of Gaston and a reluctant Pierre, who had apparently tried to head them off in another direction without success.

Jean-Paul was full of complaints about being bustled out of the way wherever he rested, always in the wrong place, hustled here and there, from room to room. He was glad to be out of it.

"These last few days have been impossible" he said. "The women talk about materials, silks and dresses the whole time. With all their squeals, whispers and giggles you cannot get a sensible conversation from anyone."

"If you are going to moan all day, then go somewhere else" Gaston remarked.

François was in no mood for any reminder of how matters were at home, and as it was his opinion had been voiced by others. They lapsed into silence. They were bored at having failed to find any entertainment elsewhere, and could only content themselves by wasting the rest of the afternoon away lazing in the hot sunshine.

"I wish this wedding was over" commented Jean-Paul.

"You wait until it is your turn. What a nervous bridegroom you will be" joked Gaston, who proceeded to pull up tufts of grass and throw them at Jean-Paul.

"Who would have him?" teased Pierre.

"You were very keen on Marie" taunted Gaston.

François felt himself tense up. If he was goaded enough, he knew Jean-Paul would react badly and there would be no stopping his evil tongue.

"Weren't we all" came Jean's cryptic reply, although the glance between him and François, who had now opened his eyes, spoke volumes.

"Why should she look at any of us?" Pierre sighed.

"Why indeed? She has a castle and an estate in Scotland to look forward to" said Jean- Paul.

François realised only too well the game his brother was playing and steeled himself to control the urge to choke him.

"How can you be so nasty?" interceded Pierre swiftly, hoping to divert trouble.

"That was uncalled for. We all realised she was betrothed when she arrived, however we might have dreamed otherwise" agreed Gaston.

"Grow up Jean-Paul. How could she ever be interested in any of us?" snapped Pierre.

"She only cares for a wealthy future" insisted Jean-Paul.

François could not take much more. How dare he insult Marie? How dare he say these horrid things about her? It was more than jealousy, it was pure spite. But before François could lay a hand on him, Gaston had already dealt with his brother by pushing him into the long grass and attempting to smother him as the only remedy to shut him up.

Whatever Pierre might have guessed about François and his affection for Marie, he had not realised the seriousness of the case until François confided his purpose that evening. It explained such a lot. François, the gallivanting carefree François, was utterly lost and likewise doomed. Pierre had never seen him like this before. He was shocked.

"I have to see her" said François. "I have to try once more."

"It is impossible, tonight of all nights. The wedding is tomorrow. You cannot go there now!"

"I must."

"Give it up! You will only make it worse for Marie as well as yourself."

"Worse? How could anything be worse than this?"

"Why break her heart? She has a new life to go to. Think of her happiness François, not your own."

"It is all I have been trying to do over these last weeks. But I cannot not stop the way I feel about her!" cried François.

"François! It just seems like that now. But you are wrong to pursue this any more."

François did not want logic or reasoning to argue with, and Pierre could do nothing to dissuade him from his latest course of action. He would not heed his friend's warnings as to the risk he took. Finally Pierre shook his head and gave up.

Marie advanced nervously to the shadows where he waited.

"I should not have come" she whispered.

Despite all the difficulties, François had known she would come if she could, just as she had known he would be there. To begin with they could not speak, content to stand together in each other's gentle embrace under the night sky. But for François there was no more time to dream of what might have been' he was in a state of panic. She had given him no encouragement or hope, yet he could not help himself. How could he make her stay? She belonged in France. She belonged with him.

"I want you to stay" he declared, keeping hold of her.

"I know, I know" she whispered as he pulled her to him, determined and strong.

This time she resisted and pushed away, wanting to be free, but eventually she relented enough to rest against his chest, to have him bend close kissing her. She was near to tears as he tilted her chin to look at her once more. She could see the battle within him, understanding that he did not want to let her leave him.

"Your love for me is too much" she said. "It deserves its equal in return, and its equal I cannot give you, must not give you."

She had to end this, to make the final break, to finish with François. She had to put him out of her life, or never know another day's peace.

"You will find someone else. You will."

"For God's sake, Marie!"

He smarted under her words. They were too objective, too clear. He was shocked, and his jaw set heavy with sorrow and his eyelids lowered. He pulled her closer, murmuring her name, his arm trapping her tight, very tight against him. His heart and body told him he needed her, whilst his head thought of her words, of what she wanted, and it was not him. His eyes were distant and dim. His face strained as he bit his lip to curb the awful groan which threatened to confirm his total despair. Time would not stand still, however he wished it. How could he stop tomorrow coming? Tomorrow was the wedding day, tomorrow she would be gone, gone back to Belmonde with the wedding party and then – to a husband in Scotland. There she would be held, kissed and made love to by someone else. She would wake every morning with someone else lying by her side. Turmoil raged within him. There was a lump in his throat, knots in his stomach, a heaviness in his whole body. He could barely breathe. There was nothing he could do – nothing.

Suddenly he put her from him, held her at arm's length and quickly pushed her towards the house. He could not take any more. His eyes were already blurred as he turned his back on it all. Disillusioned and dejected beyond understanding, he strode away from the merry lights, flowers and decorations into the darkness of the night and the coldness of his own mind.

Neither solace nor comfort could be found as François wandered the lanes, unable to consider sleep. The hopelessness and total futility of his love would not be shaken off. Restless and tireless, he walked on, trying to find some consolation, but nothing stirred his senses enough to make his pain any easier.

Finally he returned to Pierre's house, because he could think of nothing else to do with himself. It was very late, and all was quiet and in complete darkness. No one waited up for him here. Pierre stirred, grunted and went back to sleep as his friend came in. François could not find sleep at all. He stared for ages at the ceiling and then at the moonlight from the window. He was tired, sore-eyed, lifeless and dreading the day. How could he just stand there and watch her go? How could he find the urgency or energy to join the hordes of excited friends who would collect at his home today?

Yet as Pierre set out for the celebrations the next day, François found himself silently following. Here amidst all his family and friends, each bursting with exuberance and goodwill, his flagging spirits grew worse. He found no pleasure in their company or the day, although he tried to for his sister's sake. His sweet sister was a radiant bride – that much he was aware of – but the continual whirlwind of activity seemed a haze. The beaming smiles, the tears of joy, congratulations, hugs and kisses and friendly banter drove his brain mad with deafening noise and threatened to crowd out his ability to think properly.

The hours flew and the celebrations were over. Then, before anyone realised it, it was time for the wedding party to leave. François ached for the sight of Marie. This was his last chance to see her beautiful face, her gentle features, his last chance to catch for eternity the bewitching expression he loved. He wished a thousand times this day had never had to come.

There amongst the others, Marie sat silent as people made their parting wishes to them all, until François could stand it no longer. He found himself by her side, unable to speak, haunted and dumbfounded that she would really go. He needed her in his life, in his arms.

"It was never meant to be, François" she whispered.

He shook his head, not in agreement, but in disbelief. His sturdy frame sagged with every prolonged moment of agony within. There was a tightness in his throat, a pain in his head and a heaviness which took hold of every limb of his body. He could do nothing except look at his lost love.

Marie stretched forward to touch the hand, which held her reins so tightly and was startled to feel his skin so cold, almost like ice. He remained like a statue. His strange stillness made her shiver. Then there was no more time between them. He was pushed aside by others bidding their farewells. Lost, he stood back, unable to respond even to her wave as the procession slowly wound its way along the road and out of sight. Even now, with the empty landscape before him, long after all the others had retired back to the house, he stood alone watching the horizon and waited into the dusk, refusing to let go of her.

How could he accept that he would never touch her again, never see her or hear her voice? His life was nothing without her. Surely the world would stop. Nothing made sense.

CHAPTER SIX

In the weeks following Marie's departure, François often rode carelessly, letting his horse wander at will. When it stopped he would slide to the ground to lean dejectedly against his magnificent beast, absently stroking the beautiful dark velvet coat, and when the horse nuzzled him and looked at him with those trusting brown eyes, it was more than he could handle.

Desperately he sought solace in their secret meeting place, the meadow where they had sat and talked, but he found that did not help. The idea of seeing the same seasons return year after year without her there made his head throb. He could not shake off this silent, sombre depression. He had never experienced such intense emotions before.

Evasive of other company, he buried himself in work on the farm as he tried to deal with his frustration. How could he accept this? If only he had managed to change her mind, to stop her, but he had not. His thoughts were still full of her as he ploughed alone one day in the distant fields, but he straightened up as Pierre galloped towards him with unusual speed. His friend had arrived with startling news which had spread from village to village as quickly as it had crossed the channel itself.

"Have you heard? The King is dead!"

"Louis?"

"No, the King of Scotland! There has been a disastrous battle at Flodden with many men lost."

François stared at him. How could it be true? How could he be dead? King James! His mind flashed back to the man he had met only briefly, the voice and the face of the man he had left alive and well, that energetic, dominant personality. A hero of Scotland, James the man, James the King who had loved his country so much it was his life's work. François could not take it in.

Apparently the King had invaded England in late August, and in early September he had led his Scottish armies against the English at Flodden Edge in Northumberland. James had repaid the loyalty of his men, who loved and admired him, by charging with them into the first of the danger, a costly act of heroism. The death of the King, together with members of every prominent family, had created a national disaster.

"They say his body was never found."

Never found, how could that be?

Having once known James, he could not be forgotten, the kindness of his voice, the firmness of his hand. There was no denying he had fallen under the spell of James's personal magnetism. Yet nothing could bring him back, and the very thought of Flodden dwelt heavy in his heart. Convinced he had finished with Scotland, he had given little thought to the King, but now he could think of nothing else. Even Marie was briefly forgotten.

Naturally there was much talk at the meal table, and it was not long before someone asked him if he had ever seen the King. François saw his father raise his head, and, unnoticed by the rest, glance his way.

"Only from a distance, as his party passed me on the road" he lied.

"They say he was the most handsome King in the world."

"Rumours tell he had quite a reputation with the ladies" came another comment.

"I was not there long enough or in the right company to hear that mentioned" said François.

"I thought you were there so long you were staying there permanently" interrupted Jean-Paul, totally bored with the whole conversation.

François somehow managed to force a prudent laugh to offset his own reluctance to debate the matter further, as his family and friend continued to discuss the disaster. Their lively chatter crowded and pushed out his own thoughts, making him anxious for the sanctuary of the outside and his own company.

The memory of James had left its mark. His sadness for the man outweighed any relief he should have felt concerning his own safety. Instead he saw only the loss of a distant friend and one he still could not talk about.

Much as François tried to cope with all his thoughts, Jean-Paul could hardly contain his impatience to antagonize his elder brother. He had no scruples when it came to baiting or hurting François, for he considered him fair game, it was sweet revenge for the past.

"You were never good enough for Marie" he sneered. "The most charming of charmers, yet you couldn't win her over, could you? No wonder, with your reputation. What did you have to offer?"

François snarled at his brother, who enjoyed the response he had provoked.

"Marie never loved you. She proved that when she left."

François could have killed him with his bare hands; there was a blackness in his heart which blotted out all reason. This boy was no brother to him. He felt no bond to justify forgiveness for his behaviour. To make matters worse, Jean-Paul did not have the sense to let the matter drop, constantly reminding him of Marie, just to revel in seeing how far he could push François, how well he could keep his self-control in company and how far he would tolerate the deliberate double meaning and innuendo.

All this resulted in François developing a violent side to his nature where his brother was concerned and using him as an outlet for his anger, so that Jean-Paul began to suffer the full force of François's physical strength. Jean-Paul was getting hurt. He collected cuts and bruises daily as he was brushed aside by a supposed casual blow whenever the mood suited François. Jean-Paul soon found it was no longer fun to test his brother's temper. It was no longer a game, for François meant every blow.

Having brought the trouble on himself by starting the problem, Jean-Paul had no one else to blame, as he had little choice but to retaliate to defend himself, which always ended in a brawl with him on the losing end. After a time he began to avoid François; he had learnt his lesson.

Jacques despaired at the lack of tolerance between them, the hostile moods and the series of incidents which left marks on his youngest son's face. Just as he was considering separating them, the problem solved itself when François announced it would be better if he found work somewhere else for a while. He did not care where, just somewhere else.

Although he was free of the invisible curse of Scotland, his freedom was of no use; it was too late. There was nothing he wanted. Marie was out of reach, gone, and he could not change matters. He could have handled the rejection of any other woman, but not the one he really loved and who had loved him. François could not help himself; the pain of her loss grew worse every day and he could not shake himself free. He was angry at everything and angry at himself for letting it happen. The rest of the world made no allowance for his suffering. The sky, the sun and the moon were still there, day followed day and he resented it for being the same.

He restlessly drifted from place to place; he punished himself endlessly, rode too often in the rain, saturated and chilled, hoping to submit to the rigours of the climate. He dreaded the endless days. He did not want time to think or memories to drive him mad; he had to shake off the remorse eating away at him. He had to exhaust his mind and body, to obliterate and burn out the immense anger which filled him. Fate had dealt its blow with a vengeance, it sent him over the edge of normal reasoning. His spirit ached for relief, anything which would end this phase of his life. To engulf himself in a whole melee of madness, to ruin or save his life, he did not care which.

With the end of 1513 drawing to a close, he went south to toil in the harsh conditions of the stone quarries, his body pushed to the limits, his every limb and muscle complaining, but it was never enough to stop his mind from thinking. Next he tried the sweaty heat of the royal foundry, where he worked every hour until he dropped, day after day, but this also failed to achieve its purpose.

Somehow, in January, he found himself installed at his sister's establishment. What did he expect here? How could Suzanne make any difference to his state of mind? But she greeted him as cheerfully as ever, determined to bring him back to his old self. Here, with no distractions, she meant to heal this weary frame, for who else could gently get close enough to him, to tempt him to confide in her? He had always been her strength and support, picking her up when she fell, cheering her up when she was sad or unwell, and now he needed her quiet softness.

Sweet Suzanne felt so sorry for him and wished matters had turned out better, it was so unfair. None of them had realised the depth of his feelings, his suffering and his unhappiness. She knew her brother well and knew he would always pine for Marie. She doubted he would ever settle for anyone else, that there would be no one else.

"Dear François, you must pull yourself together" she would say.

What was the point? How could he deal with the emptiness in him that Marie had left?

"Do you think she is happy?" he had to ask.

"Oh, François. We all thought you would find someone else. You were never short of female admirers."

"Just tell me she is happy in Scotland, that at least one of us is happy!" he pleaded, hoping that Raoul or his parents might have heard something from her by now. But they had received no communication as yet, her new home was isolated and they had not expected regular contact. And what could she tell him that would make any difference, even if they had? He was tormenting himself.

"I should never have come back from Scotland. I wish I had never have seen her."

"Never have held her in your arms, touched her or loved her? François how can you deny yourself that? How can you wish that? No one can take those special moments away."

She had tried to cheer him and for a while they fell silent, he staring into the wall and she concentrating on her stitching.

"She would hate to think she was responsible for this terrible change in you."

"Stop please. She knew how much I loved her. Did she think I could just forget her that easily and be the same?"

"She would have expected better of you. She would have

wanted you to remember her with a secret smile, a light in your eyes."

"Life doesn't work like that" he muttered.

Here with his sister, he had finally managed to talk about Marie, whereas before he could not tolerate anyone speaking her name.

Suzanne had other solutions to keep him busy; she made him escort her in the gardens, made him drive her to the market and involved him in every normal event, then insisting he help Raoul about the estate. A ploy François soon recognised, but since she was the only female he allowed himself to be manipulated by, it was ungracious of him not to comply with her whims as a reward for her patience over his moods.

Maybe he could get through this after all, he kidded himself. Unfortunately, as soon as he had left and was on his own again, he knew there was no way to wipe out this dreadful ache in his system. At the beginning of February he announced to his friend Pierre his intention to return to Paris for another futile attempt to find a solution to his suffering. Pierre did not want to believe François meant it, remembering all he had complained of last time.

"You are crazy! You abandoned Paris before. You said it was too easy to lose everything in that fickle place."

"I want to lose everything, especially myself in a city full of strangers." "Oh François. Don't go. You know it is a mistake." Pierre sighed, knowing there would be no persuading him. His mind was set.

There was plenty of work to be found on the wharfs, unloading and loading cargoes, to fill his days with demanding hard physical labour. As for his nights, there was an abundance of other activities in the dangerous back streets of the city, where to win favour of one faction was to fall foul of another. Moodily he ignored the outside world, frequenting taverns. Sometimes he sat silent and stared all night into the same drink and then left without taking one sip; other nights he would drink non-stop. When it came to women, at first he avoided them, had no interest, then he would buy them a drink in return for a few hours of their company, to confirm the lack of effect they had on him. Indifferent to their touch or enticing smell, he used them without seeing them, for none of them were of his choosing. He played the fool, the light-hearted fickle romancer, flirted unconvincingly, flattered them and then wickedly ignored them, caring little for the consequences and scarcely noticing their wrath or scorn in return. Although all this was not enough to drive his emotions into oblivion, he carelessly broke many a heart.

Paris was the city he remembered, and in the weeks he wasted there, his wildness allowed little care for his life. He lived and existed by his wits, and more often by sheer luck. He gambled with his life, for besides women and drinking his favourite sport seemed to be fighting. He threw himself into any venture, and his appetite increased with the pursuit of reckless amusement. Brawling and sword play he did not mind, nor who with. Any unfortunate who happened to be in the same place as he soon became the victim of his attention, especially any elegant young buck who considered this country yokel needed to be taught a lesson.

But François played a dangerous game, for he soon fell in with those who could arrange illegal fights for money at secret locations. Opponents were easily found until his reputation dispelled any favourable betting. No matter how he tempted the fates he seemed to have a charmed life, as the danger and risk excited and exhilarated his whole being. It sent the adrenaline pumping in his veins and he never felt more alive than when he was facing deadly steel. The harder the fight, the more skilful the opponent and the nearer the flashing blade to his skin, the better he liked it. There was always the temptation to drop his guard and let the sword bite deep into his flesh, to have an end to his madness. But as many times as he saw the point about to pierce the skin and wanted its touch, at the last second his reflexes would not let him have that satisfaction. He remained unscathed.

One such occasion occurred when François picked on and eventually pushed another reluctant fellow into a contest of skill and strength, much to the landlord's annoyance and the customers' disapproval. François interrupted their peaceful repose as he leapt energetically between the tables, pausing to tantalise and urge his opponent on, angering the man further by his mocked laughter. "Come my fine gentleman. You can do better than that" he said.

Avoiding the stabbing sword which dented the woodwork once more, François sidestepped and ducked around the far side of the beam out of reach. The man was hot, flustered and annoyed at his own inability to curb this tiresome prankster, while François discovered little pleasure at fighting someone who was no match for him. He offered his hand in friendship, but the man would have none of it and pushed him back.

"Stand and fight, damn you." he panted.

François blocked the tired blows as the man refused to quit, until a familiar voice interrupted them.

"Have you nothing better to do?" the voice complained loudly

François grabbed Pierre's arm, glad to see him, and good-humouredly abandoned the fight, thus allowing the stranger, who finally saw little point in continuing a fight he could not win, to depart thankfully back to his own business.

The stranger returned to his master, dishevelled, ruffled and shaken from his ordeal. Rochin did not like his manservant being mishandled by some common ruffian and meant to have recompense, if not in payment for the torn clothing, then certainly in kind. Therefore, with a goodly escort for his purpose Rochin and his men stationed themselves around the tavern the next evening. François entered alone and was duly pointed out, but as the men awaited their signal, their master postponed his original intention. His hand remained on the table. He was interested in François' unusual desire to throw his life away. He might be able to use someone with such an obvious death wish.

Pierre had come to Paris on business, to see lawyers and settle the estate of some distant cousin, hoping the small inheritance would boost the small income his farm provided. His arrival naturally provided François with welcome company at his lodgings, although sadly Pierre's influence did nothing to change François' ways.

In the following days Pierre failed to be amused by his bad behaviour, lost his temper with him and complained bitterly at the way his friend was heading. All to no avail; François continued his antics and a worried Pierre felt that disaster was only a short step away. He did not like the type of people he had mixed with lately. He implored François to leave Paris, even to go home, but his friend took no notice. François continued to roam the streets, despite the fact that the city had lost its previous allure.

At home, Jacques fretted over the extended absence as the weeks changed to months with still no communication from François, until he sadly accepted that this son had no intention of coming home. He wanted him home for his own good and would have gone to Paris himself to drag him back if he could have left the farm at that time. He had no other choice; he had to send Jean-Paul to complete the task for him.

The last thing Jean-Paul wanted to do was chase around Paris for a brother who would resent his appearance and would immediately send him packing. Knowing François of late, he expected an awkward reception and thought their father's message would be ignored. But with his father's dire warning not to return without François, a weary Jean-Paul arrived at the rooms where François lodged, glad to find Pierre there and relieved to find his brother out.

Later, on the way to find his brother's latest favourite haunt, having been warned by Pierre of its dubious nature, he braved himself for the difficult meeting by taking refreshment in several taverns on the way, with the result that after a few hours he began to feel much happier about it. His reception was as expected. François begrudgingly watching his approach and commented sarcastically as to his arrival.

Jean-Paul stared from François to his new friends, who all looked like villains and thieves, and thought how well they deserved each other. Still, it was not his worry, and if François did not care to listen to his message yet, then that too was his problem.

It was much later as they all supped together at the lodgings that Jean managed to relay their father's command, despite the fact that it was obvious that François was annoyed at the nuisance of having his brother staying at the same rooms.

"I cannot return home without you. Those are my instructions" he said.

"Then prepare yourself for a long wait."

"Suit yourself!" Jean-Paul snapped at his brother's attitude.

"Just stay out of my way" François growled.

His only consolation was that once his younger brother had settled into the pleasures of the city, he would see little of him. The assumption proved correct, as Jean-Paul indeed soon found himself a very pretty companion to capture his affection and fill his days.

Rochin had a use for François and sent others to fetch him quietly to him, at their first opportunity, for his offer of employment was not for others to overhear. But on arrival at his rooms, after first ensuring that his friend and his brother were occupied elsewhere, they discovered François was out of the city.

Pierre had been in the street, bringing back some bread, cheese and wine for his own supper, when he noticed men he did not recognise at their door. Naturally cautious, he hung back and waited until they were gone before enquiring from a neighbouring stallholder what they were after. They were trying to find François. It did not bode well. What had François done now? He waited outside for a while longer, but they did not return, Pierre was uneasy; he had to warn François. He knew where to find Jean-Paul – he would be with Louisa – but where was François?

Jean-Paul laughed at Pierre's enquiry, amazed that he even expected him to know anything that his brother did.

"He told me to stay out of his way. Remember?"

Only on his way back did Pierre remember François mentioning something about being out of the city due to a wager he meant to win; typical of François not to give too much detail, either as to where he was or the type of wager involved, had it been simple gambling or something more dangerous? How he wished he could get François to go home.

Louisa was sulking because Jean-Paul had refused to take her to tomorrow night's entertainment in the river gardens. He did not have the money, but he pretended instead that he considered the event most unsuitable for young ladies. Louisa had other ideas, arguing that if the nobility could attend in their thinly-disguised masks and snigger at the performance, she did not see why she could not. It made no difference to his decision; he would not take her, he repeated. No, not for all the tears and pleading she could muster.

Thus outdone over this, Louisa plotted her revenge. Her quick mind and remarkable memory for anything she heard were now put to good use against him. All she had to do was mention François.

"Your brother would not be so prudish. Your brother knows how to enjoy life."

"Louisa, you don't know him. He is no fit company for you, he is no gentleman. Besides, he is too busy destroying himself in one tavern after another."

"Not always" she purred, deliberately smirking and flashing her eyes mischievously at him.

"I have enjoyed his company."

She thought she had won because he scowled furiously at her, but she was mistaken as to his reason.

"You are a wicked minx! I do not believe you."

Louisa hated the look of satisfaction on his face. So he thought he had the better of her, did he? Well, she would shake him yet, but how far dare she go?

"He has dark auburn hair and the most marvellous hazel eyes."

"Maybe he has, that does not prove you were together" Jean-Paul scoffed.

Louisa was determined not to lose face. She intended to make him suffer.

"You cannot tell me where he was last night though, can you?"

"And neither can you" he smiled.

She pouted, thought again and tossed her head confidently.

"Then ask him the next time you see him. See what he says."

"Very clever, Louisa. You know we can hardly be civil to each other. Also that he would never tell me either way, just to annoy me further."

"He may tell you. He has no reason to protect your feelings" she gloated sarcastically.

She smiled gleefully to herself. Although he had tried not to take her jest seriously, she could see there were doubts in his mind and he would brood miserably, until she relented and told him the truth.

François hummed a little tune to himself. It had been a profitable few days in the country and he was delighted to have won his fight and have a few extra coins in his pocket. Through the many archways he strode, his jacket slung casually over his shoulder, his steps steady and athletically paced, fearless in the gloom of night.

When the assassin struck from behind, the impact of the knife slashing into his back sent François reeling to the ground. The thrust had been deep and hard and he lay crumpled in crippling pain, in surprise and disbelief. Meanwhile his attacker, who spoke no words, made no other move to finish him off and seemed out of breath.

"Finish what you intended" François gasped at his attacker.

But whoever the man was, it seemed he could not; he could not take one step nearer to complete the task, despite his victim's complete vulnerability. There were no last fatal stabbing thrusts delivered. Finally, throwing the knife aside, the fellow ran off into the night.

Confused, François lay on the cold cobbles waiting for the intensifying pain to ease, trying to convince himself that movement was bearable. He could not lie here like this forever, waiting for someone else to find the knife and finish him off. Such weapons could not be carelessly left around for someone else to commit another crime. He had no idea where the knife had been thrown, but he must find it. He lifted his head and pushed himself to rest on his arm, gritting his teeth against the fire which tore across his back. Courage, he told himself, as he slowly turned his body in order to look around. Eventually he saw it and he clawed his way forward, his fingers scratching in the dirt until he had it safe in his hand.

With his jacket a fingertip away, he pulled it towards him and placed the knife inside the garment and rolled it up. Then he rested, for the pain was taking over his senses. He was aware he was beginning to feel shaky, and he needed to lean against something solid, to sit up before hauling himself to his feet. If he could stand, he could walk, he told himself. He must get his legs to work. He must reach the lodgings and Pierre. So, clutching his jacket tightly, he staggered forward, from one supportive structure to another, often having to pause and rest. He did not see too clearly and his back was sticky, hot and sore where the blood-soaked jerkin stuck to his skin. He knew he was losing blood fast, but dared not stop, dared not slow, for he made an easy target for any other predator who roamed the streets. Yet stop he had to, when the company of guards which made up the night patrol came by, forcing him to hide in a recess. He could not afford to be found by them either; they would ask too many questions, questions which François could not afford to answer.

Weakened, he stumbled on after they had passed, somehow making his way through the streets to those wooden stairs he would normally have leapt so effortlessly. Now they seemed impossible to climb. With the last once of energy, he dragged himself, hand over hand, up the handrail to the door.

Pierre was horrified at the sight of François, and unable to contain his questions despite François being too weak to answer. Pierre carefully helped him remove his jerkin before setting about peeling his saturated shirt from his back. He did not notice the already discarded jacket kicked out of sight. There was blood everywhere, and as Pierre struggled to stem the flow, it drenched the cloths he used, covering his hands and staining the water, causing Pierre to despair as all his efforts had no effect. Where on earth was Jean-Paul when he needed him? He could have sent him for the surgeon whilst he had been tending to this.

"It's no good" he said. "You need sewing up. I shall have to leave you to find a physician. For God's sake, don't move about."

François wasn't about to rush around. His only exertion, the moment his friend had left to dash off into the night, was to remove the knife to a safer hiding place. After that François lay listless and still, resting as his past experiences had taught him. Taking slow shallow breaths, he waited for the return of help.

The physician asked no questions of them, but swiftly completed his work of stitching up the wound and was gone. The payment of François's extra coins was enough to end any curiosity.

The next morning Pierre sent a message to Louisa for Jean-Paul to come to the lodgings urgently, but he waited in vain. With no response to his request, Pierre cursed the boy. Did he think he would have sent such a message for no reason? Where was the damn boy?

François was restless, hot, clammy and sweating, indicating a setback in his recovery which caused Pierre to seek further medicine. He returned from the apothecary concealing another potion, besides the ointment he had acquired for treating the infected wounds. Pierre had a game of his own to play, although it meant abusing his friend's trust and tricking him into drinking the potion, so it was something he could get away with only once. When Pierre offered him the draught François pulled a face at the taste, but he drank it down because Pierre insisted it was medicine. Then he slept, deeply and soundly enough for Pierre to safely leave him.

"I had better find Jean-Paul" Pierre sighed.

Jean-Paul was with Louisa as usual when Pierre found him. He grabbed him dramatically by the shoulders.

"Where have you been? Why did you ignore the messages I sent? François is in a serious condition. You had better come at once."

"Did he ask for me?" the youngster asked coyly, reluctant to move.

"He is not in any condition to ask for anyone!" Pierre snapped. He was furious at Jean-Paul's total lack of concern and yanked him to his feet, then pushed him unceremoniously to the door.

Jean-Paul had been agitated for days, dreading this visit, despite his attempt to pretend otherwise. He glared at Pierre, but was forced to accompany him for the sake of appearances. If only he had some idea what awaited him.

He soon found out. François lay very still, almost too still in the flickering light. Jean-Paul was pushed forward into the room and then pushed forward again, closer to his brother. Jean-Paul was afraid. Pierre gave him no time to recover from the shock of seeing François's condition.

"He has taken a turn for the worse" Pierre commented. He was been incensed by the way Jean-Paul had reacted to the news and he meant to make this callous youth more dutiful to his brother.

"You will have to stay and watch over him" Pierre insisted.

Jean-Paul gulped and wanted to leave, but Pierre was having none of it. Pierre merely raised an eyebrow. Jean-Paul would care; he would be made to care.

"I have been days tending to him and I have legal matters to attend to which cannot wait any longer" said Pierre. In between his appointments he made sure Jean-Paul was kept busy, making him fetch and carry, keeping a constant supply of the wood for the fire and water from the pump. That was the least he could do, Pierre had decided.

Jean-Paul hated being there, hated looking at the still figure of his brother. He could not believe he had been responsible for this. This was all Louisa's fault. If only she had not made him so jealous, not tormented him into believing that she had after all accompanied his brother to the riverside gardens. She had taunted him with his brother's reputation, and had made too much of their evening together. Was her joke not a joke — only a joke on him? The more he had brooded about it, the more convinced he became that they had been together.

Again he had hated François, for all his charmed life, his adventures, his easy skills. He had hated the thought that François had been with Louisa, and he had hated her taunting so much that he had stalked and attacked his own brother. He had slashed out with such force that it left him breathless. Then, looking down at his brother's crumpled body, he could not finish the job. Suddenly he had felt sick and with the bloody knife in his hand, he had realised the awful thing he had done. But there was no undoing the terrible crime. He had run away, carelessly tossing the knife from his sight and trying to forget the image he had left on the ground.

All too soon Pierre's game was over and François regained consciousness without any ill effects. Indeed his fever had gone, and the only discomfort, as expected was a stiff neck and tight back. He was surprised at his brother's presence there and could not fail to question it, although Jean-Paul seemed reluctant to speak at all. François surveyed him placidly, without a hint of sarcasm or recrimination.

"What have I done to upset you this time?" François sighed.

"Louisa." He could not help himself, he had to blurt it out.

François shrugged, waiting for clarification.

"Don't pretend you don't know. She told me. She confessed."

"Confessed to what? I don't know the girl. Heavens, she certainly has your measure if she can twist you around her finger and make you jealous as easily as that."

Jean-Paul went silent, unwilling and unable to believe he had been so easily duped by Louisa. Although since that night she had not taunted him with reference to either François or the riverside entertainment. And he had not asked her anything, out of pique, not wanting to know how much she had enjoyed herself. He had readily believed her, because of his natural instinct to believe the worst of his brother, a characteristic she was too certainly aware of. But had it been mischief on her part to make him jealous? What if she had tricked him? Then that was even worse, because her words, her lies, had almost made him kill his brother. He had committed a terrible act and he was ashamed. Not that he was about to confess it to anyone, especially the victim.

François was philosophical about his life. Let fate take his hand and lead it where it may, he had no say in the matter. The wound turned out to be nothing more than an inconvenience which slowed him down. He had not cared that Jean had attacked him, because it could have been one of so many others who held a grudge against his recent antagonistic stupidity. He felt no anger. It was his own fault, no doubt, for he had not been kind to his brother of late and he felt no need to rebuke or threaten him. He was content to let it pass without acknowledging to Jean-Paul that he knew. The knife had been removed from the scene. There was no need for anyone to know.

Ever since Rochin had first glimpsed the wild-eyed, unshaven, unkempt François, he had instigated his own discreet investigation about this youth and found his task was made easy by the simple trust of honest country people. Rochin grinned that sly grin; no prick of conscience troubled his dealings. Methodically they checked his irregular pattern of behaviour, and wherever he had gone he had been followed. Therefore the cause of his disappearance from the streets had not puzzled them long. They knew where he lay, the physician, the apothecary, those who attended him and his progress as the days passed.

Jean-Paul found it increasingly hard to talk to his brother. He kept his gaze to the floor and his voice stubbornly silent.

"Go home Jean, you must go home" François insisted, grabbing his wrist. "You do not need to stay for my sake. I do not need watching over or nursing any longer."

"Pierre thinks otherwise."

François looked at his downcast expression, accepting that Pierre had indeed pressed him into staying against his will.

"It does not matter what Pierre thinks. Our father will need help on the farm at this time of year. He will be pleased to see you. Better one son at home than none. Today would be a good day to set off" François encouraged him.

It did not take long for Jean-Paul to consider his brother's suggestion, and he began collecting his belongings. Then he paused.

"Father wanted you home most of all. He will not be pleased if I return alone."

"What good am I in this state? Tell him I will return soon."

There were moments like this when Jean recognised that there was no real animosity between them, and he regretted having hated his brother and was truly sorry for what he had done. He wanted to confess, to own up; he owed François that, however difficult it was. He fidgeted about the room, glancing at his brother indecisively, then out of the window and then back at François. He was annoyed with his own inadequacy with words.

François slowly recognised what was bothering him and wanted Jean-Paul safely out of the city and on his way home, as soon as possible. He did not want anyone knowing.

"Finish packing" François insisted, waving him away.

His brother smiled gratefully. He did not need telling twice. He was glad to go and glad to put off his declaration, for indeed he would rather leave it until a better time altogether.

In the days after his brother's departure, François felt better in himself. Maybe this jolt of reality had been just what he needed. He began to think of home, the house, and how selfish he had been to his family. He had wallowed in self-pity too long. He had been of no use to anyone; he had failed his brother and almost ruined his friendship with Pierre. Loyal Pierre! He deeply regretted the anguish he had caused his friend. Maybe he should go home, work on the farm and then – what? He should not think of the 'what'.

Later as François lay resting, Pierre could not help returning to the question of who might have attacked his friend. Having informed François previously about the men in the street asking about him, he wondered if they might have been responsible.

"No, it was more likely a past opponent wanting revenge."

"Aren't you bothered about them, worried about who they were?"

"No" answered François with conviction.

Pierre let the matter drop for the moment, assuming that it was because of his wounds that François had no interest in much else. He certainly had no interest in trying to guess who was responsible. Nor could he come up with a reason why the attacker had run off without stealing his friend's money.

"Do you know who attacked you?" Pierre had asked again sometime later.

"Some jealous lover, I expect."

Pierre was shocked not only at his reply, but the casualness François showed, as if it did not matter. François showed no anger, no sense of wanting justice or revenge.

"I cannot blame whoever it was. I asked for it. It was almost a death wish. I had to get Marie out of my system. I tried everything to forget her. I deserved the attack, I wanted an end, the darkness to end it all."

"In that case, why did you crawl back here after you were attacked? Why not just lie there and die?"

A very good question, one he would not answer to anyone without betraying his brother. He had done it for no other reason except to save his brother from the blame, to protect him by finding and hiding the knife. He could not let even his best friend know who was responsible.

Pierre watched him, thinking, waiting for an answer. Suddenly the penny dropped.

"You know your assassin!" he exclaimed. "That was why it was so important. Oh François, you have always known! It was your brother! Say it!" Pierre ordered.

François remained expressionless. Never. Not to a living soul, he promised himself silently.

Although François refused to confirm or deny Pierre's suspicions, Pierre was shocked at his own conclusions. He hated the idea that Jean-Paul had tried to kill François. Pierre wanted his friend returned to normal health, to sanity, to be the François he knew. Although he acknowledged that this instinct to protect his brother since the attack proved at least that François was thinking logically. Maybe he was cured.

No sooner had Jean-Paul arrived home and reluctantly made the excuse that François was too injured to return home yet than his father set out to collect him, especially after reading the letter Pierre had sent with Jean-Paul. He arrived to be greeted by a tired Pierre and a son who looked pale, weak and very shaky on his feet. He was horrified.

"François you are ill. Look at you. One puff of wind and you would fall over."

Unable to argue, François sat down and leaned back against the wall for support.

"I have a chill" he muttered.

"Rubbish. You had a fever. I also understand you were injured recently."

François knew Pierre was responsible for his father's arrival, guessing he must have sent a letter back with Jean-Paul, because he had already made his brother promise not to tell his parents too much, a promise he knew he would have kept. He understood why Pierre had been frightened for him, frightened of his apathy and of his remaining in the city.

"It was nothing. I hurt my back, I fell and cut it. Nothing more."

"I remember you saying that once before, of another injury" Jacques reminded him forcefully.

Pierre also remembered the faded long scar on François which he had only recently discovered, whilst tending to his other wound. Scotland had a lot to answer for, in his opinion, Pierre concluded before imploring Jacques to take him home without delay. He did not trust François alone in this city. There had already been several requests for him to contact people who had certain unspecified propositions for him. He did not want François drawn back into fighting again.

"I want you home, where I can keep an eye on you" his father demanded.

"No. Not yet" François pleaded. He needed more time to adjust, to pull himself together. Most of all, time to ride out into the country and bury that knife, without anyone knowing.

"I sent your brother to bring you home."

"Father, when did I ever take any notice of him? I always please myself. I am a bad example, I invite trouble and am not worth the effort."

"So if you know your own faults, at least you can correct them."

François nodded and promised to come home soon, which seemed to satisfy both his father and Pierre.

"I admit, I would rather your mother did not see you in this condition. Once you are stronger…"

François repeated his promise, refusing to be fussed over any more.

Pierre had left to get back to his own farm, leaving François to reflect on his own stupidity over Marie. He felt strangely calm. At last he had shaken off his overwhelming misery and regret. He was cured of his madness and bored with Paris; he knew it was time to leave.

Summer was coming and François looked forward to going home, to being at peace with himself. He would even renew his tentative friendship with Colette. He smiled to himself, for she had the ability to please him and it had been a long time since they had shared an evening together. He hoped she had missed him too much to reproach him about Marie. She knew better than to remind him or drive him away by any signs of jealousy. He was content to renew their old, undemanding relationship without having to make excuses for the past.

Thus, with his thoughts in a brighter mood, he completed his task of disposing of the knife and headed back towards the city. Passing through one of the marketplaces, he took little notice of the people, until a stranger spoke to him directly.

"Ah, monsieur. I must take this opportunity to thank you."

François was taken aback by the man's familiarity as he was shaken warmly by the hand, for surely this man had made some mistake, yet the man seemed in no doubt as to his identity.

"Forgive me sir. I am at some disadvantage" explained François.

The man slapped him on the shoulder, understanding his bewilderment and asked his forgiveness instead, explaining that François had indirectly been of great service.

"Having placed a large wager on your duel at Migsalle, I am now much wealthier" he explained.

François eyed him sceptically, for there were few who had been party to that event; it had been illegal and held at a secret location. Not even Pierre had known of the cause for his absence from the city for those few days. He had never spoken of it to anyone, so to find someone who had specifically sought him out on such an excuse was suspicious.

Shaking his hand again, the man made to leave, and then changed his mind and offered to provide a fine meal at the tavern as a reward. Although nothing seemed more natural than to be sidetracked on a whim, François made his profound apologies. This time his brain was working and his instincts were back in control. Common sense told him that the sooner he reached Paris and his lodgings, collected his belongings and headed for home, the better.

CHAPTER SEVEN

In the dark of night François was forcibly dragged off the streets of Paris and bundled into a coach, where he was disarmed, bound and held down on the floor of the coach as it began its journey. Unable to shake off his assailants' grip, despite all his determined efforts he remained face down on the hard floor. He demanded an explanation. Who were they? Where were they going? His questions were answered only by more blows, each harder than the last. They were enjoying this, a winded, groaning François realized. He had assumed that his recent brawling antics had led to this arrest, and he could only await arrival at some ramshackle prison, where he would hear his punishment. The idea of a spell in prison did not greatly worry him; it would only delay his return home a little longer. However, by dawn he was still lying uncomfortably on the floor of the carriage as it slowed.

As François was hauled out of the coach he found himself in front of an impressive country mansion. The men smirked at his ignorance and efficiently ushered him up the steps and inside. As he was being dragged along the magnificent corridors by these ugly men, an astute François had no doubt that this was more serious than he first imagined. Was this someone's revenge for one of his recent more irresponsible fights?

Rochin had waited patiently to see François close up again and had not been too pleased by the delay caused by the attack in Paris. Rochin had set his agents to work, both in Paris and in the outskirts, whilst keeping a low profile himself. He knew the character of men and made the best use of them. He appreciated that he would need to calm and control this one if he was to be bent into his service. Rochin had discovered the one perfect mission for which François was made and he meant to use him for this important matter, whatever it took.

Rochin moved through France unobtrusively and effectively, an undistinguished figure. He served only one master, whilst being the master of many men. As an emissary of the Duke of Albany, the merest whisper of his name would have ruined all their plans. Demure and patient when necessary, he was also devious and unscrupulous. His methods went unchallenged in the performance of his task.

"Like a lamb to the slaughter" muttered Rochin to himself.

François was shown into a large room, where he saw a man sitting at a desk. The man instructed that the bindings be cut from the prisoner's arms, and for a moment François stood free of his escorts' restraining clutches. The sun shone outside the window, the place was beautiful and this was French soil, so why was he nervous? Why did he suddenly shiver?

His answer came when a large door opened at the other end of room and a nobleman entered to join them.

If François had not been cured of his earlier madness of the past few months, then this moment would have achieved the same result. This moment, this place and this complete stranger, whose features were too familiar, haunted his very soul and caused his whole body to drain of energy. His heart almost stopped. A lead weight rooted him to the spot, a chill shot down his spine and darted out to every nerve and fiber in his body. He knew he was done for. His whole skin went cold and his heart cried out – No, no, not again, not again. He had never seen this man before, knew not his name or rank, yet François needed no title or introduction to know him as another royal personage – another royal Stuart.

"Well – you have been obstinate in the extreme ignoring the numerous invitations I sent you" the man behind the desk began.

François did not answer and the man thumped the desk with a heavy paperweight to gain his attention. Had François looked too long at the stranger, shown too much interest already, to be his undoing? He must find something else to concentrate on.

"You were not even curious about the regularity of my communications?" the man facing him commented.

François shrugged. The letters and notes had meant nothing except another minor interruption to the oblivion he had sought. Nothing had seemed important. He had been on a mission of self-destruction. Why should he have cared what this man had wanted with him, whoever he was?

"I am a worthless nobody. I see no reason why I am even here" said François. "I was quite content to be wasting my life as and where I will."

"I think not. That would be a waste!"

"My lord, I am no use to you."

"But you have many talents."

"Me?"

François swallowed hard, knowing he would need to keep all his wits about him to survive this encounter and wondering how he could get out of this situation intact. Whatever this man wanted from him, he did not really want to know, he did not want to hear. What could he do to avoid the inevitable? He could see the danger, but not the solution to it.

"The manner in which I was brought here, to be dragged off the streets and forced to come here, is a strange way of offering anyone respectable employment."

The man sat back in his chair and laughed to himself. "Oh poor François."

It was not the man who had forcibly summoned him here who concerned François, but this second man who continued to stand silent for the moment, taking no part in the proceedings. His very presence here was ominous, and François knew deep down that this could only end one way. His heart beat faster. The intense scrutiny of this noble stranger confirmed the devious intention of these men. His throat dried as he tried to speak.

"I suspect, gentlemen, that the work you propose will not be to my liking, and I would rather remain ignorant of it."

"Do you think we would have gone to so much trouble to have you reject our offer?" Rochin sneered.

François remained silent.

"Your silence does you no favour. It merely conveys that you do not trust yourself to speak."

How right they were. He had to be careful.

"I believe you are well travelled. That you have been to Scotland" the man continued.

So here it was – finally they mentioned Scotland! And whatever he said would be wrong. To pass it off as if it meant little would confirm their information, yet to deny it would involve him in a series of lies, and he would eventually be caught out.

"I do not know who would have told you that" François offered instead. He tried to sound bored and tired, attempting to stay calm because he knew full well what was coming next.

Rochin stared at him afresh, searching for something in his expression, something which would give a clue to the past. There was nothing. However he wished to move on with the proceedings and stood up, nodding towards the nobleman.

"May I present my lord the Duke of Albany, Knight of St Michael and Admiral of France."

Admiral of France he might be, but there was still the distinctive resemblance to his own features. François shook inside, but he still managed to bow with some dignity at the introduction to the prominent statesman, although every nerve in his body told him not to betray his recognition. Nothing good would come of this. His mind raced with the alternatives of escape.

"The means and the method were necessary to ensure the complete secrecy and confidentiality of our meeting. Such was vital, since talk with you I must" the Duke stated. He was well satisfied to see how closely this man resembled his cousin James, the late King of Scotland. This was their candidate, and his personal solution to the demands he received from Scotland. This man could accomplish their objective easily.

"You can be of great service to me" said the Duke.

François knew in his heart where this was leading, although he could not see why. He knew the ways of nobility, he had observed them in Paris, experienced others in Scotland. They were ruthless, cunning and cruel, and none of them could be trusted, not even this Duke.

"I have already abandoned my foolishness with the sword" said François. "I am no villain or cutthroat either."

"Why do you assume the worst? You are too suspicious of us."

"It is exactly because you avoid telling me the nature of the task you propose for me that I know it is not simple or straightforward. The careful way you have contrived my presence here is proof enough."

"Your brain is sharp."

Not sharp enough to prevent the situation he now found himself in. There was no escape from these unpleasant discussions and ahead lay a battle of wits for which he feared he was unprepared. Their meticulous planning indicated the worst. He knew it led to disaster. These people were too clever. He dreaded every word that followed.

He wondered just how much these men truly knew, for they gave no indication of the extent of their knowledge and he in return meant to give no conformation on any point. He had been so very stupid to believe everything was over, forgotten and settled with James' death. They had not referred to any connection with Scotland – yet. Dare he hope?

"I would make a poor servant" laughed François as convincingly as possible, continuing his pretence of total ignorance. How could he convince these men that he would not do their bidding, when they were equally determined that he should?

Rochin interrupted, for it was imperative that François understand the authority he faced. He disliked the game of words between him and the Duke, which was getting nowhere, although his master seemed to be enjoying it.

"My lord, with respect. I think you are being too subtle for our guest. I think he would appreciate a more direct explanation concerning what we expect of him."

"Indeed."

"The simplicity of it is, François, that you have a likeness to the Duke which could be useful."

"Wait! What are you saying? You are mistaken."

"François, your every action proves our choice is correct. You hold yourself in reserve, you refuse to offer either opinion or information, deciding carefully the words you give and therefore concealing your true self from us."

They had seen enough to condemn him. How had he managed to fall into this trap? Too easily, François scolded himself. He had thrown his life away recently as he deliberately courted danger. He had ceased to care, yet he had found no satisfaction in the chaos, fights or drinking of late. His own useless stupidity had brought him to their attention and this futile situation.

"You misjudge my character. I am a poor choice."

"Nevertheless, you are the only person who suits us."

"And I beg to refuse, before I learn too much."

There was no way he was going back to Scotland, not for anything, never. They had not mentioned it yet, but he knew it was there, in the tense silence, in the glance between these two men.

"I believe our guest is too well aware of the danger he is in" said the Duke. He smiled again, confident that they had found a careful man for this venture.

François suddenly realised that he need no longer be frightened, because he had overlooked the most important and significant fact. They needed him living and breathing. No one else could take his place. Whatever it was, without him their plot must fail; he was no use dead. That was his only weapon.

"I wish to leave, gentlemen. Your attention and this place are not to my liking. To detain me will gain you nothing. Even if it is at the request of nobility." he faced them both unflinchingly, his words deliberately provoking.

"You could be punished for such impudence!" snapped the Duke, with anger on his face.

"In normal circumstances, maybe, but not when you have been to such lengths to tell me how important I am to you."

The Duke stopped short. He had tried to weigh François up earlier and had failed. This man was not as he had expected. The youth mystified him. He had scrutinised every gesture of reaction, or in this case the lack of reaction, as their meeting had progressed. François puzzled him; he was too guarded, too careful of his words and often seemed to play safe by not speaking at all. There was something he kept from them, something which bothered him, because he could not imagine what it could be. He had shown no curiosity about his likeness to himself. What did he know? What had happened in Scotland?

The Duke retired to the far side of the room and left it to Rochin to handle the stubborn François. If they failed to encourage him to volunteer, they would have to force him.

"You will act for us. You have no choice in the matter." Rochin instructed.

"I think I do."

"You really have no idea of the predicament you are in. You think you can refuse?"

François frowned. He could not think what was coming next.

Rochin had waited to play his hand. He would change François' mind, he only needed a few words to influence their unwilling hero. His approach was much more direct. He produced a piece of mutilated material, François' own bloodstained shirt, and flung it dramatically at him.

"Yours, I believe. Someone tried to murder you in Paris. I have a report from the physician who attended you."

François made no to attempt to answer or even look at the material which lay on the floor before him.

Rochin then jangled a few coins in his hand before tossing them across the table, although François did not immediately understand their significance.

"The physician has since been paid in gold, so he does not need your coins."

François made no attempt to pick them up.

Then Rochin showed his final piece of evidence – Jean-Paul's knife. François was shocked. He had been absolutely sure he had hidden it where it could never be found. He had taken such great pains to conceal it. Now it was in the wrong hands. Had someone followed him?

"The very weapon used in the attack."

"Really? It could belong to anyone" François pointed out, refusing to acknowledge it.

"We have the knife. Someone will identify it as the one your brother owned. If necessary they will also swear they saw the attack, even if they were not there. Do you understand?"

François was silent. He was worried about where Jean-Paul was at this moment. Was he safe?

"The guilty will be brought to justice, even if the victim does not wish it. I can have your brother arrested any time I wish and witnesses can always be provided. I am just explaining the alternative if you do not co-operate."

François felt physically sick. He now fully understood the lengths these people would go to. Who would be next, and where would they stop? They would harm anyone to make him agree. What could he do? Little except curse them.

He stared at the knife on the desk in front of him, the sharp blade so close and the solution so crystal clear. Dead he was no use to them, dead there was no blackmail, no suffering and no threats to his family. So swift a death, his only escape and the only way out. It was an easy decision, there was no reasoning against it, all he needed was the determination and the speed before sanity or fear changed his mind.

But François had stared at the inviting blade too long, for Rochin, reading his intention, knocked it from his grasp the instant

François' hand had reached it. Rochin had not gone to all this trouble to be beaten by the idiot taking his own life now. The knife slid harmlessly across the floor out of the way.

Albany did not blame François; he even felt sorry for him. The youth had a certain kind of courage within his impulsive frame, but alas, it was a courage which would be wasted. He sighed, for it was best to forget such unpleasantness.

Rochin had François held while he composed himself and regained his breath. His eyes narrowed towards this still struggling figure who showed no sign of giving in to these men. He was full of fight, intent on doing something deliberately foolish to force them to kill him. Rochin could see it in his eyes, read it in his expression. He refused to respect him for his clear-headed resolve. This would not do. He cursed François for his attempt to defeat them, promising revenge if he should attempt that course again.

"Know this François, the sweet success of killing yourself will not help your brother. You will not cheat us. Let me clarify the position. It can be arranged that your dear brother could be arrested at any minute for his attack on you. He could be conscripted into the army and sent to fight in the War of the Holy League, to enjoy the prospect of certain death."

Rochin paused deliberately to allow his words to sink in before continuing.

"If that will not persuade you, let me add that your family could find themselves homeless and without money. Their title to their land could so easily be taken away. All this I promise you, if you dare to take your own life."

François was worn out. He was beaten, his energy sapped. His upright figure sagged visibly as he slumped forward to lean against a chair. François had lost the battle, not only with them but with himself. His despair was overwhelming, because he knew they had won. He could not forgive himself if he was responsible for any harm coming to his family or friends and he cursed his shameful luck. It was a simple choice between his agreement or the lives of his whole family. Rochin had his answer.

"Now you see the truth as it is. However unwilling, you will comply with our wishes. Do not doubt that."

"What do you expect of me?" François asked, dreading the answer.

"To go to Scotland."

The words pounded his brain. Deep down he had known, the moment he had seen the Duke, that it had to be Scotland, the last place on earth he ever wished to see again. The dark memories, the fearful shadows and the danger. These memories obliterated all else about him. He stood enveloped in another time, in that other place where an old woman's warning voice pounded his confused brain. To return meant fresh suffering and certain death; it haunted and frightened him. He could not be rational about death, even though he had wanted it so recently – that death was a different death to the one which now awaited him. Regret, sorrow and blind fear took over. He could not move, only shake from head to toe. He had promised James he would never return. He had wanted to keep that promise.

"How can I survive in Scotland?"

Albany suddenly realised that François knew, knew more than they did. It was obvious that he was no ignorant innocent. How could he have been to Scotland and not known? He possibly knew too well that he resembled the late King. He already knew the danger because he had suffered from it before. He had courted the worst and had by some miracle survived to be here now. Yes, he knew the enemies he faced there and would be more careful. The youth was worth his weight in gold.

"Why should you expect me to go to that barbaric country? You may as well kill me now. It will not be your life at risk, not you who will suffer if caught. Why does it have to be me? I am no good at secrets and intrigue."

Albany smiled. There was no one better at keeping secrets, because he suspected François kept a very important one from them. One which would never be spoken of.

The Duke fully understood his reluctance to go; he had felt the same when he had been asked to leave his own beloved home in France. Albany was French by upbringing, a knight of St Michael and an Admiral of France, married to the beautiful Anne de la Tour and on excellent terms with the French court. He had been perfectly content with his life until the messenger from Scotland had arrived. As a cousin to the late King James, the pro-French Scottish nobles had secretly offered him the regency of Scotland because they considered the Queen weak and liable to bring up the young prince to the benefit of the pro-English and England itself. Albany had wanted no involvement, having tried to live down his own father's infamous reputation in the affairs of that country all his life. The last thing Albany wanted was the power or the position these troublesome Scots offered.

Thus unsure of the true feeling and situation in Scotland, he had made his excuses and sent his friend Anthony d'Arcy de la Bastie as his deputy. It had solved nothing, for the Scottish council continued to communicate, each time more urgently requesting his acceptance of their proposals. The council considered Margaret unstable and unpopular, and the cause of constant power struggles between the nobles. It was reported that during the late stages of her pregnancy and the birth of the King's posthumous son, Alexander Duke of Ross, in April, it had been increasingly difficult for Queen Margaret to maintain political control. Forced to rely on the traditionally pro-English house of Douglas for support, Margaret was now infatuated with young Angus of that family, which caused further concern amongst her nobles. Fearing the rise of that family to such a powerful position, where they would control the young king through his mother, the most powerful members of the council now favoured the Duke of Albany to replace her as Regent.

Still Albany did not wish to go. His lovely wife was ill and he could not, would not, leave her. Again he received reports; Margaret intended marriage and he was needed more than ever. Having delayed his departure several times, he knew that sooner or later he would have to go to Scotland; it was inevitable. He had struggled with a solution and thanks to Rochin, he had been handed François – a gift from the gods, a gift to be used.

Dismissing the others from the room, the Duke and Rochin unveiled their weak and desperate plan to François. The basis of their idea had come from a ruse the Queen herself had used prior to the battle of Flodden, to deter James from going to war. She had sent a servant to appear as a supernatural vision at the Abbey Church of St Michael where the King and his ministers were praying for a successful venture. But this and the mysterious voice at Markets Cross had failed to persuade the King to change his mind. After the battle of Flodden it was known that the Queen had suffered many bad dreams about James and it was this they intended to play on, to prevent her marrying the Earl of Angus. Yet knowing she would not be so easily tricked herself after attempting a similar stunt, the ghost they presented must be no vague shadow; only an undisputed replica of James could succeed.

They went on to explain that this haunting could work because it would exploit the belief by his subjects that because his body had never been found, the King had survived to escape the battlefield.

This belief was further substantiated by claims of spasmodic sightings of their beloved King by people in various parts of the land.

Sightings? François wondered how much gold it had cost and who had paid it, but the question, like so many others, remained silent in his head.

"Because of your resemblance to the Duke here and the late King, your presence alone can influence the Queen" Rochin went on. "Your face is the key factor. Your mission is to persuade her against the mistake of an alliance with Angus which could ruin so much the King had worked for."

"My friend De la Bastie is already at the Scottish Court and watches the climate closely. You will join him, be under his guidance and follow his instructions" added the Duke.

They made it sound so easy, but François was not vain or stupid enough to think he could influence a queen, even if he could reach her unseen. How did they expect him to achieve any of this, he wanted to ask, but he knew better than to waste his time. And what of the people who had seen him before, those who would remember him and know he was not James? They would hunt him down again. He had learnt the dark side of men in that foreign country. He was not the same person as that reckless carefree youth who had gone on the earlier adventure. Too much had happened. Death was easier, preferable.

Their words drifted over his head. He knew they would not take any notice of his fears or arguments; they had made up their minds. There was nothing he could do to change what they had in store for him. François resented their willingness to sacrifice him for their own interests. Even if these people had suspected any previous contact between him and the Royal House of Scotland, it was of no importance and made no difference. The utter futility of his situation tore him apart.

He poured himself a drink, gulped it down, poured another and stared at the Duke, while Albany congratulated himself that his own problem was settled for the moment.

"And if I fail to influence her or to survive the attempt, what happens to my family then? Will they still be made to suffer?" he asked.

"No, François. That you do your best is all we ask. That will secure their continued wellbeing."

François wanted to believe them, wanted to trust them to keep their word. What exactly would they judge to be doing his best? And afterwards? No one had mentioned the conclusion of this venture. Deep down he knew the answer. Once they had finished with him, he would know too much.

François dreaded his return home. He had intended to go yesterday before this nightmare had overtaken him. He would never be his old self again. In such a short space of time his mind had become burdened beyond belief. He needed to collect himself and prepare to face those at home. To delay the moment he headed for the village inn, where a sulky and impatient Colette waited.

Colette had been disappointed in him for not coming back from Paris earlier, but her pleasure and delight at his arrival soon turned to anger when he scarcely noticed her. Because he did not hear her speak, she slammed the table with the jug to attract his attention, yet although he raised his eyes he failed to acknowledge her existence, returning his concentration to the table. She swung away in a huff, determined to ignore him, but as she observed the solitary figure still sitting in the same spot in the failing evening light, she could not help forgiving him any slight. He seemed unhappy and she threw her arms about him, longing for the return of his more cheerful expression, until with some little promising, caressing and coaxing, she drew him away to join her in the loft. But once there, his preoccupation continued as they sat side by side in the warm night, which did nothing to keep her temper sweet.

"To be too busy for your brother I can understand, but to be too busy thinking of other matters when you are with me is an insult" she snapped.

He kissed her fiercely, but she bit him in her anger and without thinking he hit her in retaliation. She had never acted like this before, but then he was no better; he was responsible for her reaction. He did not know what he was doing here, only that it was wrong to use her as a remedy for his ill mood. They sat staring at each other, no longer friends and yet not enemies, and neither spoke as he left.

Jacques had been puzzled by François' delayed return, and although initially pleased to find him well, he held his son back from riding to the house. He related the appearance of some stranger enquiring after him, but François laughed, dismissing it convincingly as the result of a misplaced fondness he had shown for a wealthy merchant's daughter, a matter which was now settled and forgotten. What else could he have said to the dear man, who breathed a sigh of relief as they then rode on.

In the following weeks at home, François prayed for a miracle to save him and spent hours in deep thought trying to find an answer to his burden. There must be a way out, but no matter how he tried there was no solution and no reprieve. As his beard grew, so did his heartache and dejection. How could he protect his family? Would these men keep their word once he was in Scotland? How would he know? Torment struggled within him as wide-eyed he paced the floor, wondering how events had come to this.

At night he lay on the bed, not even trying to sleep, staring out at the night sky. How many more nights would he lie here wondering if he could keep up this pretence of normal behaviour? He had to force himself to keep to a routine, while every fibre screamed at him to run away. His head ached continually with the nightmares of Scotland, the memories tumbling into his mind. Fate had made him the King's double, and demanded a sacrifice. Although he had survived before, this time he knew he could not. It seemed unfair. He had wanted so little from life.

Often he would disappear to roam the surrounding countryside, savouring the sights and sounds that were part of him. They were French and for a while longer, he could tread French soil. He dreaded every day that passed, because each day was one less he had to be here. He could hardly bear it, knowing this time he would never return, never touch, never love these special places as much as he did now.

He tried to block out the rest of the world, but could not stop it invading his mind. For him there was no future, no expectations. He was an unwilling pawn in others' games, a ghost which they could not afford to acknowledge. He would end up alone in a foreign country and probably dead. To succeed or fail meant nothing glorious or memorable. Fear shook his very soul and anguish filled him afresh. He had no one to help him, no one to confide in and no one to know the truth of his going.

"Who will protect me?" he cried aloud.

"What did you say?" came his father's voice as he approached from the field.

François turned away abruptly, making excuses to be elsewhere.

François had been quite content to let everyone assume his mood swings were the result of his continuing disappointment over Marie, because it had suited him in the beginning. It made it easier.

Thankfully, even his closest sibling and friends could not see it as anything else. They had all been sympathetic and undemanding. How could he have told them the terrible truth of the situation?

"The shadow of Marie still casts its shadow on his tormented soul" Pierre had said. How could he let any of them know his intention to go back to Scotland? He would never have withstood their combined arguments or pressure. As for Pierre, he would have broken every bone in his body to prevent him leaving for Scotland, if he had even been given a hint of where François was soon going. Thank goodness Pierre was away at the horse sales.

It was strange how odd things came into his mind. Useless thoughts, such as those concerning his grandmother. If only she had still been at court here in France, where she might have seen this duke, then she could have warned him about the likeness to his face. If she had not come here and filled his head with the romantic and fond memories of her home. If he had not dreamed of adventure. If he had not been born… Useless thoughts.

And then there was Jean-Paul. He was so different, so uncomplicated. If only he had dealt a better blow that night, if only he had ended it then, that night in Paris. He had known his step well enough. Didn't his brother realise he would not have let anyone else get that close without defending himself?

Then Scotland again! Remember your promises, he had been told the last time he had been there. He remembered the promise he had made to himself on his return from Scotland never to leave his home, never to stray from the beautiful valley, with all its familiar warmth and comfort. The promise he had made to Marie, never to forget her. The one to his best friend Pierre, to be less reckless. And the promise he made to the Abbott and to the King - most of all, the one to the King.

He remembered his useless attempt to question their venture.

Would the shock of his face succeed in blanking out any noticeable voice difference? Would the stubble on his face age him sufficiently? How could he be King James? "Your clean-shaven appearance is too distinctive for your arrival and your hair should be longer before you leave" had been the parting words he had received from Rochin.

Despite the warm day, the coldness overtook him again and he pulled his jacket closer around his body and nestled his face into the upturned collar. He had stubbornly refused to be what people had wanted him to be all his life, and now he was having to do exactly as he was bid.

François reluctantly paid a visit to see Suzanne at Belmonde, where he found his sister had grown more beautiful and was as happy as anyone he had ever seen. She had criticised his beard as soon as she saw him.

"It makes you look old" she complained kindly.

"I am old" he replied.

"Never!" she smiled, kissing him.

She would always be his little sister, always be herself, and yet her joy at being with him again made his own suffering worse, because there was little doubt that this leaving of her would be final.

As the days passed, François had no zest or emotion. He could barely speak and withdrew more and more into himself. Concentrate as he might, words and people faded away from him. He would smile weakly, hoping to hide the torment he must bear alone. There were moments when he felt he could not prolong this charade and that he could not stay one more hour in their company. He no longer belonged here, he felt distant, not really part of them any more. He had not slept properly, and he was overtired and dark-eyed.

He sat in his private favourite spot in the hills, where he had so often sat and pondered things. With his back against the tree, he buried his head in his arms. His head could not cope; he wanted an end to this utter futile situation.

Jean-Paul finally found him. He wanted to talk to his brother desperately, despite the difficulty and awkwardness of the subject. He had to confess. He approached slowly, almost changing his mind.

"François" he whispered to the still figure. There was no response, no sign he had heard. "François" he said again, a little more firmly.

"What?" came a muffled solemn reply.

"I – I want to talk."

While everyone else had assumed François's mood was connected to his despair over Marie, his brother knew differently. No one had noticed that François barely spoke to his brother, that he had been indifferent to his presence. He seemed to ignore his very existence, and Jean-Paul knew why. Although François had never said anything, never mentioned or accused him, it was clear that he knew who had attacked him. Although François refused to blame him, Jean-Paul had come to confess.

"François, I – am sorry" he gulped.

Jean-Paul saw it fell on deaf ears, but he wasn't going to give up. Now he had gathered the courage to speak, he had to continue.

"I am sorry for what happened in Paris. I was jealous, I hated you for being more attractive, more charming, more everything than me. I have learnt my lesson. I let a lie, a simple lie make me so angry that I wanted to kill you. How could I have done that? That I was capable of such a crime, is something I will never forget."

There – he had got it out. He had managed to voice the guilt he had carried for ages. The animosity towards his brother had ended that night, he could only hope François would feel the same, understand and accept his apology.

"Please forgive me" he went on.

François slowly lifted his head, to stare ahead, unwilling to let his brother see his sore eyes.

"Oh Jean-Paul. It is forgiven, forgotten. It was a mistake, we all make mistakes. You are wiser now in a lot of ways, more of an adult. All I ask is that you are more careful in future and try to keep away from trouble."

There was only concern in his voice, for who was he to lecture his brother about controlling his emotions when he had let the same emotional madness control and ruin his life?

Jean-Paul was hugely relieved, but puzzled that it had been dismissed so lightly. It should not have been this easy. He looked at François sitting there, unable to fathom why his brother was still in the same sorry mood, until he saw the tears in his eyes. Had he been wrong about the extent of his brother's real feelings for Marie? It shocked him. He had never realised that there was truly no one else for him. Despite his fickle flirtations, it was a sham, an act. Now he did not envy François so much.

"Did you love Marie that much?" he asked afresh.

François had not wanted to be reminded of Marie on top of his other burdens. If only it had been for Marie, then he would gladly have gone to Scotland.

"Grab happiness whenever you can" was all François added, without diverting his gaze.

Thus they parted with a comfortable acceptance between them. Jean-Paul intending to go fishing and promised to make him proud of his catch, not that François seemed interested.

François spent his last nights with Colette, because he could not face going home. Colette would not turn him away, despite their last quarrel. Yet it was not the François of old who lay beside her. She could feel his heart beating as she touched his chest, his hands held still over hers. His eyes were cast to the ceiling, lost and needing her comfort and warmth. She was glad of his company, although she could not cheer him or make conversation. At last he kissed her and held her close to him.

"Thank you" he murmured. He had needed someone to hold, someone to hold him.

Now there were no more days left. Today he would be gone, he would be collected from the meeting point and escorted to the coast. The day itself dawned bright and clear, the sun only heightening the guilt he felt for the pain he must shortly inflict upon his parents. Today there would be no smiles. He would leave no happiness here. Today he would face their anger, disbelief and curses.

At first he had considered not telling them where he was going, but they deserved something of the truth, rather than letting them worry endlessly about his disappearance. He had to make this parting sharp and quick. Let them think the worst of their heartless son; that would make his eventual loss easier.

He stood alone in the yard absorbing the familiar surroundings before walking to the fields where his father worked. His steps were laboured, yet he soon stood by the man's side. He knew what to expect, but there was no more time to delay this moment.

Jacques stopped work immediately. He had known there had been something terribly wrong of late and hoped that François had now come to confide in him. Carefully he attempted to coax the difficulty from him.

"What makes you walk all this way out here after me?" he began kindly.

"I leave for Scotland today" François blurted out.

There was a long silence as the words struck home. Jacques did not believe what he was hearing. He shook his head. This could not be! Yet as he looked at his son's expression he saw it was true.

"What madness is this? How can you go back after what happened to you last time? You barely survived. Why, François? Why? This is not some rash notion over Marie, is it? I thought you had come to terms with that."

Marie! It would be natural that everyone assume his plans were connected with Marie. He was plagued by her name. Marie, who had gone from him. It was hard to think of her. There was no place left for her when his whole being ached only for life itself.

"I promise, it has nothing to do with Marie" he answered forlornly.

"Then why go?" Jacques asked.

It was a perfectly reasonable question, but one he could never reply to. He could give his father no reason for his going, nor could he lie to him.

"This is nothing to do with Marie" he said.

"Then in God's name, give me the true reason. I thought you were cured of all this gallivanting of yours. There are a thousand other places better than Scotland to satisfy your thirst for excitement."

François felt so cold, as if the bitter winter frost had filled his being. He could only stand firm and accept the verbal abuse. He did not defend himself, it was unbearable, but if his father had seen beyond his own blurred rage, he would have recognised the pained eyes which betrayed his son's feelings.

"I do not understand you. What is behind this? Do I have to beat the truth out of you? Where is your common sense?"

There was a tense silence as he searched for the right words to change his son's mind. His hand was heavy on François's shoulder, which François covered with his own, because he had no words to ease his father's grief or tell him how much he cared for him. François was wretched in his deceit. He could not stand much more of it.

"I thought I knew you. How can you be so cruel as to put your mother through this again? "

"Stop! For God's sake, please" François pleaded. His muscles tense and knotted, he shook himself free and fled with his father's voice calling after him.

At the house, he expected the same scene with his mother. Here he was equally blunt and evasive in his announcement, and he accepted the ferocity of her emotions as she clung to his chest imploring and pleading.

"Damn your stubbornness!" she cried. She ran out of words and collapsed into heart-rending sobs, just as Jacques entered the room. His father scowled and François stood there helpless as a distraught Eleanor fled into her husband's arms. They both glared at him.

"I must go" François said impatiently.

"Must?" his father instantly queried. François did not answer. He could not look at either of them any longer and lowering his head, he turned wearily for the door. Yet within that moment he found his father had moved swiftly to stand blocking the door way.

"I will not have you make another mistake" roared Jacques.

"Nothing will change my plans. I am going." François answered.

"No, by heavens, No! I will stop you this time."

François drew a long deep breath, for he knew his father meant to stop him by force. He had never hit his father or tested his strength against him before, but now it seemed unavoidable. François shook his head. How could this day get any worse?

"Please stand aside. There is no need for anyone to get hurt" François pleaded.

Jacques was a big man, a strong man and the one more likely to win, but François was the more desperate, the more determined, for leave he must if his family were to remain safe. He steeled himself mentally, for speed was his only chance.

"I'm so sorry I have to do this" he whispered, before he swung the punch. He had not wanted to inflict any pain, but the unexpected blow put his father groaning on the floor before he could defend himself. It was the only way. It made him feel hollow and empty to his core. What sort of person had he become?

When the stunned Jacques looked up he found François standing close to him, his fists still clenched. Jacques had no inclination to move. Instead he looked at his son, silently questioning the change in him.

"I am sorry" François said sadly. Then he lowered his arms, stepped over his father and walked out of the door, not daring to look back. His life as he knew it was over.

CHAPTER EIGHT

On an early morning in July 1514, François came face to face with the cold reality of the Scottish shore once more. His boots sank into the cold wet sand as he strode across the small cove to the path, where another stranger awaited him. They did not speak; there was no need, each knew the purpose of the other. Hooded and cloaked, a cloth wrapped around the lower part of his face, he rode at full speed with his escort towards de la Bastie, passing from stranger to stranger and smuggled from one dark place to another, until he completed his journey.

The town of Linlithgow was always particularly busy whenever the royal entourage was in residence at the palace, which easily gave François the opportunity to make contact with the Duke's envoy. De la Bastie greeted him silently before telling the nearest serf, in this case François, to load a basket of wood and follow him back to his rooms.

Once securely settled in the French diplomat's quarters in the town, François freely criticized these latest arrangements in his journey. Aching from his prolonged bent position, he felt angry as he put the wood on the fire. It surprised him that he had reached here in one piece, but he was worried by the number of people he had met en route, too many in his opinion. Too many who could turn out to be his own assassins in the end, but that he kept to himself.

De la Bastie frowned at his guest's frank remarks, but what bothered him more was that François obviously expected and valued the same degree of honesty from him, forcing the unprepared man to agree with his observations for the moment. François made it clear that he had no intention of being intimidated by his new master. He was here under sufferance and made no pretence otherwise. Here he faced only one man, who had to be as careful as he.

François had already taken stock of the Palace and surrounding town from the other side of the loch before his arrival. The imposing structure, built with solid defensive walls, stood on a mound with terraced land around it, the lower terrace housing several timber stables and workshops and areas used for archery, jousting and hawking. Unfortunately he could only see one entrance gate, the rectangular panel above displaying the royal arms, in the centre of the east side, with a drawbridge and ramp. Guards would sleep there, patrol the premises and operate the drawbridge and the portcullis. With a clear open space on the sloping access through parkland, the guards who controlled access into Palace had an excellent view of those approaching. There was his first problem.

For his own peace of mind François needed some idea of the routine and the inside layout of the palace, in case he needed to take evasive action. He was horrified at the information de la Bastie gave him. The palace consisted of an open courtyard in the centre surrounded by the enclosed quadrangle of actual palace itself. Then the four circular staircases which were built in each corner of the open courtyard, gave only narrow vertical access to all areas above, including the important first floor of the elaborate royal lodgings along the west side. François sighed. With guards checking the credentials of any visitor, he faced another problem.

He was further alarmed to learn that the main rooms of the royal lodgings only led directly into each other; there were no corridors on any side. On the first floor the king's apartments consisted of three rooms, each room graded in importance. The King's Hall, where court ushers vetted visitors, led into the Presence Chamber, a reception room where visitors were received and music was performed. This in turn led into the most private bedchamber, which also had three closets or side chambers.

The Queen's own private quarters had a similar arrangement directly above those of the late King. There personal servants normally slept close to the Queen, often in canvas beds in her bedchamber or one of the small side closets, while other staff bedded down in warm spaces, in the great hall, the kitchens and the bakehouse. This was utterly hopeless. François groaned.

Indeed there were few corridors elsewhere for him to escape through. There was a three-tier gallery along the south range, which provided sheltered corridors between the great hall and royal lodgings, but it put him on the wrong side of the building as he understood it. There was also an outer enclosure on this side and a doorway and path leading to St Michael's Church. None of these figured in his strategies.

Linlithgow Palace was a retreat away from Edinburgh and Stirling, where in the past their majesties could enjoy themselves, be waited on and entertained. When they were in residence, there were a vast number of people residing there, to handle the scale of banquets in the splendour of the Great Hall. The townspeople themselves busily provided a variety of goods and services, supplies of food, table vessels, rushes for the chambers, horses and hay. Even the local women brewed ale for the huge household. This constant activity could be an advantage, since the drawbridge was constantly left down because of the number of carts and deliveries arriving and departing.

François had to consider all his options. At the foot of the kitchen turnpike stairs was the lower kitchen, which complemented the court kitchen in providing food for their banquets. The kitchen area would be the best place to mingle and as far as he could see the one postern, a backdoor used by servants at ground level on the north front, would be easy to reach.

The other possibility had been to mix with the scruffy rustic labourers delivering barrels to the cellar, on the ground floor in the west range. Once down the steps in the cellar he could hide and then later find the stair way built into the thickness of wall which led directly up to a window bay in the Kings hall above. But then what? There would have been an usher there guarding the door way into the presence chamber. He would still have had to reach the Queen's apartment on the floor above that.

François could not understand how they expected him to perform this miracle. Besides which, how could he know where the Queen would be in the palace at any moment? He couldn't simply go searching for her. She might even be in that small room towering above the palace in the north east corner, known as Queen Margaret's bower, where she had sat waiting for her husband's return from the battle of Flodden. Just how could he reach the Queen undetected? De la Bastie had promised it could be achieved, but François did not see how. Be patient, he had been told. Patience was not one of his virtues. Why wouldn't de la Bastie share his own strategy?

Occasionally François stole a look from the window towards Linlithgow Palace. Stifled by the lack of fresh air and exercise and confined to his hiding place, he could only brood and wait. He had let James down. There was no way to calm or suppress the haunting fears which dominated his long hours here. He cursed his awful destiny and the lack of his ability to change it. Inside he was a man in torment, a man possessed by his concern for the safety of his family.

Would Rochin or the Duke keep to the bargain? They had promised that if he played his part as best he could, if he had tried to talk to her, tried to prevent her intended marriage or just delay her, then no harm would come to his family. He hated these people who had broken and changed him. They had made him someone else. He made no secret of his doubt over the success of their venture. How could he contrive to meet the Queen? There would be few chances, and once the chances were gone, what were their plans for him? Would he ever escape again?

To impersonate the King was treason; there would be no mercy. No doubt Rochin and de la Bastie would ensure he was never able to talk. He would be killed first, he had no illusions. He felt he was already a dead man. He was sick to the stomach. He could hardly eat anything and all he kept being told was that they merely had to wait for the right opportunity. What opportunity?

"My God! You are James in every detail" gasped de la Bastie, once Francis had shaved and trimmed his hair in readiness to perform his deception. François made no comment, what had the man expected? Yet surely this man had viewed only a few portraits of the King to compare him with. He doubted if he had never seen the King in person, although obviously his resemblance to the Duke had stunned his host for a moment. François ignored his stare. He was impatient to get this ridiculous task over and done with.

The opportunity came sooner than either of them expected, for the Queen announced a banquet and masque for the visiting ambassadors, her friends from the English court. De la Bastie, as the

French representative, knew he would be invited, although he expected to be deliberately placed on a lower table that evening, in an attempt to antagonise him and ignore him, thus demonstrating her public opinion of the French. Not that de la Bastie would give her any indication of being thus shunned tonight; there would be no display of anger or frustration. Diplomatic experience meant he would make the best of it, talking and eating as if he enjoyed every moment of the company he was seated with.

On the day, prior to the elaborate banquet, a hotchpotch of people filled the palace, jugglers, tumblers, players, dancers and musicians, as a host of merriment resounded within. Garlands of flowers and greenery hung about the walls, tables and chairs, while the entertainers and giggling courtiers alike paraded in their fancy dress, teasing and tormenting each other into guessing who was behind the elaborate masks and disguises. Even outside the girls and boys, squealing, raced and chased about the courtyard in between the displays, nearly colliding with the barrels being rolled from the store. It was a day to be foolish and take advantage of the relaxed etiquette of court procedure, as people roamed unhindered through every passage and room, in all types of outrageous and brightly-coloured robes.

His nerves tingling with fear, his heart in his mouth, his throat dry, François made himself walk into the centre of the frivolous enjoyment. His mask deliberately at an angle and his cloak swung jauntily over his shoulder, he bowed and acknowledged other revellers as if they were well acquainted. Everyone was too busy enjoying themselves to question another costume in their midst. François had his one golden chance to cross the courtyard directly and to pass through the palace unchallenged. Maybe this would be his only chance to gain adequate access to the royal apartments.

Margaret had slipped away from her attendants below to relax, and dismissed her ladies to contemplate her recent developments in her life, she had never been so elated and so excited by her own power and freedom.

She was twenty-four years old and the ruler of Scotland. Despite the custom, she had by James' will and in his honour been created Regent. Her thoughts wandered from the proposal of a joint Regency with the Duke of Albany, as urged by her council, to her brother Henry's warning and then to the satisfaction of a more suitable solution for her future. She was in love with the handsome young Archibald Douglas, the recently-created Earl of Angus, constantly commanding his company. She was convinced he felt the same and she was determined to marry him, because it was the only answer to the passion and desire which obsessed her. Margaret was deeply aware of her position and her royalty, realising the council would never consent, but after her proposed secret marriage in Kinnoul Church she would have the backing of the Douglas's to support her. None would dare criticise or condemn her actions then.

She was unsuccessful at hiding her pleasure as she occupied her mind with the thought of the boy soon to be her husband. Her eyes were bright with excitement at her dangerous secret, and her pulse raced with wild thoughts and dreams. She smiled to herself, eager and expectant, the smile exaggerating her plump, round cheeks. She blushed deeply and lowered her eyes as the sun dazzled her. She felt glowing and content, knowing how attractive she looked this moment with her long red hair flowing loose about her shoulders and setting off her elaborate gown. And tonight she would dazzle her guests.

François had no specific plan for his confrontation with this woman. He had learned everything about her, her temper, her moods, and he had even caught a glimpse of her as she had passed through the town. He felt no guilt or compassion about his task, there was no sentiment to weaken his resolve. Her stupidity had been the reason for his forced presence here and that anger gave him the courage to speak. It was easy to be James, to rebuke, blame and command her. He hated this Queen; she was small and plump, with a white complexion and long red hair, and he found her features quite unexceptional.

As expected, he found her alone in her chamber. Removing his disguise in the empty stairwell outside, he stepped unseen into the room behind her, the deliberate swish of his cloak causing Margaret to look around curiously at the slight sound.

She stopped and stood transfixed, unable to speak or move, her eyes staring unbelievably at him, growing wider and wider until they ceased to focus. A shiver brought her back to normality as she began to gulp for air so she could breathe again.

Was it James? It could not be. James was dead! She knew he was dead. It had taken months of nightmares after Flodden to finally accept his death. A dreadful period filled with remorseful tears, emptiness and resentment until she ceased to think of him. Yet as he moved nearer she saw this man was real; this was no ghost. There were those charming hazel eyes, the auburn hair and that smile that had won her heart so long ago as he said her name, then warned her. Warned her against her infatuation with the young Earl, warned her that Angus would not be a good husband.

He opened his arms to take her into them, to hold her, they reached out and brushed her hair. She shook her head, her eyes pleading, her tears falling unrestricted down her face. But when she wiped them away, he was gone.

Frantically she called his name, searching the room, unable to understand where he had gone. He had been here, she had seen him and touched him – hadn't she? He had spoken to her, not that she could remember what he had said. She sat shaking.

Oh, James, her fickle beloved husband, the seducer of women, too many women, but she would forgive him anything to be in his arms once more. She longed for his magnificent body, and her senses quivered, remembering the pleasures and response he aroused in her. She easily forgot Angus and cried out again for the man who had mastered her Tudor pride and temper.

Sobbing, she trembled, not knowing which way to turn. If James were alive, he would not have waited this long before showing himself. It had been two years since he had died. What game was he playing? Who else knew? Was it him, or just her imagination? If it was real the news would have been heralded throughout the palace, the whole country. There would be such celebrations, yet she could hear only the sound of normal festivities echoing through the building, nothing more.

Was she going mad? To make sure she did not make a fool of herself to the council especially, she decided not to mention the incident to anyone. Besides, who would believe her, and whom could she trust? Indeed, as she slowly regained her regal composure, she decided she would do nothing. She must wait to see if it happened again.

Meanwhile, because of the passing courtiers, François had secured himself safely in a hiding place by the shadowed recess of a tall cupboard, where he had no option but to listen to the whispered promises she made to the empty room, her passionate innermost confessions shocking him. Trapped for the moment, his heart pounded at the risk of discovery as this impulsive woman beat her fists in anguish on the panels near him, causing him to hold his breath in case she heard him. It seemed like ages as he waited for her to calm that Tudor temper and restore the regal composure, for only then could he take his chance of escape.

Eventually she exhausted her energy and quietly left the room, allowing François to retrieve his plumed headdress and robe from the chest and make good his own escape. Not that it proved as easy or as quick as he would have liked, as he had to fall in with various groups of fellow revellers he encountered. Someone slapped him on the back and joked about something he did not quite understand, to which he tactfully laughed to avoid suspicion. Then another man, already well intoxicated, threw his arms around him and offered him half a cup of wine, before collapsing against him. Pretending to be in the same condition and playing the jester, he was forced to walk some way supporting the fellow until they were out of sight, when he swiftly propped him in a corner to leave him contentedly singing to himself. He felt obliged to use this seemingly acceptable act to slowly stagger back to the lodgings, where de la Bastie grabbed him urgently, excited to hear news of how it had gone.

"She was too shocked and frightened to hear my words" François reported. He was in no mood for questions. Still recovering from the ordeal himself, all he wanted was to forget, but his co-conspirator would not allow that.

"Did she believe who you were?"

"How could she not? Am I not James?" came the dispassionate answer, unwilling to commit anything of value to the conversation.

"Is that all?" demanded de la Bastie.

"Isn't that enough to begin with? At least I have her attention. She is worried by my appearance. What did you expect?"

"Results! That is why you are here."

They lapsed into a disagreeable silence, each resenting the other. François commented upon the Queen's plain and unattractive features as he settled down to his concealed existence again. De la Bastie for his part had stopped listening, instead concentrating on the evening ahead. Wearing a scarlet satin doublet, a thick black velvet cloak edged with rich black fur and a black velvet cap to match, edged with brocade, he was confident that he would not be outdone by the English for style. He could withstand their animosity and pique. Besides, apart from the political purpose of this evening's banquet, it was the perfect chance to observe any signs of the effect François might have had on the Queen.

Margaret had managed to hide her uneasy preoccupation sufficiently that night, the falseness of her gaiety evident to those few who were close to her, not that they dared question it. Although in the following days, others were puzzled by the Queen's behaviour as she kept her ladies unusually close to her, hoping that should James come again she would have witnesses to confirm his manifestation. Days passed, and with each one she had expected his return, until since he came no more, she began to doubt her mind. She had thought there had been no mistake, but dreams were as real as reality and she eventually dismissed the idea, chastising herself for allowing her imagination to play such tricks.

Her continual attentive retinue did not allow an opportunity for François to repeat his performance, not that he minded, although it frustrated de la Bastie, who understood that their success depended upon frequent confrontations.

"Every encounter must be effective, memorable, dramatic" he urged François. "You must frighten her out of this marriage. Lord Drummond, Archibald's grandfather sees the advantage of this match, he has already spoken with Angus's uncles about it. If the marriage takes place, the Douglases and their connections will rule Scotland through Angus and the Queen."

François did not want to be embroiled in politics, explanations or historical facts; he did not want to know anything. He was merely a pawn, controlled by others, just as James had warned.

"The council will not believe my words. I am only a foreigner interfering. Besides to show our hand and let the Douglases suspect our intelligence would mean them having us removed from court."

François did not need reminding how vulnerable they all were, because he was the one most at risk.

A few hours after the midnight bell, de la Bastie let François out through the rear door of their apartment. Carefully he made his way the short distance through the town to the park grounds, where he used an overgrown shrubbery to give him good cover to begin with. François could not believe he was actually doing this after all his sceptical arguments, and was terrified by every step he took.

Crossing the open ground, he skirted around the base of the palace, his progress slow as he judged his movements in between the routine tour of the sentry. He had a key for the postern door - goodness know how it had been acquired - which opened easily, if noisily, causing him to stop. He waited and held his breath, but no one called out. Inside the door there was a space facing a large archway leading to storage and rooms towards the kitchen, plus, more importantly, a short, small, narrow corridor with steps leading to the turnpike staircase and eventually the Queen's apartments.

The whole place was quiet and empty, the stairs deserted. No guards appeared and even as he reached the first floor near the entrance to the King's bedchamber, there were no guards stationed there either. This was unreal. His heart was thumping nervously in his ears. It was too easy, too quiet. He suspected he was walking straight into a trap, yet he could not turn back. Slowly he made his way up to the next floor.

Somehow he reached the Queen's apartments, and on tip toe he quietly passed sleeping attendants and footmen. He paused outside the door. She should be on her own in her bedchamber. This was it. He had no quick escape, no way out if it went wrong.

In the darkness of night James had come again, the candle in his hand, its light flickering before his face as he shook his Queen awake. She thought she had dreamed of Angus, and when she saw it was not him, she still smiled dreamily. She was not afraid as she continued to look affectionately at him, she reached to touch him, her fingers caressing the contours of his face, and in wonderment she stroked the lips she remembered.

"Oh, James" she sighed, softly aching for satisfaction.

He drew close and she felt his breath on her skin, which thrilled her to expect more. Her arms were about his neck and urgently fumbling his hair as she closed her eyes for the demand of his lips on hers.

François felt the inviting warmth of her body and the lusty desire of this young widow and he panicked, suddenly throwing her back. He had not expected this kind of response.

"Why should I please you now, when you seek to take another to your bed? Was I not enough to satisfy you? Was I not all you wished?" he hissed at her.

Margaret was instantly enraged. How dare he, of all people, question her fidelity or loyalty, when he had taken so many other women even after their marriage! She sat up sharply, but he had retreated from her reach. Then a sound from outside distracted them both, a sound which instantly resulted in darkness as François put the candle out. One of the servants had stirred.

"James?" she called, demanding his attention, but she could see nothing even when his voice brushed by her ear.

"Do not marry the Earl of Angus!" he whispered.

She had had enough of his games and demanded he relight the candles, but she received no answer. Angrily she struggled to find the tinder, unsuccessfully, all the while cursing his stubborn refusal to help, until she had to make her way to the curtains to allow the dim light to fill the chamber. About to rebuke him, she stopped short, because he had disappeared yet again. Defiantly she glared around the room, wondering where he could have gone, what game he was playing. As before, he did not return. Bewildered by the event, she had no intention of being made a fool of either. James appeared and vanished without a sign, a feat impossible by anything human, so she concluded this was his ghost, a jealous ghost who sought to keep her for himself.

She laughed out loud; at last she had sweet revenge on him. Let him suffer her previous anguish and torment, for now she could enjoy this new love to spite him. She smiled and lay back, vowing to tease him further the next time he came.

"See how easily I fall prey to his ways now!" she said to herself.

She had not cried out for assistance, nor shouted for her ladies; indeed she had made no attempt to draw attention to what had just occurred. François had expected mayhem to break loose. Instead there was only silence after he had closed the door, which made it more unnerving. The servant who had stirred before had obviously gone back to sleep, indicated by the occasional snoring he heard.

He stopped and drew another deep breath. He wanted to run, to get out as fast as he could, but he forced himself, very slowly, in stages, to retrace his earlier route exactly. His alertness on a knife's edge, his whole body tight with tension, he eventually made it back to safety.

As if this nervous spent energy were not enough to recover from, François was mentally exhausted. He had been shaken by the Queen's unexpected behaviour. Not that he wished to divulge this to the man who faced him. He had nearly been caught out by her sexuality, her mere closeness. The obvious love and passion she had exhibited were almost too much, and he had barely saved himself. She had revitalised his own suppressed emotions, stirred that desire for life, his own life. It ran riot through his veins and he wanted freedom from this place. Not that he would tell de la Bastie that either.

"You must go back tomorrow. You must try again" de la Bastie said, interrupting his thoughts.

"No. Not tomorrow! Not ever again! I am in no state. I am a quivering mess. It cannot be done again. I have done my best. It is suicidal to continue. Surely twice is more than you ever expected me to achieve. Do you want me to get caught? Do you want them to find out about this scheme and the Duke's complicity?"

This made de la Bastie stop for a moment, his frown deepening as he considered the problem. He could not risk his master's reputation.

"The whole task of reaching her unseen is impossible now" François insisted.

"Have you frightened her enough? Do you think you have made a difference?"

Had he? he did not really care. He was merely thankful she had not woken her attendants and that he was still in one piece.

"We must make sure we have the advantage. In two days' time there will be a market in the town. Selected merchants will be allowed to set up stalls in the courtyard. The place will be busy with people. It might be possible. Their attention will be based only on the courtyard" de la Bastie pondered, ignoring François' assessment.

"No!" screamed François at him. Wasn't de la Bastie taking notice of anything he had said? Each confrontation was fraught with more danger, the arrangement and the achievement more difficult.

Slowly his panic subsided and reason returned. He might yet outsmart his masters. Was there another way to end this charade?

He had done his part. He had been James. He had scared her. Could he frighten her enough to leave Linlithgow? And even if she did marry Angus, whether the Duke of Albany became Regent now or later, the council would ensure that the young prince would become King, nothing could change that. Why was he really here?

François meant to end this. He would visit the Queen one last time, without asking or waiting for approval. He would go the very next night, and make it one she would not forget. This time there would be no doubt. He would be James in full flow, an angry James, James the King. Except this time François had to be extra careful. He wanted to survive, he wanted to live to spite them all. Thus forced to wait longer in between his movements, he became the unwilling participant to other conversations as he remained trapped and often impatient as the steps sauntered by, and voices passed or stood directly beside him. Much he did not understand or take notice of; they confused him with words and names he did not know. He was only relieved that they had not discovered him.

At their next meeting Margaret openly laughed at his commands and he found he was getting nowhere. He could not believe she was not frightened of him.

"You cannot win, James, there is nothing you can do to prevent my marriage" she said. "You can be as jealous as you like. You are only a ghost and you can come as often as you like. You cannot hurt me."

Taunted by her, François became indignant, seeing the wisdom of the men who sought to replace her as Regent. Anger and pride commanded him, and he truly became James in mind and heart. With no regret he advanced to hit her hard across the face, accompanied by words not of his own, threatening to deliver the punishment she deserved.

"Did that not hurt? I can deliver more." Showing no pity for the frightened creature who cowered against the wall away from him, François continued. "Shall I come every night to beat you? Shall I shake you from your sleep? Shall I follow you around this palace, although none else can see or hear me? Shall I make your days miserable? This I shall do, until you abandon the idea of your marriage."

Margaret's face stung from his blow, and she was shaking at the memory of what had taken place. What ghost could inflict physical pain? What evil force had she encountered? Whether this was some supernatural being or not, Margaret had no intention of meeting it again. Terrified, she fled from the room, unable to speak. She rushed around the lavish reception rooms in circles, unsure of what to do. Soon her attendants began to wake.

François had swiftly hurried in the opposite direction, down the stairs and out of the palace, without looking back. Breathless, he arrived back at the lodgings to be confronted by a distraught de La Bastie.

"Where have you been?"

"To finish it" François declared, his jaw set with determination. "This time she is so alarmed that she will want this mischief stopped. She will have her soldiers be extra careful and diligent in their duty. She may even have the whole palace searched on some pretext. It is done with."

François was convinced that he had managed to put an end to the whole stupid plot and his participation in it. His actions were bound to drive the Queen from these walls, which pleased him, for then their schemes would be suspended. Then he would, as far as he was concerned, have completed his task; even de la Bastie could not deny that. Although he had no intention of mentioning his part in manipulating the situation to his advantage. Neither would he mention the other whispers and secrets he had overheard during his various concealments, for it could only lead to further complications. De la Bastie had his own sources of information and it was not for François to act as one of them.

Indeed François was correct in his assumption. No longer welcoming her nights alone and desiring to be free of the malevolent spirit which had left a bruise on her face, Margaret left no time in preparing to leave the palace. Leaving all the cares of the court behind and thinking only of Angus who waited there for her, she rode out to Stobhall, the home of Lord Drummond. Soon she would be married.

The court was dull without the Queen, and the council were slow to realise the danger of her prolonged absence, unlike de la Bastie, who was annoyed and worried by her sudden departure. François, on the other hand, was delighted, glad she had gone as he tried to convince de la Bastie his charade was finished. Yet frustratingly, de la Bastie refused to acknowledge the possibility of defeat.

Annoyed by the restricted confines of the place, François was daily tempted to break out, inspired by the relentless activity beyond its walls. Watching others revel in that which was forbidden to him naturally made the situation worse, and he threw himself dejectedly back on to the bed. The hours of solitude and boredom gave him little else to do but think, the thing which suited him least. François longed to be free.

He settled instead for a cool breeze, and quietly opened the window slightly. Reaching a comfortable position on the cushions, his relaxation soon changed to apprehension when almost immediately his quiet seclusion was interrupted by a conversation below. This time he listened as each word became clear and precise.

"The word from the Highlands confirms they are preparing to act."

"Open rebellion will result in their property and lands becoming forfeit to the Crown."

"Exactly what I want!" one laughed.

"An adequate reward for our services!" another joked.

"That young Lord Innes is a fool. He involves himself deep and deeper. Nothing will save him, and his people will be turned out onto the hills to starve."

Innes? François knew that name. His mind was racing. Marie! François ducked to each side of the window to try to see who these men were, but he could not see anyone and the voices had moved away. He had to see who they were; he had to find another vantage point.

He unlocked the door and stole a quick look outside. The alleyway was empty. The other occupants were normally engaged elsewhere on business at this period of the day and trusting to providence, François grabbed his hooded cloak and ran to the first corner. From the top of the cobbled slope he overlooked the scene beyond. It was full of strolling groups, people unhurried in their activities, and their movement gave nothing away. How could he tell who the conspirators were? He felt cheated.

He knew nothing about them, except that by threatening Lord Innes, they threatened Marie. Marie, whom he had forgotten. Marie, whose memory hurt him again, but more importantly it stirred because of his fear for her safety. Shocked and stunned, he was scrambling back towards safety when he felt a hand grab his shoulder and the sharp coldness of a blade at his throat. Thrust into a recess as men marched by, François found de la Bastie glaring at him.

"What the devil are you doing?" he hissed.

François let out a relieved sigh and easily shook himself free, heading hastily back to their sanctuary. Once there he hardly listened to his reprimand, his thoughts occupied by Marie, her husband and these other men. Her predicament dominated his mind, obliterating his own problems, as he struggled to think what he could do. His first instinct had been to set out immediately to find and warn her, but de la Bastie would prevent him. He had to come up with a plausible reason which allowed his departure.

"I was listening to speculation about the Queen" he lied. "Don't you know she is with Angus? She has had enough of the tiresome ghost who haunts her here. She has run away from James. Margaret has beaten you all. She is under Lord Drummond's protection, where she spends her days with Angus, shut away from court and their eyes. I suspect by now she is already secretly married, and there is nothing anyone can do about it."

De la Bastie stood open mouthed.

"Yes, married. I assure you" François insisted with conviction. It was a desperate idea, but one which he knew would worry de la Bastie, because there was no evidence to contradict his words. Thus having sown the seeds of doubt, François continued with his views, insistent that there could be no other reason for her continued absence.

"What is the point of my remaining when she shows little sign of returning?" François argued. "Once the Queen returns with her husband, I will be unable to escape this palace unnoticed. You cannot afford my capture. Or even my dead body to be found so close, if that is your solution to the problem. I must be housed elsewhere immediately."

"Not until I am sure it is necessary" de la Bastie protested.

"That may be too late" François pointed out. He was desperate to persuade this man to let him leave before the Queen returned and de la Bastie discovered his ruse. François was torn by haste, yet he could do nothing. Any stealthy attempts to escape were impossible, as without the Queen in residence, the household roamed the town at their pleasure, their presence a constant threat to his plans.

François did not know how near the truth his own words had been. Queen Margaret meanwhile considered herself in heaven. She had married Angus in Kinnol Church and was content to be at her husband's side living a normal married life, giving no thought to the problems she would face when the council heard news of her marriage.

"Why didn't you stop her?" de la Bastie stormed at François, when he received confirmation of the secret marriage. François was not really surprised, and managed to sound calmly offhand with his reply.

"I told you how difficult she was, but you would not believe me" he replied. "There was always a risk as to how she would react to James. There was never a certainty this scheme would work the way you wanted. Why should it? You and your friends in France refused to admit that too. At the most it would only ever be a delay, to allow the Duke to remain in France a little longer. No one could prevent the Queen from marrying exactly whom she pleased, when she pleased. It has been a complete waste of time, and you have all put my life in danger for no reason."

His companion was not listening. He was thinking, mumbling his thoughts aloud, aware that the council were still ignorant and not even suspicious. It gave him time to send word to the Duke to find out what could be done.

"Done! There is nothing to be done except get me out of here. It is too late for anything else."

At last de la Bastie saw the wisdom of moving François to a safer destination for the moment. Although he could not leave court himself, he did not intend to let François stray too far out of his sight or control for long. So alternative plans were swiftly made; plans to hold François in close confinement and out of sight from the public. He did not account for François not being in total agreement with the detail, not that François had divulged his own sùspicions until now.

"I have completed my part of the bargain" François told him. "You are finished with my talents, which means that I am now expendable. So I will be extra cautious of any of your plans for me. I do not trust any of you. Especially your masters in France."

They had made no plans for his return, he was well aware of that. And he left de la Bastie in no doubts as to his instinct for self-preservation. His outburst in the short exchange which followed clearly showed they had underestimated their man. They had made him King James, and something of the real King had rubbed off on him. He had become harder and stronger mentally. They might have beaten him into submission earlier this year and forced him to do this, but now they would regret it. His anger had built up until it had finally obliterated his previous fear and the trauma of their threats. He had passed the point where they could control his mind. He was changed by what they done to him and all the clever words of de la Bastie, were no match for his own determination.

As planned, François concealed himself among the slow, sleepy travellers grumbling at their early departure in the poor morning light. The smoke from the night fires lingered to swirl around the company of strangers which made their way from the noisy cobbled yard, cartwheels creaking, onto the open dirt road beyond.

His contact had no intention of letting François ride off on his own, but this time François waved his protest aside, this time there would be no stopping him. His temper flared and his hand fingered his sword, making it evident that he was prepared to fight to get his own way. Thus having achieved his intent, he set off, knowing that within hours, de la Bastie would have men searching the countryside for him, terrified in case he fell into the wrong hands.

Urgently he rode, the wind stinging his face, his billowing cloak tugging behind him and his sword bouncing against him with every rhythmic stride as he forced the horse onwards.

Well into the day, he reigned the animal to a halt, hoping he had travelled far enough to deter any inquisitive followers. Satisfied that he had, he changed direction for the abbey.

The Abbot was the one man in the whole of Scotland François could trust, the one man who might help when François needed help. He vowed to have Marie safe, if not back in France, then somewhere else, and would kill anyone who stood in his way. In his rush he had not given enough thought to the conclusion to his plan; he simply knew that he needed advice and assistance, and had to reach the Abbot.

The tolling bell called all to prayer as François paused cautiously, considering the possibility of entering the abbey unseen. Everyone would be in the chapel. As he checked around for travellers, he saw only a small boy working in the gardens, who offered little danger. Yet as he approached François appreciated the protection of his deep upturned collar, because the boy's eyes seemed to follow every step he took. Uncomfortably François stopped. He had not expected to attract the interest of an unworldly child, nor had he expected the boy to lay aside his tools and come towards him.

The boy remembered, the boy glared at him, the past memories stirring that dormant hate to the surface. He had not forgotten him, not forgotten or forgiven any who were responsible for the old woman's terrible death. He had coveted the dark powers, the charms, the potions and the poisons he had learnt from her, and he meant to use them to have his revenge one day. He had grown quickly in the two years into a lanky, awkward boy, which benefited his purpose, because few would recognise him as the urchin he had been. He tended the monastery gardens, in order to collect the herbs and berries he required, keeping his secrets and biding his time. For despite all the pious conditioning he received from the monks in Dunfermline and the kindness of the Abbot in letting him return, it was only the burning determination for revenge which kept him sane.

Finally François recognised the expression, if not the appearance, of the boy, and before he could exchange any word or make any other move, the boy signalled him to follow him into the abbey. The Abbot was stunned at his arrival and hurriedly ushered him into that familiar room François had long ago occupied. François saw it had not changed, the mere sameness of it being a comfort to his racing heart. Here he felt safe; only the Abbot's complaints were harsh on him. As he expected, for he deserved every angry curse.

"So much for your promises. How dare you return to Scotland? How dare you come here? James let you go in friendship and you betrayed his trust in you. I am distressed to see you dishonour him so easily." The old man was really angry.

"I had no choice. I did not return willingly" he said, without going into detail.

"I do not want your excuses."

François stood humble, guilty and repentant before the Abbot. There was much to explain and at all costs he must win his sympathy and support.

"I know I am in the wrong, but whatever you think of me and what you see as my disloyalty, I am not here for myself."

The Abbot was in no mood to listen as he paced the floor in front of Francois, trying to calm the violence he felt towards the young man.

"After all that was done to save your life and make you safe, you threw it away. You were warned! James made it perfectly clear. You are not wanted in Scotland. You should not be here. So why have you come here to me? I owe you nothing except the curses James would vent on you. I will not harbour criminals or conspirators."

"I ask nothing for myself, but I make no apology for wanting to save an innocent life. The Lady Innes, my sister-in-law, will be in need of safety and protection. She will need to return to France quietly without fuss or attention. Who else can I trust except you?"

"Oh, François! It cannot be done" the Abbot sighed, the sadness in his voice hard to hide. "I am only a priest, I have no contact with men who arrange such matters. I know nothing of the organizations the late King commanded. I have no authority to instigate any furtive missions. It is not in my jurisdiction."

François could not believe that the Abbot would have been unable to solve his problems. Had he expected too much, based upon what had happened before? Had he been foolish to assume help would be that easy? He sank into the chair, head in hands, then dragged himself to his feet again.

"Then I must go. I still have to warn her of the trouble her husband is in" he mumbled.

"Where did you learn of this threat to your sister-in-law?" the Abbot asked. "For what purpose were you in Scotland?"

"I cannot tell you" he replied honestly.

"No, I thought not" the Abbot sighed, almost resigned to the fact. "Yet you come as James, bearing his face again."

François hung his head in shame and silence, for he dare not reveal anything about it.

The Abbot made him sit again, while he poured François and himself a drink.

"Before you set off on your quest, there are several other issues I am curious about. You insist in talking only of Marie, never of both of them. What if they both want to escape to France?"

"Then Marie will not need my assistance, will she? Her husband has men and resources enough to arrange their passage without me."

"Will you help him if he asks it?"

Her husband! François had not given him any thought at all. What did he matter? He was the one who had put her life in danger, and he cursed him for it. He did not know the man, and he did not want to.

"Personally I think not, by the look on your face."

The man meant nothing to François compared to his fear for Marie. She was his only concern. He would not let her suffer any hardship when the fault was none of her own.

"First she must be told of the risk of remaining there" François argued.

"And how do you mean to approach the Lady Innes or her husband? I doubt he will welcome any stranger who arrives with no proof to substantiate his claims to the warning he brings. Especially when that someone has only his wife's safety on his mind."

François had not thought this through properly. His aim had been to get there first before any of the conspirators could act against Innes. Then what were the chances of seeing Marie alone? Just because he had achieved the impossible at Linlithgow, it did not mean he could repeat the feat anywhere else. Yet this was the more important.

"There is something else you have not considered. They might both believe in the cause he is involved in. They may not want your interference. Also, she may not want to leave her lawful husband or abandon her home. She may love him so much that she does not wish to go back to France, either for her own safety or for you. I am surprised that you expect her to leave her husband when you have not seen her since before her marriage."

"She deserves the choice, whether her husband wishes it or not."

"And if she will not leave – what will you do?"

"Accept her decision, as I did before."

"Hmm. I am tempted to suggest otherwise. Do you hope for the lady's affection in any way?"

François could not afford the luxury of reflecting on the past and had no intention of debating the trivial morals of the matter. He did not have time for argument to redirect his actions.

"I am not so stupid as to hope for that. Especially when the likelihood of my life lasting much longer in this country is less every day. I may use my resemblance to the late King to rescue her, but they will work against me once that is done. The longer I travel with her, the more difficult I make her escape. Yet I can draw them away from her, once she is safe."

"Very noble, but a little too – self-righteous."

They fell silent.

They were interrupted by the boy reminding the Abbot of his next appointment, at which the Abbot nodded and patted the lad affectionately on the shoulder.

"Thank you, I had not forgotten. I will be there" he murmured.

"Is there anyone who can help?" François pleaded, as the Abbot made to leave the room.

The Abbot studied him long and hard, and saw there was no way to dissuade François from this venture. Was François asking too much? Admittedly it was not for himself, but even so it was not the

Abbot's place to interfere or have any part in such actions. He was out of the royal service, retired and would be leaving this abbey soon, to settle elsewhere in a small chapel near the coast. Ayles, who had been a King's man more than he, was his only chance.

"There is one person who might help you, but I fear he will be even angrier at your return. He may refuse because you have broken your promise, after he went to such lengths to save your life originally."

This was all fresh news to François.

"Who is he?"

"For safety's sake I will mention no names. The best I can do is to send the boy to find him."

"Are you willing to do this?" François asked of the boy. The boy readily agreed to deliver the message the Abbot could not put into writing, keeping his excitement well hidden, for he was keen to travel the countryside once more. He promised to find the Abbot's friend, knowing from others that he still continued his trade as a pedlar out of habit and would be at regular locations at certain times of the month.

"How long will it take?"

"To get there and back, while he considers his answer, it may be several days. Maybe even more."

"I cannot wait several days. Any delay could be vital."

The Abbot tried to work out the number of days in which this could be managed. "I shall suggest the boy will meet you, with news or the necessary guide for the lady's onward journey. Can you achieve your rescue and return to a rendezvous in say fifteen days?"

"If you can provide me with a good map to show me the route. I can."

The Abbot pulled out a roll of parchments from the cupboard and left them on the table for François to study while he attended to his other appointment. François eagerly scanned them in detail, for this could make such a difference to his journey. He was still memorising the finely-drawn maps when the Abbot returned.

"They are accurate" The Abbot promised.

"Thank you."

"Remember, it will be for this man to decide if he wishes to assist in this rash development. If he does, then you may have to adapt your plans to suit. He will decide the best action to be taken. You will do as he says, Thistledown. Whatever it is, do you understand?"

François hugged the Abbot with spontaneous relief and set out with new fire in his spirit. He sped through the hostile landscape as if the devil was at his heels. Time was important and he had none to waste. He was secure in the knowledge that as 'King James of Scotland' he could do anything, because this time he had nothing to lose by using his talents to their full advantage. It might just tip the balance in his favour and make the difference where he might otherwise fail. Here, where fear, suspicion and rumour were rife, he hoped a royal ghost would daunt even the most determined opponents long enough for him to succeed.

CHAPTER NINE

François entered the great valley at night and picked his way slowly through the dark landscape, careful of every step and sound. He had thought the whole valley empty of human habitation as he followed the single wide track along the twists and turns of the hillside, until he was suddenly confronted by men in his path. Their swords glinted in the moonlight and François feared he would get no further than this very spot, when a bonneted head appeared at his side.

"Gods, Frenchie! You made enough noise for an army coming along the trail" came the friendly voice.

François could not believe his luck as the man clasped him firmly by the hand.

"Lachlan! What are you doing here?"

"I could ask you the same! But not now. Like you, I am somewhere I should not be. I have come to steal some of the young laird's cattle. An easy task, provided you do not go blundering into the rest of my men."

François looked around, seeing nothing of any other men, nor even those who had previously blocked his path. Lachlan smiled at his searching gaze.

"You had better not see them, or they have failed. Come the morrow this valley will be in uproar, my friend. Innes will have his men scouring the hills for us, so you had best find a good place to hide. It will be a bad time for a stranger to be caught here."

François sighed despondently at the news of his intentions.

"You do nothing to help my plans, then."

"And what plans did you have in mind in this valley?"

"Me – I have come to steal his wife, if she will consent" François joked.

Lachlan opened his eyes wide in admiration, laughed and thought the whole idea tremendous.

"Well Frenchie. I would never have thought it of you. These years have changed you. Do you need my men? We would be glad to help" he asked, full of excited enthusiasm.

"Thank you, but no. My first task is to somehow meet her secretly, to sound her out. Not to have an army take her by force."

Lachlan understood without further explanation that his friend was engaged in a delicate matter which was best accomplished by his own stealth.

"My actions will not hamper your task, indeed they may help. They will not be looking close to the castle. Hide yourself close on the hillside there and you may have your chance while we attract all the attention."

"Will Lord Innes ride with them?"

"Sadly no. He has guests staying there these last few days, and he will not abandon them. He will leave his men to hunt us."

Guests – François feared the worst, that he was already too late. Anxiously he questioned his friend, but Lachlan had no more information to assist him with or time to give him.

"I have mouths to feed with this meat and must hasten this departure. At least I shall have the extra satisfaction of drawing his men out of your way."

Then he too disappeared, as silently as his men had.

Left alone on the hillside, François later heard the night cry of some creature and guessed it signalled that Lachlan and his band were moving on. Taking the advice Lachlan had offered, François concealed himself high in the rocks to wait through the long hours of darkness. There he allowed himself a little of the food the Abbot had given him, aware he would have to ration his supplies for an extra mouth on the return.

The next morning, he finally saw the pursuers head along the valley and once all seemed quieter, he set about surveying the possible approaches to this ancestral stronghold. It was a daunting building, half fortress, half manor, and built into and on the very rock the mountains were made of. It held a strong commanding position above the fast-flowing river, the only entrance being by a bridge from the open road, with rough pasture fronting its length to disappear along the short valley floor. No doubt this was where the cattle had recently grazed, until today. Trees sparsely covered the immediate rugged slopes to the side and back, before stretching into a magnificent forest which merged far into the steep hills beyond.

François glanced once more towards the castle grounds and sighed. He would have to climb up the near-vertical crevices towards the rear, to find out if there were any better opportunities for a stealthy entry. Hobbling his horse at a fair distance into the forest, he set about the long difficult climb to the plateau at the rear. From here, hidden in the treeline, he discovered he could overlook the walled garden which provided a sheltered hollow from the strong winds that gushed down from the hill tops. A place which would surely be suitable for Marie to spend her time.

Unobserved as he was amid the tall trees, he was satisfied he had found the ideal spot from where to watch for any sign of her. Settling down as best he could with the awkward prickly branches digging into him, he huddled close to the gnarled solid trunk, his cloak close about him, to keep his vigil. In the hours that followed hours he waited, desperate for a sign of her and remembering all the obstacles and pitfalls the Abbot had mentioned in this task ahead. Would Marie believe him?

Marie had sat by the window missing the treasured company of her maid, who had been summoned below. She picked up her quill, more out of boredom than any willingness to write, for there was no point when this isolated place made any communication with her family difficult. Distracted, she watched the birds, envying their freedom to fly so far and found herself crying, the tears rolling down her cheeks onto her still hands in her lap. Then, stirred by the commotion of her husband and his friends in the hall below, she grabbed her shawl to escape to the sanity of the garden while she could.

Here she found some small pleasure in the flowers, which reminded her of home far away in France. She had made such a mistake in coming to this country, but she could not change that now. The beginning had been so different. She had been fascinated by her surroundings and her bridegroom had been the most delightful young man she had ever met, and had swept her off her feet the moment she had arrived. He had seemed perfect; he had made such a fuss of her, but her romantic dreams were soon shattered as she began to find he had no understanding of her education. She was brought up in an affectionate, sharing family environment, but he never discussed matters; he simply expected her to accept his decisions without question. She had tried hard to soften his manner, hoping to make their life together better, but her displays of affection were rebuffed. She could not help but compare this miserable existence here with the idyllic times she had spent in France. France, and – François. It hurt to think of him. It only made her more miserable.

At a distance François mistook the slim figure walking aimlessly over the lawns for a maid. He climbed higher to keep the figure in sight, expecting the girl's mistress to join her. Only when he heard a voice bellow her name from the building and she hurried to its command did he look more closely.

It could not be!. He stared after her. This was not the girl he had left. There was no lightness or gaiety in her steps, no gentle smile as she nervously faltered in her rush. François was shaken.

He could hardly wait for her return to the garden, but when he at last saw her again, her red, puffed eyes worried him. She did not look well. His impulse was to call out to her, but prudently he held back. His voice would never have reached her, and if he had shouted loud enough, he would have been heard by others besides Marie.

Silently he willed her to come to the bottom of the garden, nearer to him, but she remained stubbornly beyond his reach. He realised he was too far away to attract her attention; he would have to be close to the wall to make sure she alone heard him.

He leapt down from his perch, hurried down the rocky slope, scrambled through the wet narrow gulley and climbed up the jagged outcrop to reach the corner of the outer garden wall. Out of breath and bent double for a time, he began his examination of this annoying obstacle to find a way to talk to her. The wall was solid, and too tall close up. The remaining parts of the original outer wall, great masses of collapsed stone, lay scattered around the more recent rebuilt outer wall, deliberately left to deter any unwelcome approach such as his. It slowed him in his search, and he soon found that the former openings had been filled in to re-strengthen the defence, except for one doorway which had been blocked by fallen turret slabs. It was all he could do to squeeze into the space between the wooden door and the stone blocks.

Marie had wandered to the lower terrace of the garden,

desperate for the peace and solitude of her sheltered favourite spot in the sun. The wind rustled through the trees and Marie fancied she heard the voice dearest to her heart. For all the world she wished she had never left his side, never been foolish enough to think anyone could have taken his place. Duty had kept her from following her heart. Now, regretfully, she realised how much she loved him and remembered guiltily how she had ignored his desperate pleading. She had ignored her heart and had no one to blame but herself for her present unhappiness. There was no way out, no future except this.

"Marie! Marie!"

Marie shook her head. There was the wind playing tricks again, that voice in her memory gently calling to her, as it had done so often in the past. Marie smiled ruefully to herself, keeping that precious sound within her head for a while longer.

Then a scratching and tapping from outside the garden door startled her, making her jump back. She stared at the solid wooden door, wondering if some wild creature lurked there to threaten her in her last refuge.

And then she heard a voice – a French voice. His voice.

"Marie! Marie! Don't run away! Please, it is François!"

She shook her head. This was madness, her imagination playing tricks again or some cruel spirit using his voice and name. The voice whispered to her again, calling for her to open the door. She covered her ears, blocking out he tormenting voice, for how could it be real, François could not be here. More miserable then before, she ran back to the house, to wipe out the disturbing hallucination.

François could not understand. He tapped on the door, and still she did not answer his gentle whispers. He could not see inside, yet he felt she had gone, run away from him. He wondered if in her loneliness she had truly forgotten him. Dejected, he turned back to await another opportunity, facing another delay which neither of them could afford.

François found no other place of access through this solid defensive wall, which at intervals had been raised to form battlement walkways. He returned to the buried doorway once more and again squeezed himself into the gap. The door with its metal stays, studs and hinges looked as solid as the stone it was set in. Yet there was nowhere else to try. He set about pushing and pulling the smaller pieces of stone away from the door to give himself more room to investigate its resistance. Wedging his back against the stones and placing his feet on the door, he pushed hard, trying to use himself as a lever. Although it was too thick to break through, the door creaked and groaned, and at last showed slight signs of giving way in places. As he moved his feet around the whole door, testing the pressure in this manner, he concluded that only the bolts at the top and bottom inside really prevented it from opening.

His work had not finished. Using his knife, he worked away at a splinter at the top of the door to widen it enough to form a spy hole, a useful aid to confirming if Marie was alone the next time she came to the garden. Finally, when it was almost too dark to see any more, he moved more stones to make the space outside the door large enough for a person to squeeze through.

He could do no more here until tomorrow. He settled down by the door for the night, for the space he made also gave him shelter from the cool winds. Although it was still autumn, it already felt like winter up here. Come the dawn, he knew he could only wait, occasionally peeking through the crack he had widened to watch for her.

The next day Marie returned to the garden. Calmer now, she

allowed herself to settle down to a little sewing to keep her mind occupied. Carefully she unpicked the old worn lace, not noticing that the replacement pieces and silks she had brought with her had fallen to the ground, where they lay until caught by the light breeze. Little by little they were dragged and tossed about, finally coming to rest, rustling and fluttering but firmly lodged by the far garden door. After a while Marie put aside her material and began searching for the missing lace, the search bringing her further and further along the garden.

Marie heard François' voice calling her, always calling her from beyond the wall, but not trusting the tempting sounds, she made no attempt to answer, preferring to rescue her treasured lace instead. François was watching the performance, and as she reached the half-overgrown locked door, he saw his chance. As she bent to pick up the lace, there came a tremendous banging against the door, which shook on its hinges, followed by a desperate cry which stopped her alarmed flight.

"For God's sake, Marie don't run away. It's me – It is François!" he pleaded.

Marie stood facing the door, trembling as his frantic words tried to persuade her to he was real.

"Marie, come to the door!"

François! Dare she hope? Somehow an invisible force moved her towards it, and her hand touching the wood. Was he really there? He kept talking, gently reassuring her, telling her that he could see her through the slit in the door, and if she looked up she would see him wave a piece of twig through it. Now she had no doubt, but how could she reach him?

His words were soft now, telling her what she must do. Nervously she bent to the bottom bolt. It was heavy, rusty and stiff and it took all her strength to pull it little by little along its housing until it was free. He praised her efforts and reassured her as she stretched to the top bolt, but her fingers could not reach it, let alone move it.

"It's no good, it's out of reach!" she cried to him.

"Is there anything in the garden you can use? A spade, a hoe?"

She nervously checked behind her towards the house, then rushed around the garden and returned with a hoe. She set about prodding and pushing the top bolt, stopping every time it slipped noisily off the metal in her attempts. At last it slid free and she threw the hoe aside to help pull the heavy door as François pushed it from the outside. The stiff and rusty hinges made it difficult to move, but it opened enough for a person to slip through the small space.

She was desperate to reach François, to see him, to be with him, if only for a short while. She looked at this person who beckoned her urgently towards him, but as he advanced to assist her, she pulled back in horror.

This was not François. She did not know this scruffy stranger who had used his voice to fool and frighten her. Panic-stricken, she stepped back inside to lean shaking against the sturdy door, trying to shut it against whatever trick this was. But it would not move for her, and she cried, frightened at her frustration, expecting the strange man to burst in and grab her.

François protested that it was he, despite the change of appearance. How could she reject him so swiftly without taking time to look properly? Surely she trusted him. Would she not look again?

Marie recognised the change of his tone, the choice of words. Cautiously she put her head through the archway to consider this apparition. At last she saw past the attire, through the unkempt hair and stubbled face. It was indeed François. She was not mistaken.

He had meant to pick up her lost silk which fluttered near his feet, to offer it gently back into her hands, but the idea was forgotten when she came up to him. She clutched his hands, whispered his name and laid her head on his chest. As she felt those strong arms about her, she wished she could melted into his heart and never exist again, except in him. To feel his strength and security left her numb and exhausted with gratitude. Just to touch him was all the joy she needed. Her warm, gentle smile was echoed in his, the smile she had almost forgotten. She did not know what miracle had brought him here; she did not care, only that he was truly here and that was enough to cope with for the moment.

Suddenly he took her in his arms, and held her as he had never believed he would again. Marie was still his.

"Oh François! Tell me I am not dreaming" she sighed.

"You are not dreaming." His own words choked in his throat. "You cannot know how much I missed you."

She glanced towards the open garden door, fearing discovery every second she remained. Frightened for herself as she was, she was suddenly more frightened for François.

"I cannot be too long out of sight. The open door will be suspicious. It was so foolish of you to come."

"I had to, Marie. I have important news. I have come to warn you. Your husband has put you both in danger. He must be warned against his associates. Their conspiracy has reached certain ears at court."

He had wondered if she would believe him or simply dismiss his accusation as too fanciful. Even worse, he hoped that she wouldn't see as some poor excuse to destroy her marriage. In fact François was surprised at her lack of concern for her husband's activities. There was little reaction to his devastating news. She seemed to accept this impending disaster easily.

"Do you understand?" he asked.

"I am not surprised. He makes no secret of his complaints against the lowland lords. He only listens to those who agree with him. It will not stop him."

"The penalties are severe."

"It will make no difference" she sighed.

François did not need to be told twice. Her husband deserved everything that was coming. But not so Marie.

"Then what will you do?" he asked.

"What choice do I have? I must stay." Her sadness was evident.

She was married, duty bound to stay with her husband, bound by her marriage vows and respectability. Her upbringing allowed nothing else.

"Why should you share his punishment? Wouldn't you prefer to go home to France and your family?"

"Oh, François, if only it were possible" she answered wistfully, for this was too much to hope or expect.

"Marie, listen to me. Listen carefully to what I say. There is something I have to tell you, and it is very important you understand this before you make your decision. I will help you leave here, but I cannot come with you to France."

"What?"

"I came to Scotland for another reason and because of that, I may put your life in greater danger. I will take you to safety. That is all I can do. If you leave you husband, it must be for the right reason, because you want to go home, not because of any fondness you may still have for me. I will not return to France with you, I can never return there. We can never be together."

"You expect me to go without you? Why give me hope and then take all my hopes away? Is this your revenge for the past?"

"You know me better than that."

"Do I?"

Marie knew she had wounded him. She saw him catch his breath, yet he held his tongue, obviously he did not blame her for her reaction. There was an awkward silence before he returned to the matter at hand.

"Go now, quickly, and come again tomorrow. If you sit in the garden sewing at this end, that way we can talk from either side of the door without anyone knowing."

Luckily neither the slightly open garden gate nor her long absence from the garden had been noticed, and Marie managed to return to the house safely, to ponder on the extraordinary episode. She had dreamt of leaving, it was what she wanted the most; but was she brave enough to risk such a wanton act?

Words, ideas, thoughts and dreams were fine, they kept her sane at times, but she was realistic. Positive action was a completely different matter when to succeed meant everything and failure meant dreadful punishment for them both. Dear reckless François! Looking at his serious face, she knew he meant his promise, he would try to achieve it, knew his determination but also the opposition he faced. How dare he give her hope, when she had none? Hope was a sharp contrast to her misery, which could not be contained any longer. The truth of her unhappiness poured out amid tears she had not dared shed until now. She cried softly at first and then with great sobs as the stress she had withheld was finally released.

She had made her decision. Didn't he realise she would go with him anywhere, for an hour, a day, forever? Whatever he asked of her she would do. She could hardly wait to return to the garden the next day to tell him.

"I will help you return to France – if that is what you wish" he repeated.

"I do. I want to go home. But they will never let me leave!" she pleaded.

"Then we shall not ask them" François joked, trying to make light of the matter.

Yet all the while the need for urgency ponded in his brain, an urgency he still had to convey to Marie. They must go soon, or her courage might fail at the very moment she had to be strong.

"This is your only chance" he urged her. "You must be sure. I cannot wait another day. It will not be easy. Will you trust me? Are you sure you want this and all the danger it entails?"

With François at her side, what else mattered? She trusted him completely. To be with him again was a prayer answered.

"Even if we fail" she promised, because she had begun to believe they could manage even this.

He had spent the previous night working out his plan. The uneven ground at the rear would be impossible to cross in the dark. No, he would have to use the main entrance, before the other men returned to the castle or those from the court arrived.

"We have to go this very night, when the darkness hides our flight" he told her. As they made their rushed plans, there was one last warning he had to give her.

"No matter what I say to your husband and his guests, do not be surprised. Do not question anything. You must not stop, you must follow our plans regardless."

François was all that was precious to her, all she had. It was only his dependability which gave her the courage to return for these last few hours.

How could she hide her fear of what she must do? She kept to her room until she was summoned to join her husband and guests for the evening meal. Silently she sat picking at her food, not daring to glance up, while her husband, obsessed with his friends, took little notice of her disposition. For once she was glad to be excluded from their conversation, their thick accents and local colloquialisms making it hard to understand them at times. Of all his friends she feared Murdo of Uist and Lord Neil the most.

As they remained immersed in their conversation, Marie slipped away. Her heart pounding, she searched out her warmest clothes and pushed the rest of the tangled, discarded garments out of the way. She listened in between her hurried movements for the slightest sound of anyone coming. No one came, not even her maid, for she was still busy in the kitchen, helping keep their visitors supplied in the great hall.

Once dressed, Marie paused, glancing at her few jewels and the silver hand mirror her parents had given her. The jewels would fetch money to help them on their way and she quickly bundled them into her jacket pocket. There was nothing else here she valued or cherished a fraction as much as the freedom she craved. She was ready, and she must not let him down. He had risked so much. Dare she think of home? No, not yet, she must concentrate on one thing at a time. First she must escape. Surely that was enough to begin with.

She fidgeted at the top of the stairs before creeping quietly down a few steps at a time, to gradually edge herself into position where she could see the front door to the main courtyard, whilst staying hidden from those who passed below. Safety seemed so far away as she stared at the door. Somewhere beyond was François.

Meanwhile, against an ominous fiery pink sky which reflected its colour across the countryside, François had scrambled back up the valley to find his horse, which had been patiently grazing all this time. He could not ride in along that open road as he would be spotted and challenged long before he reached the bridge or the main building, so he would regrettably have to leave the animal here. He prayed he could acquire horses easily from the stables. God what was he doing? How was this going to work! He was putting them both at risk.

There was no undetectable approach to the inner courtyard, so he would have to rely on stealth to reach it. He shivered as the night obliterated the features of the landscape, and the wind howled as he crept along the river bank towards the front of the castle and the main gateway. Two sentries stood outside, forcing him to crawl on his front until he reached the bridge buttresses, where for a moment he could stand unseen. Suddenly he felt a hand on his shoulder, but even as he turned, prepared to fight, he was relieved to find it was Lachlan who stood before him.

"You took long enough to get here! I have been here for at least an hour" hissed Lachlan at François.

François grinned, delighted to see his friend and have his help. For now, if he did not get out of the great hall alive, Lachlan could get Marie to safety.

With very little noise or effort they managed between them to overpower the two sentries, bind them and lock them in the gatehouse, where they would not be heard. They entered the courtyard and made their way to the stables. They watched the lanterns slowly being lit in the main building, the candles burning brightly in the great hall, and tried to estimate how long the evening meal and refreshments would go on for. Satisfied they had time, they began their preparations by turning all but three horses loose from the stalls. Quietly they ushered the rest of them out over the bridge to the pasture, where, despite their frantic waving of arms, they obstinately refused to wander any further, content to graze where they were. Unable to waste any further time on them, they returned to the still, quiet, empty courtyard.

François looked for Marie's shadow at her window as she

moved about upstairs, then the darkness as the candles were snuffed out. Listening and watching for danger, they led the horses to the main door, glad that the deafening wind would drown their movements over the last stretch of gravel to the entrance. Lachlan stood keeping close hold of the reins as François softly crossed the steps.

His hand on the latch, he paused, then lifted the lever and pushed gently against it, testing to see if the lock had been turned against him. It had not, and the door opened a crack. Inside he could hear the sounds of the gentlemen engaged in drinking. Slowly he pushed open the door a little more, quickly glanced about him and with no sign of anything amiss, he stepped through the gap and closed the door behind him, to avoid the draught being felt or noticed within. Flattened against the wall, he checked his surroundings. In front of him were the stairs, to the left the way to the kitchens and to the right the large archway into the great hall.

Marie's frightened face peered at François from the shadows of the stairs, and when he beckoned her forward, she flew down the remaining steps, never taking his eyes from his, and ran to his outstretched hand. Relieved, she had hardly clutched his arm for support when her husband's voice bellowed after her, telling them both she had been seen. Marie stared hopelessly at François, not daring to turn around, but François barely flinched. He guided her behind him and, indicating silence, made her remain by the main front door.

François knew he was committed now to his next act. There was no turning back, he had no other choice; their one chance lay in his own hands. He had been King James before and he would be James again, an angry commanding James, provided the fates were kind enough to allow at least one of these Highland lords to recognise the royal Stuart features. They had not seen him yet; only

Innes had caught sight of Marie and made to move from his chair. François stepped forward into the great hall, in full view of its occupants, rounding on his heel to face them squarely, his head up, his shoulders thrown back, his body tense as he stared defiantly at them. His hand rested on his sword, prepared to use it if necessary.

Chairs were noisily pushed aside and turned over in the rush of men scrambling to their feet, surprised at an intruder so brash as to enter their midst. Their hands were drawing weapons, their faces snarling as they advanced on this solitary intruder, but François hardly blinked as he watched them. Indeed the glance between the two men at the front and their hesitation, which spread to the others, told François all he needed. His face had worked to his own advantage for once. He prepared to deliver a regal performance, upright and proud, fearless and strong, his eyes fixed upon them.

"In the name of James IV, King of Scotland, you will stay your weapons!" he growled.

Sir Neil, nervous of their plotting, grabbed Murdo, unable to believe his eyes. Like the whole of Scotland, he had been sure the King was dead, and Murdo, a fighting man, for all his cunning instinct, did not understand what was happening. They both halted sharply in their tracks, blocking the rest of the men from making a fatal mistake and commanding them to obey this man. That build, the bearing and those features subdued them. They did not dare lay hand on the dirt and dust-stained figure of their late King. Alive or dead, who knew how many men he had at his call, either human or from another world? Superstition and fear held them back.

"What nonsense is this? Who gives orders in my own house?" Innes demanded.

"Let it be" threatened Murdo, holding his arm.

Their host was taken aback and rendered speechless as all voices died away and a deadly silence enveloped them all. They had not yet realised that Marie was connected to this sudden apparition in their midst; she had been forgotten in all this, and equally she did not understand the trance which held these men.

"What is wrong?" she whispered.

"I'll explain. The horses are outside. Go quickly, Lachlan will help you" François answered under his breath. He pushed her backwards towards the door, while remaining in the entrance to deter any reaction from those inside until he could be sure she was safely in the saddle. He said no more to the company facing him. A vicious draught from the door swirled cold around them, flickering and extinguishing most of the candles. Then he was gone. Swiftly sprinting to his horse and leaping astride, he joined Marie and Lachlan as they raced into the night.

Pandemonium followed their departure, and raised voices fetched servants from their chores as loud disagreement raged through the castle. Everyone was demanding to be heard. Who was this man who had challenged them and held them at bay with such authority? This man who had spoken in the King's name, fearless of them?

"How does he act for the late King, without being the King?"

"How could it be the King? The King is dead. Yet I doubt there is any other man alive who bears those features."

"Then it was his spirit."

"I will have no dealings with dead spirits, of Kings or any other kind."

"He appeared like a ghost, I agree. But no spirit needs to take horses, and the Lady Innes seemed willing and prepared to go with him."

"Then what did he know, and why did he come?"

"He came alone, unannounced and without an escort. There

has been no intelligence to warn us of any worrying rumours at court."

None of them knew of the reason for this event, only that, ghost or not, whoever the intruder might be, it was obvious it had been planned and that Marie was party to it. She was an unknown quantity and the extent of her knowledge about them was uncertain, but however little she understood, in the right ears it would be enough to implicate them all. Would she go straight to Parliament and court?

Kenneth Innes scowled. Marie had made him look a fool and he cursed the man who had the nerve to help her. Unlike the others, the identity of the stranger was irrelevant to him. How had they communicated when she had seen no one, nor had any correspondence? How dare she run away, his wife, that chit of a girl, that coy French miss with all her female sensibilities, that timid creature, mild manners and frightened obedience? What a convincing act. She had fooled him, deceived him.

Desperately they rode into the night, diverting only briefly to collect François' other horse to prevent it falling into the wrong hands, then onward they raced until they had left the valley floor and gained the advantage of the wooded slopes. Here they paused to catch their breath and look at each other, unable to believe that they had actually succeeded in this outlandish, improbable plan. So far no one was chasing them. Here Lachlan left them, keen to catch up with his own men. They exchanged a warm handshake, their friendship reflected in their expression.

"Thank you for coming to help me" said François.

"It was my pleasure. I did not see how you could manage it alone."

"I don't think I could have" François agreed, as Lachlan prepared to ride away.

With that the pair of them continued their journey through the darkness, listening for any sound of pursuit or danger, until eventually they were forced to rest, both for themselves and the horses, in a well-hidden gulley. Marie was exhausted by the hard ride and she fell into his arms as he lifted her down. Shakily she clung to him, unable to talk or comprehend exactly what had happened and François buried her into him, wrapping his cloak around them both and holding her warm from the night chill. He let her sleep snuggled up against him, her head nestled into his neck as it had done so often in the past, and he took joy from all the things he had missed. She was in his arms again, and his heart burned to have her close to his body again.

She slept peacefully and reassured there, while he remained alert for any sound of danger. He held her, reluctant to wake her as he knew he should. Much later, she raised her head and slipped her arms about his chest to hug him. This was so real that she wanted to cry. It was wonderful to see him there, and she hoped that every future waking moment she would find him there beside her, looking as he did this moment. His expression so completely lost in hers.

"How could I have been so blind?" she reflected.

"We cannot dwell on regrets and the past. You are on your way to France" he murmured into her ear.

"To France!" she whispered, feeling content to stay like this forever.

Yes, she could see it as she spoke. The memory of France, the memory of how her life used to be - and how it would soon be again. She looked up, her dark eyes watching his expression. Her only regret was that they had wasted so much time apart.

As the days passed, Marie was impatient for the dream to become reality and without care to herself, she rode urgently beside him, determined to match his energy to reach France the sooner. They ate only twice a day to preserve their rations and when they rested the horses she sank to the ground, fighting the lethargy which seeped into her tired body. She must not weaken, she told herself, nor complain, for fear François would slow their progress. Instead she smiled at him and François, seeing her smile, was satisfied to push on further, heading east and then south, hoping they would meet the Abbot's man somewhere on the road in the next day or so. Engrossed in their need for speed they rode silently, their mounts bouncing along at an easy gait and covering the ground effortlessly. Even the spare horse, which had originally jostled about being led, had settled into the routine.

Sir Kenneth Innes had scoured the night and the next day, chasing shadows and searching every scrub, thicket, old ruin and hut, finding no clues or sign of their quarry. For him, finding Marie would exonerate his own faults. He remembered with discomfort her natural questions. He had resented her intelligent interest in his affairs and disliked the way she had disturbed his conscience from the beginning. Innes felt unhappy about not finding them, but eventually agreed with his friend's decision to join Murdo, who had set out in a completely different direction.

Murdo of Uist was a clever man, important to these Highland lords. He needed no excuse to exploit their stupidity. He had no time for fruitless searches, assuming the two had either gone to ground or more logically gone to court to testify against them, so he set out to contact such people as had ears to the court. There he meant to intercept the rumours and prevent them from reaching the wrong people.

François and Marie covered much ground without any sign of

pursuit, and François could not believe their luck. Tired from the hours of constant anxiety, he slept briefly by her side while she sat watching the road, but mostly looking at him. She found it impossible not to touch him, her hand resting lightly on his thick auburn hair, absently fingering the wisps ruffled at his collar. She saw him as he had always been, carefree and energetic, but also kind and considerate to her. His expressive, charming features were strangely serious on the journey and his infectious smile rarely seen. Yet despite this, she felt happy at this moment.

They continued their hasty flight, their horizons ever changing as they avoided settlements and other casual travellers in an effort to remain undetected. Suddenly Marie shuddered and pulled her horse to a halt, startling François.

"I thought I heard something" she whispered.

They both listened, François for the sounds of danger and Marie for the faint cry she thought she had heard. Then he heard it too, a scream of pain breaking the silence some way off. Marie was agitated, her small hands clutching and pulling at the edge of her cloak as she looked fearfully at him for some solution. They could take no chances. François turned them from the track across the springy turf and enter the cover of the woods, cursing the necessity of another diversion and delay.

"It may be nothing, sounds carry" he commented, trying to make light of the matter. But their attempt to avoid discovery had brought them upon an alarming scene of violence. Unaware of being observed, two thugs were attacking an elderly man, determined to rob him of his goods and purse.

François cursed. He had to intervene, for it was not in his nature to turn his back and ride away. Pushing Marie out of sight with the horses, he leapt to the aid of the weakening victim, who doggedly held on to his purse despite the punishment he received. François let out a wild cry to attract their attention as he charged into the clearing. The men's blows were unskilled and the only flash of steel raised against him resulted in a counter-attack which left one dead and one in flight.

Marie had watched mesmerised from her place in the trees. Having witnessed her companion's deadly precision with his one accurate thrust of his sword, she could not take her eyes from the dead man, nor forget the horror she had seen François commit.

François ignored the bloody body on the ground to attended to the old man. Using few words he helped him to his feet, dusted him down and steadied the man as he stumbled. The old man grabbed his hand, mumbling his thanks repeatedly, while François tried to stop him and make sure the man could safely be left, so as to extract himself from the scene swiftly before the man saw either of them in enough detail to be able to report it later if asked.

Thus dismissing his act of charity, François walked back to Marie and they rode off without noticing the old man's reaction to his benefactor. The man crossed himself, believing he had been blessed by the great powers above for sending such a splendid knight to save this poor worthless servant. What miracle had happened! The ghost of King James himself had saved him! Although rumours of other sightings were not unknown, the old man knew that few in the village would believe him, and as the shadows from the woods rode off, he saw a vision he would never tell about. James and his lady riding together, but not the English Queen; instead he supposed it to be the ghost of Margaret Drummond, for had it not been claimed in some quarters that they had secretly married before her death?

The old man smiled sympathetically, their secret safe in his sentimental old heart, and waddled off towards his home in the village.

Marie, still shocked at the sight of bloodshed and death, stared at François as if she no longer knew him. He had taken another man's life so easily, made no reference to it and showed no qualms about the act as they resumed their travels. She brooded about it for the rest of their ride that afternoon, trying to fight the rejection and revulsion she felt.

"You killed that man! You killed him without any hesitation and thought nothing of it" she snapped.

"What else did you expect? It is either kill or be killed. This is Scotland, Marie, lawless, brutal and vicious. Men live and die by the sword here. I warned you what it was like when you wanted to come here."

"But you were so – callous!"

"Did you think your escape was going to be easy? That we could just ride away without any trouble? This sword is the only weapon we have to survive and I will do whatever is necessary."

She could not accept his justification and drew away from him, disappointed because this was the first serious flaw in the perfect hero she had always seen him to be.

It was time to move on again, and fetching the animals, he dragged her to her feet and pushed her into the saddle. They rode in hostile silence, each deep within their own thoughts.

Marie was heavy hearted. In this last day they had grown apart, and she wished for all the world they had not. She tried to dispel her previous doubts, but for all their closeness, there were moments when she did not understand François. He had been distant, held himself back; he was not the same. The brightness of his character had vanished, and his French mannerisms were replaced by the solemn seriousness of the Scottish people. There had been no laughter, no gay dancing eyes gazing into hers; instead they were sad and cast down. He was silent, shutting her out from his concerns for her safety which apparently affected him deeply. If only she could heal this rift. She felt sorry for being childish earlier, as she realised the great responsibility she put on him.

Now they had stopped again, she had time to be curious. She wanted to know more about the circumstances of his presence in Scotland and of his arrival at her husband's castle. Yet he would not answer her questions, and she could not understand why.

"There is nothing to tell" he said. "Except that being here allowed me to rescue you."

"That is no answer."

François shrugged. It was the only one he was likely to give. But Marie would not be put off. There were too many details which had begun to puzzle her.

"Why didn't my husband and his friends try to stop us leaving?"

"They were too surprised. They didn't know who else or how many were with me."

"They seemed very hesitant, almost afraid of what they saw."

"They were merely unsure of who I was. They didn't want to do anything too rashly. It was enough to make the difference."

With a sudden impulse he bent to kiss the top of her head, which put off her intention of pursuing the matter further. She forgave him for being irritable, although she saw this as another of his ways to avoid continuing the conversation, but she forgave him.

The land, still in the shadow of early morning, found François awake, reflecting as to the clearness of mind he would need today, for today they should reach the rendezvous point. He remembered the pain of their last parting, but his time he was a different person, hardened by experience, resigned to its necessity. He had put all idea of any future with Marie from his mind a long time ago. He loved her, and he would always love her wherever she was, it was something he had come to terms with. He could live with that knowledge now.

But Marie, how was he to prepare her? She had been so happy to be with him, she trusted him more than he deserved. Soon he must end this spell, yet he would be relieved to have her safely gone.

"We must soon part. I know you will not like it, but it must be this way. I depend upon you to be brave. I come no further with you. It is arranged for another to guide you to the coast and take you to France."

She did not believe he really meant it. She had never thought he would not come with her, although he had warned her right at the beginning that he could not. She had thought he would surely change his mind.

"François, do not abandon me like this! I will not go with anyone else" she cried.

"You must. For my sake and your own. It is important that I know you are safe. I need to know you are safe."

She looked at his saddened face, she did not want to lose him, she tried to understand, but those expressive eyes stared firmly ahead, avoiding hers. She was afraid to ask more and slipped her hands into his empty hand to see him close his eyes as he gently squeezed his fingers about hers. She leaned on his arm and they stood together as they had done before in France.

"I dare not start wanting what I cannot have" he confessed.

"You will never lose me!"

His heart ached, for he had no future of his own to give her. It was the one thing he could not promise her. He had denied the intensity of his love for her. He would never see her again after today. What good had their love done for either of them? His only consolation was that the memory of her was worth anything which might follow. He had tried to forget her once, but now he would never do so. He suddenly felt very tired and very old.

She accepted his decision, because she had failed him before, and she would not make that mistake again. She meant to prove she would trust him this time. Who else was there to take care of her, who else loved her enough to risk his whole life for her? She only wished she knew what power held him in this hostile country, when everything they both wanted awaited them in the warmth of their native France. When would he join her, when would he come? Once he had finished with this place he would come home eventually, despite what he thought. Despite everything he said. She had to believe that.

CHAPTER TEN

François had no doubt that the Abbot's friend, whoever he was, would have everything arranged as they approached the designated place. Although he did not know much of the man personally, the trust the Abbot put in him cast aside any doubts. Likewise, whoever was sent by this valued stranger would also be as careful as possible to achieve the safety of this clandestine appointment. None of them would be wanting any witnesses around. François prowled the area like a wild cat several times, cautiously checking the surrounding cover to make sure. Then he settled to watch for the coming of their contact.

As he stood studying the way, glad this would soon be over, he felt surprisingly calm and now the hour was almost here he found it the easiest thing of all to let Marie go. His mood was only broken by the arrival of the boy from the abbey and his companion.

The boy had been busy, having met with Ayles, who had immediately set off to make further arrangements, when he had accompanied the guide to the meeting place. Here his purpose was to identify the Frenchman to his companion and likewise to verify to François the man whom was to escort Marie. His task done and acknowledged, he left them to their discussions, for he had other plans of his own to follow, despite the Abbot's instructions.

François and the escort talked rapidly for fear of discovery, then, reassured, François returned to Marie, who clutched at him tightly, reluctant to be parted from him. He knew she did not want to go without him, but would go because he insisted. He let her hold him briefly, kissed her, a kiss to remember, a last lingering kiss which bonded the desire they felt between them. Then, to prevent any weakening on either part, he twisted her quickly around, lifted her on to her horse and slapped it solidly to set it off at a gallop.

She gasped at the suddenness of his actions, trying to cry out her protest as she clung to the saddle until she gained control at the top of the rise where the escort waited. Panting and windblown, she turned to look back for François, only to find the place empty of all but shadows and dust. He had gone already. She wanted to cry out his name aloud, to have it carry on the haunting winds to reach him, but it remained softly echoing on her lips instead.

Reluctantly she let the guide lead her away, her only consolation being that the sooner she was safe, the sooner he would come for her. She would learn to be patient.

If François imagined he heard her soft cry in the wind, he gave no visible sign, riding urgently back in the direction they had come, planning to confound his enemies. Most importantly, he intended to engage in a policy of action to occupy these men completely until Marie was out of reach. Then he would have peace one way or another.

Yet, as he reflected later, whilst he sat with his sword playing in his hand occasionally flicking the dirt at his feet, it was not so easy. Instead of being relieved that he had achieved the one task which meant the most to him, there was a deflated, sombre mood about him. He had no future except to waste time teasing and distracting his pursuers, and after he had done his best to pit his wits and strength against them, then what?

If only he could stop thinking so much; it never did him any good. Doubts always returned. There was nothing left to strive or fight for, except simply keeping his life. Each day he survived would be one more than he expected, although he had accepted that he could not outrun them all forever, there were too many of them. He wondered who would come first; Lord Innes and his friends, de la Bastie's agents or even those men who had sought him before. All of them were deadly foes.

While François had more on his mind than de la Bastie, the latter fretted, cursing the irresponsibility of François for being unable to influence the Queen. He also could not forgive his men for letting François vanish. An unwilling participant in their game from the start, he was too valuable to lose. He could not believe that he had escaped their clutches completely, but none of their vast network had reported any sign of him. Thus de la Bastie remained at court, busy to represent the Duke of Albany and hoping to make up for this failure.

Lord Lyle let out a penetrating whoop of glee at the unexpected report Thurn had brought him. Never had he been better pleased and his face beamed with unusual delight. He did not mind that the news came via that old opportunist Murdo of Uist, just as long as it was correct. With renewed desire for satisfaction after being cheated out of his quarry once before, he fetched the Frenchman's sword, which he still held, tapped the dull blade and thought once more of its owner. He had given up after they had searched in vain after the attack on him by bandits, believing he had probably perished.

So Innes and his friends were puzzled by the apparition were they? He could tell them who this mysterious stranger was. He could, but he would not. He wanted François for himself. He wanted him still able to talk. He doubted that the true purpose of the Frenchman's return was to simply abscond with the lady Innes. No it meant more. It confirmed the earlier ideas he had always suspected.

Lord Lyle smiled to himself. Yes, he would help these Highland gentlemen, offer them every hospitality, promise them any assistance in their search. He sent his messenger to urge Murdo and his companions to visit his estates, where the atmosphere was conducive to their task. By pretending friendship, he gained extra help in his own search for François.

Ayles had found François' camp without too much difficulty and stood above the clearing, listening and watching for any telltale signs of his being followed. It was good to be back in service again. He had missed the excitement and nerve-tingling sense of danger he had previously enjoyed. He had continued his pastime as a roaming pedlar because it would have been too suspicious to suddenly stop, and besides he found the habit hard to drop; it had become his way of life. He had known and served the late King well; the mysteries and intrigues, communications and unspoken messages in the service of Scotland had been his trade. Even now he knew more than most of what was going on, not that he was involved any more. When the boy relayed the message from the Abbot asking assistance for the lady, he had been surprised, until he heard of her connection to François. So the Frenchman had returned; although he guessed it had not been for the lady, it was more likely that others had forced his appearance. He knew of the council's concerns about the Queen's regency and the offer to a reluctant Duke of Albany. Yet he had had not thought the Duke of Albany to be so ruthless or clever as to find François, to use him. But someone in his service had, someone who was dangerous.

François must have been careless to attract such attention. The King would not have liked this turn of events.

"François!" It was the clear, authoritative voice of a man who knew the person he was addressing, but François, although startled by the silhouette on the skyline before him, did not move. Just because a man knew his name did not mean he could be trusted or that he should approach any nearer. Many knew his name who were not his friend. This man had evidently known where to find him and clearly knew him by sight, whilst he in return did not recognise nor remember the stranger who waited quite comfortably ahead of him.

François hesitated, neither acknowledging nor turning away from this encounter. Instead he remained facing the man, who stared back unflinchingly.

Ayles reflected that the young man had aged much since he had last seen him, and he could not help half-hating him for his continuing disconcerting resemblance to the late King. Annoyed at François, he mean to treat him harshly.

"So you return to confuse matters after all. You disregard the warnings and the trouble others took on your behalf. You scorn the sacrifice the old woman made protecting you. I am astounded at your deliberate defiance. You promised the King you would stay in France. His majesty would curse you for your treachery!"

François was dumb with astonishment. This man knew much more than his enemies could ever have found out.

"Oh, Thistledown! What have you done? To stir up such trouble again. This time it will be more than your past enemies who will search for you. There is a husband, and I suspect a certain de la Bastie, who will be more than anxious to find you."

François did not remember having seen this man before, yet he had used the King's name for him, known of the promise he had given James and their meeting. How did he know so much when he had not told the Abbot everything?

"You need not deny that he and the man he represents at court are connected to your return."

"Who are you?" he asked.

"A reluctant traveller forced from his retirement because of your reappearance in Scotland. I did not rescue your unconscious body in order to have to repeat my acquaintance with you. Your previous experiences should have been enough to keep you in France forever."

This was the man who had delivered him to the safety of the Abbot's care; this man had saved his life. François earnestly walked forward to meet his benefactor, surprised to discover that there was nothing exceptional about him.

Ayles advised adjournment from the open track and François followed, eager to thank him for his past actions, but Ayles had no time for such trivial talk. He was intent on humbling him further, on making him see sense.

"Once you were aware of the significance of your features you were expected to avoid playing into their hands, to live quietly" said Ayles.

François wanted to argue, to explain, but there was too much, too many words to find.

"I thought I was safe after James died."

"Then you should have known better."

"I admit I was reckless, I let an obsessive misery become my undoing. I tried hard to avoid this involvement."

"Enough! I did not come to hear your explanations. I came to rail against you. To curse you for your stupidity, because James cannot. You have done nothing to deserve the life the King let you keep. You dishonoured his memory by tricks and confusion. You do not serve Scotland by returning, even if it was not by your choice. You waste your time and mine. You are now in a trap of your own making, one you alone must undo."

"Undo? How do I begin?" François asked, surprised by the idea.

"By not waiting here to delay and confuse your pursuers. Do you want them to catch and punish you? To become a martyr for no good reason? What good does it do? Where is your common sense? You do not help anyone by staying. The lady is safe from here on. She nears the coast as we speak. She was not followed."

François smiled to himself. Marie was safe. What else mattered?

"Use this chance to break free of this whole mess. The French faction have no hold over you either. The Queen is married. You may be an inconvenience for them, because they do not know what to do with you, but you do not need to throw your life away. You have horses."

"Yes, one to ride and one to trade" François volunteered.

"At least you are beginning to think logically. So - leave Scotland, start afresh somewhere."

"Start afresh? That sounds so easy."

"Believe in yourself. No one can control or make you a prisoner in your own mind, unless you let them."

"I wish I could be sure Rochin would ever stop looking for me."

"Oh Thistledown! If you had not been so proud of your handsome looks, a simple remedy would have saved so much heartache" Ayles insisted as he left.

François had not understood the last comment, but Ayles' other words began to make sense. This man was right. He had been a fool, he had been wrong to wait for his enemies to find him. There was no reason to stay here and nothing to stop him from leaving Scotland. Besides, he had certainly had enough of this beard.

Suddenly he felt so much better. It was such a simple decision to make. He settled back to rest for a while, a contented smile settling upon his face, totally at peace at the acceptance of his new prospects. He could already picture somewhere soft and green, with the sun on his back and the warm earth in his hands.

De la Bastie had been alarmed by recent rumours of a spectre in the Highlands which had filtered through the lesser members of the court. He was convinced that François was responsible, but relieved that none of the stories were taken too seriously. If he could just get his hands on that rogue!

Meanwhile the gentlemen from the north, aware that their movements through the glens had aroused suspicion, had returned to geographical isolation after confirming their assessment of the situation at court. Innes, however, preferred to stay, for Lord Lyle was an excellent host and Innes enjoyed the carefree life here with all its creature comforts. It no longer mattered who amused his days or nights, he had realised how little he really cared about his missing wife. His jealous obsession had mellowed. He stayed for the thrill of the hunt and the excitement of the other entertainments he shared with Lord Lyle, letting Thurn and his men seek out the misguided lovers as they wished.

The boy from the abbey had never been far away from François since their last encounter, having followed his trail doggedly through all its various twists and variations. Even now he watched over François' latest camp. The disused charcoal burners' hut was well above the rugged valley floor and hidden by the rocky crags in the forested hills. An excellent place to avoid detection, as the boy noted, watching those searching below as they passed without deviation from the track. In and out of the dappled shadows, they had ridden straight past. Silently the boy waited, not minding the delay for he would soon ensure the Frenchman would draw out those responsible for the old lady's death. François was the bait, and amongst those same men would be the one man he sought in particular, the man Thurn.

Probability decreed that François would never know how well Marie fared, but he did not mind; he could only assume the best. He imagined the flurry of activity by the family to make everything especially nice for her, their loving attention after her traumatic journey and Marie bursting into tears as the relief hit her. This time he was happy for her.

There was a lightness in his step and a carefree swing as he strolled through the damp woods, the earth having that rich smell of autumn. Revelling in its atmosphere, he ran his hand over the bark trunk, feeling the texture and making him glad to be alive. He even still had that spare horse he could trade or sell. He tossed his head and smiled. Today he loved the world with every fibre of his mind and body. "Thank you" were the words in his head.

The ash of the fire smouldered by the rough shelter which had provided his refuge, and the clearing was quiet except for his own movement. His casual saunter betrayed the fact he had seen no danger signs.

Suddenly a yell from the surrounding undergrowth rang in his ears, and he turned to see the sun glancing off sword blades. Instinctively he drew back to gain time to draw his own sword and edged towards the trees, where he hoped the restricted space would separate them, allowing him to defend himself the better. Yet the cut and thrust of these individuals as they strove to press home their advantage inevitably drove him backwards. The frenzy of twisting and parrying their blows made his arm ache from the strength of their attack.

He side-stepped and ran between the trees, gradually improving his position as they followed him. He could not find his own horses, and his only idea was to reach theirs. Well below, he heard the animals snuffling and fled in their direction before he could be cut off, but their shouts told him they had realised his aim.

François and Thurn arrived simultaneously at the same spot, forcing the restricted area to become another battleground, each circling the other at close quarters and making the mounts restless and frightened. One horse reared and, advantageously for François, knocked his opponent off balance, allowing François to make a grab for one of the saddles. Thurn, stumbling to recover, tried to deliver a wild glancing blow. François ducked out of the way and turned in the saddle to give his adversary a boot in the face. Then, pushing the agitated animal on, he rode urgently into the forest, where the uneven ground soon made sure he was lost to sight among the trees.

After a significant distance, he swung down from the saddle, grabbed the skin water-bag and sent the horse into flight with a hard slap across its rear, hoping that the frantic mount would continue to lead his enemies on its trail for quite a time. His original idea of doubling back behind them to head in the opposite direction would have to be done quietly and on foot, and without waiting for the sounds of the following horsemen to get too close, he sprinted down the slope of the uneven hillside. There, easily hidden by the deep banks, he waded into the fast-flowing stream, walked some way down its rushing current and crossed to scramble up the opposite hill. How long the horse would keep running and how soon they would catch up with it and then turn back for him did not even enter his head. They would have no idea where the horse and rider had parted company, and any ensuing search would delay them further. He had time and distance on his side, and he meant to make good use of both as he set off at a good pace over the top of the valley.

Lord Lyle rode zestfully ahead of his guest to join his men after the news the messenger had brought him. A skirmish! They had been that close, and he was probably injured. He would have this Frenchman yet! He could feel it in his bones. He could not wait to see their prize for himself. Indeed in a short time he had caught up with his men, who, having followed swiftly in the wake of the solitary horse through the forest, were on their way back, having discovered that the rider had gone missing.

So he was on foot! How foolish, for with the hounds he had brought with him, Lord Lyle knew they would easily find his trail. The game was not over yet.

The dogs strained at their leashes as they pulled their handlers along, howling to be set free. They had the scent and Lyle instructed their release, watching them disappear into the thicket. There was no better indication of success. Diving through the brambles and undergrowth, the dogs smelt blood, and soon found the limp body of a freshly-dead animal. They circled, panting and sniffing, then growling menacingly. Their hackles rose, their lips curled back showing their teeth, eager to tear it apart. But the hounds were deprived of their game, instead to be chased squealing and yelping away by a ferocious charging wild boar which considered them too near to the meat it meant for its young.

The men instantly recognised the sounds and recalled their pack, who returned eager for reward to join the rest of the party already retreating to a safer distance. But the boar had not given up its attack. It continued his chase and now turned on them, running riot amongst the horses, causing panic and terror. The clearing was suddenly a mass of swirling, uncontrolled thrashing legs, such that the riders were at pains to remain mounted. Innes for one, his unsettled horse pawing the air, became unseated and was thrown to the ground with his leg crumbling beneath him. He cried out in vain. Jostled and pounded by hooves, Lord Innes lay still, his head smashed, dead upon the ground. The wild boar was suddenly gone, and the noise faded to whispers as all were left in stunned silence.

Lord Lyle was shocked at this turn of events. He could not believe that his young friend, who had become almost irreplaceable at his side, was dead. In the role of chief mourner, he ordered the slow and careful removal of Innes' body to the nearest chapel, where he could lie at rest in the monks' care until transportation to his ancestral home could be arranged. Lyle cursed his luck as they abandoned the search and accepting that they were destined not to win the day. Then he returned home to reassess his expectations for the morrow. He was certain François would not get far on foot, and with the benefit of numbers on his side, he was confident that they would catch him tomorrow.

Ayles urgently rode back to find François, having received a message from another source that the boy had not gone back to the abbey as instructed. He could guess at the game the boy played, and as expected he found evidence of the boy's betrayal, as he had deliberately marked the trail leading to François' camp. Ayles already knew he was too late. The hoof marks were recent, and as he arrived at the site he saw the evidence of the skirmish, but luckily no sign of François, either injured or dead. He must have escaped unharmed, since the signs indicated a chase into the forest. The Frenchman was on his own from now on and no longer his responsibility. Ayles could only pray he stayed safe, for everyone's sake.

The boy felt no guilt for his actions. The Frenchman was a foreigner – what did he care about what happened to him? He had witnessed the earlier fight and seen his long sought-after enemy Thurn battle with the Frenchman. He had seen Thurn concussed, but uninjured.

Now all he had to do was follow him and his associates back to the estates of Lord Lyle for the conclusion of his own revenge.

He knew where Thurn would be later that evening, and he found it easy to mix with the crowd around the tavern where the men drank. With a little cunning and using the knowledge he had gained from the old woman, he administered a little something extra to Thurn's ale; something slow and tasteless, but satisfyingly effective.

The next day no one resumed the hunt for François. Thurn had died early that morning, after hours of squirming, writhing agony. The household feared they had all been poisoned, and even Lord Lyle took to his bed and sent for a priest and a scribe as a precaution.

Meanwhile François could not believe there was no one chasing him. He did not know that Lord Lyle and his men were too worried for their own health to leave the estate or that Innes was dead and his Highland friends had gone back north. Nor did he know that de la Bastie had been informed that, although the council had insisted on the appointment of the Duke of Albany as Regent in place of the Queen after her secret marriage, King Henry of England had persuaded King Louis to detain the Duke a little longer in France. The Duke was delayed, but not because of anything they had achieved here.

François wondered how long his luck would hold. Ahead lay the arduous task of avoiding discovery along the endless miles of hills and trees, crossing terrain he did not know, once more. How many days did he have? From the shadow of the bank he watched a line of huge, creaking supply wagons, each pulled by a team of oxen, lumbering slowly along the valley. Dare he approach them? Would he be safe? His alternative would be to secretly conceal himself in the rear of the last wagon, to hide from sight and rest his legs.

As he stood there he saw another had already taken up his idea, for there above the dropped tailgate grinned a face he knew. Lachlan! Of all people. What a relief, what a comfort. What was it about this fellow, always springing up from nowhere to surprise him?

Lachlan waved enthusiastically from the wagon, indicating to François to join him, an offer François had no intention of refusing, if only to satisfy his own curiosity. Making a running leap as Lachlan moved over, he landed effortlessly in the correct spot alongside him. François was intrigued as to what he was up to this time, but Lachlan had just as many questions for him.

"Alone and on foot again. What has happened to the Lady Innes?"

François' explanations were simple. The lady was safe on her way to France, and he had finished his task and was bound for the west coast and a new start.

"What about you?" he asked his friend.

"We are just acting as escort for the convoy. We have men ahead on the hills, on the lookout for trouble. This is too easy a target for bandits."

François looked around, peering around the surrounding countryside, unable to understand why he could never see Lachlan's men. Lachlan winked and smirked, understanding his curiosity.

"You are welcome to travel with us if you wish" he offered. François was not foolish enough to refuse. Here with Lachlan and his men, he could relax for a while, thank goodness.

On reaching the next village a day later, Lachlan confirmed that they were now within their own lands and safe from other bandits trying to steal their goods. Here some of the wagons were unloaded and items carried into barns and other buildings, these being their winter supplies. The rest of the goods were to be delivered to each community on the way back to his uncle's stronghold.

"It will be a slow journey from now on and I am impatient to get home. I have sat too long on this hard floor, I need to stretch my legs." Lachlan jumped down and began pacing the ground, bending and stretching his limbs, a smile on his face. "I know a path from here which is a short cut. What do you think? We are both fit, and on foot we could reach our destination by nightfall."

"On foot? I have walked enough already over the past days" François complained.

"Then you should have held on to your horse longer. Or rather to both the horses you had last time I saw you" Lachlan joked.

"What happened to your horse, then?" François retaliated mildly.

"I lent it to one of the outriders, when we needed their horses in harness to help the oxen pull the carts up the steeper slopes."

"Then why not stay with wagons, until the horses can be spared again?"

"There are many settlements which have to be supplied. It will take them another two or three days."

François shrugged. He did not mind the wait.

"Aren't there any animals we can borrow?"

"Oh Frenchie! You must be tougher in the Highlands. Come on!" Lachlan urged cheerfully. Reluctantly François followed him. Having informed the others of his intention to strike out over the hills, no one seemed to object or find a reason for him not to. Lachlan, like the rest of them, had the local knowledge and saw no danger in this route, but as the long day went on, even François questioned his decision to cross the rock slide on the path in front of them as they climbed around one hillside after another. In his own limited experience he felt sure it was too loose to hold them, but Lachlan laughed and set out to prove him wrong before François could stop him.

No sooner had Lachlan's foot touched the edge of the scree than the whole section of the hill moved and he was swept away down the hillside, amid the gathering of debris in its progress and seemingly with enough noise to be heard for miles. It had all happened so quickly. Even as François dived to grab his hand, he too found himself propelled face downwards in the loose shale for a distance, before being knocked breathless as he became lodged against a boulder. His ears still resounding with the deafening rumble which had engulfed him and with his senses shaken, he found himself viewing the valley almost upside down, and it took him a while to appreciate his precarious position. Carefully he edged himself upright, as the aftermath of odd loose stones left behind bounced casually past his head, to join the dust and rocks at the bottom. His own battered and bruised body was nothing to the immediate concern he had for Lachlan, as he scanned the valley floor for any sight of him.

He could just see his friend at the bottom, draped like a piece of limp rag in the rocks, still and quiet. In the whole valley no one else had appeared. Not a soul had been roused by the noise; they were totally alone and without help.

Slowly François made his way down, terrified of slipping and sending more rocks down to bury Lachlan or add to his injuries and all the time fearful of what he would find when he got there. It seemed ages before, trembling and weak himself, he reached the half-buried body.

He gave a heartfelt deep sigh of relief to find Lachlan was still breathing, although it was a miracle that he was still alive at all. His head was bleeding, his face pale and the rest of him crumpled as François set about removing the rubble from him. As he uncovered the last few rocks he stopped. One leg was broken and so badly damaged that initially François could not look at it for more than a second without feeling sick. His head swam as he tried to focus on the bloody mess of mangled skin and bone. What on earth was he supposed to do? He was no physician.

Desperately he looked around, wondering how long would it be before one of their previous fellow travellers would appear. Or had they simply dismissed the sound, well used to the frequent rumbles which occurred in these parts? Maybe they had got too far away for the sounds to have reached them.

François could not just waste time waiting for their help. He had some idea of what was necessary, but could he do it, when every glance made him want to throw up?

Fighting nausea, he forced himself to take hold of the flesh, to move the wet oozing stickiness so that the bone lay in a line, then, taking another deep breath, closed the wound together and bound it tightly with strips torn from his shirt. He bound it over and over to strengthen it and then set about to look for the splints he would need. A few trees nearby provided several branches strong enough, and using parts of his woollen jerkin as pads, he attempted to keep the bone in place between the splints as he tied them on tight with strips cut from his jacket sleeves.

There was no way to know what other internal injuries Lachlan had, or his real condition. Similarly there was no way he could leave him here alone in this exposed spot to fetch help. If he was going to have to carry him, it would be exhausting, but it was his only choice.

It took the rest of his energy to drag Lachlan into a sitting position and then pull him half onto his feet, so he could bend to and lift him across his shoulders. Lachlan was heavy on his back and it was clear that progress was going to be difficult and too slow for comfort.

It was not long before he was exhausted, and François stumbled several times, his body aching as he dragged himself on. He did not have the physical strength to match his will to continue, and knew this was an impossible task. In the short distance he had travelled he had made too many stops already. Dizzy, he saw nothing except a blur of the landscape. He lowered Lachlan gently to the ground, where he joined him with a heavy thud. He was exhausted and cold, only the body part of his outer jacket left to wear. He closed his eyes briefly.

When he opened them, he found Lachlan had stirred and was at looking at him.

"Where are we?" Lachlan murmured.

"How would I know?" François snapped back unintentionally. Then, regretting his tone, he tried to reassure Lachlan that the situation was not as bad as it seemed and that once they had rested properly, they would soon find his fellow clansmen. Lachlan smiled weakly, not believing a word of it. François checked the state of his injuries and propped him up to give him a little water to drink. There was no point in asking his friend how he felt. He was in pain and kept closing his eyes.

"Your face is bleeding" he muttered, as François bent over to tend to him.

"Where?"

François had not noticed or felt anything. It could not be much, so he swiftly dismissed it.

"You must leave me here. I slow you down."

François had to admit that neither of them could go on like this, but he disliked the idea of leaving his friend. It would be dusk soon, and spending a night in the open wouldn't help. How long would it be before the rest of Lachlan's men reached their destination and realised Lachlan was missing? How long before they set out to find him? Lachlan had said it would take them two days to get there. He needed help before then, if only he could find shelter and start a fire; although a fire might draw attention to their location.

There were plenty of dead trees and broken branches littering the valley floor, and if François could find some sheared stones to use as a flint, he might be able to get a fire started. If they hadn't been in their own region, he would not have risked it, but Lachlan had assured him it was safe.

He gathered every twig, stick and branch there was, from as far as he could see, until he had a huge stack. Then, piling all the broken pieces of bark, small twigs and dried grass into one heap, he set about striking the stones to get a spark. Again and again the spark went out before he could light the dry grass, but then, just as he was about to give up, it caught. Slowly he nurtured it, gently adding small amounts to begin with, until as the cold began to make him shiver, a roaring fire lit the night. He added new supplies to it every time it went low, determined to keep it going as long as possible. Surely his people could not be too far away, surely someone would see the smoke curling straight up into the sky?

François had stayed awake, constantly feeding the fire until the wood was all burnt and there were only ashes and sparks left to warm themselves by. Lachlan had slept for most of the time, which was a good sign. All they could do was make the best of it until morning.

Morning came and with it the sun, gradually warming their stiff bodies, yet they could not simply sit and wait for deliverance; it could be another day or two before anyone appeared. They had to move on. François would have to carry Lachlan again, and he repeated the procedure he had used before, lifting him, carrying him for as long as his back could stand it and then resting him on the ground, each stage shorter than the last. It was time for prayer.

Then, as if someone had heard him, two men appeared scrambling down the ridge, waving as they came closer. François was taking no chances and drew his sword just in case. But their weapons remained sheathed, and they ignored him completely in their concern for Lachlan. Then one of them went back to fetch more men. With ease they took over the whole matter of transporting their injured colleague to safety and were soon setting off up the hill, leaving an exhausted François to trundle up behind them.

Much fuss was made of their arrival in the settlement. Apparently the smoke had been seen the previous night and this had been the earliest they could have set out, not being able to see the rocky path in full darkness. The two of them were soon housed in the home of their chieftain, where a physician immediately tended to Lachlan and complimented François on his actions, insisting he had done well. Apart from cleaning up the wounds, some stitching to hold everything together, fresh bandages and better splints, Lachlan needed only a long rest to heal his broken bones. He had been lucky.

"I will attend to you next" the man told François.

"There is nothing wrong with me" François laughed.

"Come over to the light" he was told. François shrugged and followed the man to the window, where he sat down. The man took his jaw, turning his face first one way and then the other in the bright sunlight.

"You have a sliver of rock embedded in your cheek, and the skin is starting to close over it. It will have to come out. It will cause blood poisoning if it doesn't."

"But I don't feel any discomfort. It has never hurt that I

noticed" François protested. He realised that the injury must have happened when he fell face down in the shale after Lachlan.

"It will do both this time. I will have to cut the skin back more to remove it. The sliver is deep. Removing it will be painful and it will bleed freely. I will have to stitch it" he warned.

François was feeling faint at the thought of it already.

"Do you want a draught to make you sleep while I perform this?"

François shook his head. He did not know if he could stand the pain nor sit still while this man put a scalpel to him, but any draught had its problems. It was not the initial taste but the effect it might have, the nightmares and hallucinations which could surface in that drugged unconscious state, to make him cry out and say something he should not. He remembered the one Pierre had given him and the ramblings during his fever, which fortunately had never made any sense.

The assistant laid out the instruments, bowls of water and cloths on the table, while François sat nervously in the chair avoiding looking at them. The physician tilted François' chin to one side and told his assistant to support his head in that position. The blade touched his skin and he tried not to flinch as it slowly traced the line of dried skin over the piece of shale in his cheek. François closed his eyes and then passed out, to the wry expression of the physician, who preferred it that way.

The surgery performed, the bleeding stopped, the stitching complete, they left François propped up and wrapped in a blanket to recover as the chieftain returned. He had come to visit his nephew who was now awake and cast a suspicious eye at the stranger in the chair, questioning Lachlan as to who he was. A good friend he might be to have helped his nephew, but what clan claimed his sword, he asked.

"None. He is a foreigner" Lachlan replied.

The old man was even more suspicious, and went to look more closely at this sleeping hero of the day. A scruffy individual and freshly marked, he thought little of him until in the middle of this François turned over on to his other side and continued sleeping. The resemblance was barely disguised to the knowing eye.

"A foreigner? Are you sure?" he questioned Lachlan. Lachlan was certain, and the old man left the room without another word.

François eventually woke to find himself in an additional bed in the same room as Lachlan. He yawned, stretched and flexed his muscles. The comfort of a proper bed was pure heaven to his tired body. There was only a slight twinge and tightness in his face to remind him of what had just occurred. Fingering the stiches, he could not wait to find out what he looked like. Pulling himself from the bed, he sauntered across the room to find a mirror and stood there for a while, turning his head this way and that.

François studied his reflection closely in the glass mirror. The stitches were a good deal neater than he had expected, but still dark with the congealed blood. It resulted in a prominent narrow ridge of skin where it was held together and it pleased him greatly. Now he understood the last comment that the man, who spoke for James, had made and laughed aloud, although it hurt. It made such a difference to his appearance. It was the best thing which could have happened. He should have realised it long ago. Anyone might remember a man with a scar, but little else about him.

"You will be marked permanently. Why are you smiling?" Lachlan asked.

"People turn away from scars. They are ugly to see and it puts them off looking too long at the rest of your face."

Lachlan did not understand, but he let it pass, impatient for other conversation to amuse his convalescence.

François refused their genuine offer to stay with them in the Highlands, because the Highlands had ceased to be his favourite place. His obsession with them had ended at least two years before.

"Where will you go?" Lachlan asked, unwilling to have his friend leave.

"To the west coast. To Ireland maybe."

"They are more uncivilised than we are!" the chieftain laughed, entering behind them.

The canny old chief sat in his large tapestry-covered wing chair by the wide open stone fireplace, listening to the two younger men discussing his options.

"To the coast then" Lachlan conceded regretfully.

The older man shook his head. There was not much of a living to be made there, but he suggested an out-of-the-way haven where there were people who would help him. It could be arranged with various letters of introduction, which he swiftly wrote, for he was honour bound to help François in gratitude for his invaluable assistance to his nephew.

By the time François prepared to set off on his next journey he was a new man, his beard trimmed, his hair cropped, fresh clothes and a good horse. What more could he hope or expect? He paid his respects to the laird, thanking him for all his kindness during these past weeks, at which the older man had only one parting comment.

"I wish you well Frenchman. I only saw the late King once, it is good that such features do not exist any more."

François smiled graciously, fully understanding his subtle inference. They both understood and were content nothing further would be said. François had much to be grateful for, especially the scar he cherished.

Lachlan hobbled to his feet, sad that he had failed to persuade his friend to stay. He took his hand and pressed into it his parting gift, the silver brooch-pin from his bonnet.

"May it serve as you as a talisman" he said.

"I think it already has."

At which they both grinned and made much of what they both knew would be their final parting, admitting that they were unlikely to forget each other for a long time.

Housed with a good family known to the Abbot, Marie had received the news of her husband's death with little regret and great relief. Now, as a young widow she was free, free to love François and to recapture and repeat those cherished memories she had of them together.

In wistful romantic mood she remembered his form drifting through the dancing sunlit rays towards her, his gentle arms about her and his soft words filling her head. There, in their favourite places, they had not dared to dream of a future together. Surely they could be together now. What was there to prevent it?

Unwilling to take the arranged boat passage back to France, her continual excuses and delay caused the Abbot some worry. Taking her aside, he tried to discuss her future travel arrangements in France, but it was no good. It was obvious her reluctance to leave was because of her hopes for François, and the Abbot would have to explain the harsh situation.

"Oh, Marie, my poor child" he began, "You must give up this idea of seeing François again. It will never happen."

"I want no one else and nothing else except to be with him. He let me go once because I did not love him enough to stay. This time I shall wait for him, to prove my love is equal as his."

"Marie, please! You cannot wait here. That is out of the question. He does not want it. You must remember what François told you.

He wanted you safe at home in France. He never promised to go with you. He meant it when he said he could never go back." The Abbot paused to make this point sink in. "He came here on another mission, a personally dangerous one, one which I know nothing about, not that I wish to. It was only during it that he discovered your plight. He has risked too much already by abandoning his assignment to rescue you."

Her dearest François had indeed done so much for her, which was why she found it so hard to believe she would never see him again. She did not want to accept he was gone forever. Yet on reflection of his words, to know she was safe had been all he really asked for himself.

"François will never be safe here or in France. Would you throw away his sacrifice, throw away his love, after he has done so much for you?"

Ayles, who had eventually completed his normal deliveries of goods on that route, had arrived at this point and was astonished to find Marie still here. He watched the Abbot trying to explain, but quickly noticed that his soft approach was failing to make any difference. It was time to step in. She must see sense and understand the truth.

"François was never the carefree youth you thought him" he said. "Yes, charming, roguish, all that, but he had already suffered more here than most men. Then he lost himself in you, loved you too much and you obliterated the memory of Scotland. When you left him to come to this country, the worst place he could think of, that drove him to despair. There are cruel, manipulative people in the world, people who will use any weakness for their own plans. François returned because of them, not because he wanted to."

Her mouth dropped open, shocked by the startling and frank information.

"You must have seen the change in him?" Ayles continued.

She had, but that had been her fault. Or had it, remembering the one brutal incident she had witnessed? One she would never forget, although he had made excuses for it.

"I saw him kill a man. I did not know him then" she admitted reluctantly.

"François has become a hardened, world-weary man, marked by experiences no one should endure. People who do not care about human life, would destroy him if they could."

"Why? What has he done wrong?"

"Nothing, except come here."

"Tell me the reason why that should be so dangerous."

"The reason is so immense that even I cannot tell you."

Marie saw there was some secret, one never to be explained, and now she was truly terrified for François. It frightened her more than she had ever been frightened before, even more than when she had waited on the stairs for him to come to her rescue. Her lip quivered and in silence she looked at the sea between her and home. It was so simple for her to continue her journey and reach the safety of her family. It was obviously not so simple for François. He could not go home. Her skin went cold, sending shivers down her spine. How dare this cursed dismal Scottish soil keep him from her!

"I have seen his heart. I thought to make a difference to his life. That we would be happy together."

She loved him, she wanted more than memories to live on.

"He faces a precarious nomadic existence. A future alone, if he survives" Ayles stated unemotionally.

"Will he ever be safe from all this trouble?"

"No, Marie. I think not."

Marie was crying, sobbing, accepting finally that she would never be with him again.

"You do understand?" the Abbot asked.

She nodded, her eyes to the ground.

"He can never go home, never be - what you would want" Ayles told her.

"I have lost him, then?"

"Forever" the Abbot concluded.

Ayles and the Abbot watched the boat taking Marie back to France from the small port and both breathed freely again. Ayles might have exaggerated François' plight rather more than he should have done, but he knew he dare not give her any hope; she must forget him. Likewise he had pretended ignorance of François' whereabouts when she had questioned him extensively.

Ayles knew François had last been seen heading west, where he would probably have met up with Lachlan, but he refused to mention this to her. Otherwise he was sure this pretty young widow would just as likely sell her jewels for gold coin to pursue a quest to find François. She had been made to go to France; it was the best for everyone. They were too old to go traipsing back and forth across the country for the sake of a romantic whim. What was the world coming to?

Likewise, the Abbot had his own answer to any enquiries concerning François, one which should surely stop any further speculation. The Abbot wrote in his great book later of another poor soul found in a terrible condition nearby, clearly just another victim, one of many brutally attacked and robbed in this lawless region: "After a few days in our care, he failed to rally and passed away, to be buried in our churchyard. He spoke only his name; François. Presumably French. A stranger in our land, nothing else is known."

Even a simple wooden cross had been supplied and carved, and some poor unknown soul from the infirmary, having passed away, was buried in the churchyard under his name. François had gone. This was the end of his story, they had decided.

CHAPTER ELEVEN

The small fishing community on the rugged coast of Argyll, below Crinan, had accepted François simply because of who had sent him, and he was content to work hard amongst them for his food and lodgings. The fishing boats came and went in endless days of toil; in almost all weathers, they plied their trade between the outer islands and the coast in calm, cold and fog, because this was their only livelihood. François began to recognise the moods of the sea, the cloud formations, the local tides and currents, but he never intended to stay during their winter.

From here the village overlooked the isles of Dura and Islay in the distance, and as François looked out at the islands, he knew this west coast was another prison of his own making and that to go to Ireland was not what he wanted; he wanted warmth. He would have to go south somehow, yet the endless inlets cutting into the coastline, with many long lochs biting back even deeper into the landscape, made the idea of following the coastline out of the question. He stood leaning on the door frame and took a deep sigh. He would have to make a move soon.

François' father had never been at peace since François had left and the unexpected return of Marie at Belmonde had caused much speculation. Apart from being upset at the news of her tragic marriage, Jacques had been confused by the part François had played in her departure from Scotland. He knew for certain that François had not gone to Scotland because of Marie, let alone to rescue her, so what had he been doing in those months prior to Marie's return to France?

Jacques was still burdened by the strangeness of his son's going, unable to think of any power on earth which could have made François go there. Someone or something must had persuaded him, or rather forced him, because he had left in silence without a hint to anyone of what was behind it. Not even Pierre, Gaston or Colette. A fact which added more to the strangeness of it the more he thought about it.

Jacques was angry with himself because on reflection, it seemed that his son needed help. He remembered the complexity of his expressions, the silence in the days before his departure. It had been as if he had never expected to return, but for what reason would he willingly make that sacrifice? Scotland was the key, but the key to what? He wished he knew the answer.

His thoughts wore him down, so he was pleased to have Suzanne request his company away from the farm on a special shopping expedition to find a present for Pierre and Colette, who were at last to get married. The pair of them set off happily enjoying each other's company, chattering away full of ideas of possible gifts, and soon arrived at one of the neighbouring towns near Suzanne's home. Upon entering the square, they found the streets full of people and were soon told of the arrival of a grand coach and an escorting retinue. Naturally curious, as were the locals, the pair of them joined the gathering crowds to stare at the sight. They had rarely seen such a display of wealth and privilege, and like the others they were interested to find out which person of importance was behind it. Having asked who it was, they were told it was the

Admiral of France, but they were none the wiser; they had never heard of him.

Rochin, the master of intrigue and manipulation, walked through the village slowly, congratulating himself that everything was in hand. The arrangements for the briefest of stops as his master the Admiral of France, the Duke of Albany, travelled back from Scotland after a year away would involve little ceremony. Rochin meant to ensure his travels were quickly done through this part of the country, since the route took them in the vicinity of the Belmonde estate. He had not forgotten that Raoul had married François' sister Suzanne, or the suspected romantic link between Raoul's sister Marie and François. And François still sat uneasy in his mind. There had been a rumour that he had helped her to leave France and then disappeared. His long absence left François's family with no information, and their simple acceptance had no secret overtones. At least Rochin had ascertained that none of the family were expected here. For one glimpse of the Duke by any of those who knew François would put their imaginations to work.

The Duke of Albany stepped down from the coach, stretching and turning his face to the sun. Then he relaxed and smiled benevolently to the crowd of onlookers, waving to acknowledge their interest as he took a short stroll to stretch his legs.

That moment had shown François' family a sight they would never forget. Jacques felt as if a lead weight had hit him in the chest, he stood like a statue, unwilling to believe his eyes. Suzanne, who had likewise been struck motionless, gasped and leaned against her father for support. He remained as silent as she, both swamped by their own racing thoughts, neither daring to blink until the man and his entourage had left.

Then Jacques quickly ushered them away from the crowds,

desperate to find somewhere private to get over their shock. They eventually found the seclusion they needed by their horses, only to stand staring at the ground, afraid to say what they thought.

"I do not understand" Jacques muttered. Who was this Duke of Albany, and why did he look so exactly like François?

Ever present where it best suited his master, Rochin had originally come ahead to satisfy his own curiosity, and he could not believe his bad luck when Suzanne and her father had come into plain view. They should have been elsewhere. The sister and the father! Others he would not have worried about, but this pair would not be misled. He desperately searched for his men to signal his instructions, but none could reach the far side of the square in time to prevent them from seeing the Duke.

Rather than make the situation worse by drawing more attention to his master, Rochin held back, contemplating the best course of action. He waited patiently for them to leave the village before deciding to make no move against them. He had observed their confusion and sadness, but besides the likeness between the Duke and François they had seen, what else did they have? Nothing. They might have guessed François had gone because of some scheme connected to his master, but they would never know the full extent of what he had been involved in, and no one in France was likely to tell them. Even that was over now, irrelevant and past history. None of it mattered. The Duke of Albany was Regent in Scotland and would remain so for many years to come. Shrugging, Rochin gathered his men and set off after the Duke.

It was Suzanne who suddenly realised who could answer their questions about the Duke of Albany and quickly she urged her father to hurry back with her to her home. Her husband's family, who still socialized occasionally with courtiers, might know something. If not, her husband himself, who always surprised her with his fount of knowledge, might have the answer.

"Can we risk asking doing anything so directly?" asked her father. "And what about Marie, what if she is there?"

"There is nothing to worry about. Marie is at the Dowager House with her parents. Besides, there is a perfectly ordinary and logical way to mention this topic."

Full of excitement and eagerness, she burst into her husband's study and relayed the details of the wonderful spectacle they had seen today to Raoul, describing the people, the carriage and atmosphere. Her curiosity overflowed as she asked him what he could tell her about the important man they had seen. Raoul was delighted to answer her questions, for he was more than pleased at her enjoyment in things; he loved to see her happy.

This information, although not often mentioned, was no secret, although it was of little concern to most people in France. Few people moved in his circle, Raoul told them. The Duke of Albany was a cousin to the late King James IV of Scotland, and also the Admiral of France. He had been made the Regent of Scotland by the Scottish Council, because the nobles there were unhappy with the widowed Queen Margaret and apparently the Duke had proved himself capable and well respected in his post.

Jacques and Suzanne did their best to hide the effect this news had on them. Although Jacques did not really want to know the details of the man's position, it was obvious that the Duke's connection to Scotland had a bearing on his son's fate.

Scotland and François! Poor François was burdened with an extraordinary resemblance to this man, and he knew somehow that because of it he had gone back to Scotland. He had hidden the menace of it during those last few weeks at home. How much else had his son kept from them? What other secrets had he buried? What had he been forced to do?

All that Marie had told them about her last meeting with François confirmed that François had undertaken some venture which had put him at risk. He had told her that he could never safely return to France. How would he survive a second time in that country – assuming he had survived? He would never know what had become of him. He had lost his eldest and dearest son. Damn this man! How cruel life was.

A short while later, Jacques and his daughter left the house in silence, arm in arm.

"It does not explain anything" she whispered.

Jacques agreed, but instinctively he realised that it would do no good to share their discovery with anyone else. How on earth were they going to be able to hide their feelings and keep the secret of what they had seen from others? But they must. However difficult, they had to keep this matter between themselves.

Suzanne felt the same and promised to say nothing. For her she realized a simpler truth, that this had made her frightened for her brother. Marie had always hoped François would return, but with this sight of the Duke, Suzanne saw that it would be impossible. She only wanted François to be safe, wherever he was. She loved him and would do anything to help him. Her father held her tight and comforted her as he wished he could have comforted his son.

Pierre had been to collect Colette from her grandmother's, where she had been given a beautiful trousseau of lace and linen. The pair of them were idling back on top of Pierre's lumbering old wagon, enjoying the scenery, as the Duke of Albany's approaching retinue came into sight, and Pierre pulled his cart off to the side of the road to let them through. They sat and waited, for they were not in any rush to be anywhere. As they watched the coachman stopped the coach immediately in front of them to collect and tighten his grip on the reins whilst one of the outriders checked the strappings.

When Colette saw the man inside the coach, she grabbed Pierre's arm and pointed, speechless. Pierre followed her finger and saw what he thought was an illusion. He shook his head and stared again. There was no doubt in their minds what they had seen. Colette's normal healthy colour had paled. They looked at each other in disbelief.

Within moments the coach had gone, all too soon to be followed by another band of riders, presumably another part of the escort. The rider at the rear stopped to look at Pierre and Colette before chasing after the rest. Pierre did not like the look of him. The hard stony face and the cruel, sharp eyes left an indelible impression, one he would not forget easily.

Rochin cursed. First François' sister and father, now his friend from Paris. Pierre was unpredictable, an unknown. The only saving virtue had been the lack of fuss any of them had made, which might have resulted in a public scene. None of them had acted in the way he had expected, and fortunately even these further complications did not warrant the necessity to control these people. That game was over. He could let them be.

At least they had part of their answer, while he would never know the truth about François, not the whole truth. Even his long absence was no proof that he had not survived, and Rochin hated uncertainty.

Not that Rochin should really care any more, because François had ceased to be of use the moment the Duke had sailed to Scotland. The whole scheme was long past and no longer relevant.

François was redundant; even the knowledge he had would be useless. Rochin would not have to worry about keeping him quiet. There was no need, because François' own fear would keep him out of both Scotland and France, and keep him running for the rest of his life. No, François would not be stupid enough to come back. His face would never give him peace. Rochin was not going to waste time in looking for him. He had the satisfaction that François would be on edge every moment of every day for the rest of his life, that he lived looking over his shoulder, unable to find anywhere he felt safe. That was a suitable punishment.

Jacques rode away from Belmonde, his whole body sagging with misery, because he could not stop his mind from thinking darker, more sinister thoughts. Was it only this man François looked like, or someone else in the same family? Someone even more important, in Scotland? No! Please no! He gulped and shivered as the ideas became more vivid, ideas which he wanted to dismiss, but couldn't. Now Jacques understood the difference in his son after his first adventure there, his reluctance to talk about his travels or his wounds. How he had avoided mentioning any reference to the King, even when casually questioned by the family after the King's death. He had given nothing away.

What had really happened in Scotland? He could only guess at the terrible plight François might have found himself in. Had his reckless son kept a most dangerous secret and held his tongue, against all odds? This son he had cursed for his stupidity in Paris, for his raw emotion as he fought his own demons, was a better man than he had thought. He had underestimated him.

Jacques halted his horse as he neared the farm, knowing he could not go home yet because of the state he was in. He had to find something else to concentrate on, to find some explanation for his obvious low spirits. If only his mother-in-law had not filled his son's head with the romantic stories of Scotland as a child, he would not have been so obsessed with seeing that country for himself. Then this might never have happened.

But who was he kidding? It was in his son's character to find adventure. If it had not been this, then something else would have dragged him away from the safety of their home. There was no one to blame.

It was five years since François had left Argyll, five years of traveling and varied employment, before he found the warmer climate he wanted. From the north Ayrshire coast, through the Nithsdale valley, he had crossed through northern England, gradually coming south to the east coast. He had worked at anything which took him south; he had become a drover, led pack horses and took panniers to market, transporting everything and anything. As a crew member on the boats which criss-crossed the Channel, he had touched the soil of his homeland and felt its beckoning allure. Yet even here in France, he wandered aimlessly between various wharfs and ports, unloading and loading cargo. Each time he had known this was not what he wanted, and moved on.

He now stood in the doorway looking at another harbour. There had been so many doorways, so many views, in his long travels. The deep tone of his auburn hair had faded and had lost it startling colour. His skin was now weatherbeaten and tanned, although the purple scar was still distinguishable on his face. In a way he was content, because he had no need to prove himself to anyone and he did not live in fear any more.

François had finished unloading the latest cargo and sat with the other labourers on the wharf, resting their tired limbs and enjoying the sun on their backs and a drink in their hands.

"François!" came an excited voice from a short distance. "François. François. It is you. How wonderful. I cannot believe it!" the sheer delight sounding in every word, as the steps bounded towards him.

It was his old friend Gaston. François smiled to himself before even turning around, having recognised the familiar voice, surprised to find that the appearance of a childhood friend after all this time felt quite wonderful.

"You are alive!" Gaston continued. Then the steps and voice halted.

"Oh, my God! Your face."

François still smiled, a wide, genuine grin as he grabbed Gaston's hand and hugged him affectionately. He was so pleased to see anyone from home; he had not realised how much he actually missed them.

"What happened?" Gaston asked, always to the point and never subtle, staring closely.

"It is nothing too serious" François answered, dismissing it casually. "But what are you doing here of all places?"

"I am working for Colette's father. I am buying into the business. I am here to look at some new wine."

"You! Of course, who else, since you must have drunk every type of wine there was" François laughed.

They joked about the past and their childhood, the normal trivia between friends, both reluctant to talk about the present situation.

"François, you do know everyone thinks you are dead?" Gaston gushed, unable to put it off any more.

François smiled weakly. Of course they would, that was exactly what he had hoped would happen. To remember him in the past tense was fine.

"When are you coming home?" Gaston went on. "Your family will be delighted to see you. Especially your father, he has not been the same since you left and these past few years he seems to have aged more than normal."

"I am never coming home. I am no use to them. I don't want them to know I am here in France" François stated calmly.

"But they need to know you are alive at least. They will be so relieved, so happy."

"Please Gaston, don't go upsetting them by saying them you have seen me. Please promise you will not tell them."

Gaston did not understand. Not come home, to where everyone longed to see him again? Was he mad?

"I mean it, Gaston. I have changed, I am not the same person. Too much has happened. Please accept I have reasons for staying away. I don't want them to find me. They are better off without me. They will expect too much. I am making a new life."

"I miss you" Gaston said glumly.

"Likewise" François nodded, a little subdued.

Gaston had not asked any more questions, because he knew François would not explain any further. Above all François was his friend, a cherished friend and he would not ruin that trust. Accordingly he promised he would not tell the family, if that was what his friend really wanted, and they parted on good terms. Gaston waving cheerfully and expressed his hope that François would still be around here the next time he came back this way.

François watched him go, nodding at his last suggestion. He had been tempted to ask a host of questions about his family, but he had not dared to get drawn back into that previously-contented world. He had dared not ask about Marie either, although it was on the tip of his tongue, for it would only open old emotions and regrets. He had thought of her kindly. Sometimes his mouth and eyes would crinkle at a memory, a memory which sat comfortably in his heart. How often in the past a turn of the head or a skipping step had played tricks in his mind to remind him of Marie. Then he would sigh, satisfied that she was happy and safe at Belmonde.

François was still at the same location a few months later, because the port was busy and the work had come on a regular basis. Money in his pocket was vital, to help him save for the future and keep food on the table and a roof over his head. He was mildly content, and he quite liked the idea of Gaston reappearing at some point; it would be a welcome change in his days.

As he walked along the beach he ignored the figures along the edge of the shore. He was heading for his lodgings, eager for rest. A man waved to him, and François closed his eyes in disbelief. It was his friend Pierre.

"Before you start, Gaston only promised not to tell your family" Pierre explained bluntly.

"Why have you come?" François challenged.

"I had to see you for myself. To know it was true. Thank God it is."

"Is this some conspiracy between you?" François asked.

Pierre shook his head, while his eyes stayed firmly fixed on François, unable to stop looking at him. He was studying him from head to toe.

"Thank God you are safe" he said. "We have been so worried about you. "

Here was his best friend, a friend he had put out of his mind, like the rest of his old life. But he could not deny the ache it stirred in him or the bond he felt. Dear Pierre, who smiled a forgiving grin, tilting his head as the familiar expression to indicate that he had merely come to renew their old companionship.

"No one else knows I came looking for you" Pierre assured him.

"There was no need to come."

"But there was! I have something important to tell you."

"What?"

"I should warn you that I saw someone a few years ago, quite by accident, which made my blood run cold."

François took a deep breath, almost afraid of his next words.

"I saw the Duke of Albany, close up."

There was a long, deliberate pause as Pierre searched his friend's face for his response. François said nothing, nor did he give any indication of understanding the relevance of such a comment. Not one twinge or flinch gave anything away.

"So?" he eventually shrugged.

"François! For God's sake! The resemblance cannot be ignored. It frightened me."

"You imagine too much."

"I made further enquiries. He is cousin to the late King of Scotland."

"And now you think you know something?"

"Yes I do. Your strange decision to leave France and your home again did not make sense until I saw this man. Tell me there is no coincidence!"

"There is nothing I can say." There was nothing he could tell Pierre, nothing he wanted to remember or make public.

"Marie was convinced you were in mortal danger" Pierre continued in a hushed tone, leaning close.

"I had to exaggerate matters to make her come home without me."

"Why? Why stay behind?"

"It seemed the best idea. To confuse those chasing us."

Pierre was still sceptical about all his replies.

"At least assure me that there are no silent men of power threatening you or deliberately seeking you out for some cause?"

"Not as far as I know. Besides I wouldn't be of much use to them, looking as I do now. Would I?" he joked.

"Hmm. So that is why you are back in France and living where no one will find you."

"I prefer to live quietly and avoid complications."

"What complications? My lawyers in Paris tell me that the Duke of Albany has been Regent in Scotland for several years. Occasionally he returns to France because of his wife's ill health, but never for long. He will be staying in Scotland for the foreseeable future."

"You have been busy with your time" François smiled, still not admitting anything. Trust his best friend to have tried so hard to find the answer, and to get very close to finding it.

"Surely you do not need to hide any more?" Pierre enquired.

"I am not hiding" François laughed, correcting him.

"Then come home with me!"

François did not want to face his family or see their pain and anguish. Besides, the farm had not been his home for such a long time that he felt he did not belong there any more.

"No. Too much has happened. It would not be fair on anyone."

"Rubbish! You are making excuses. Your family need to see you, just as I did."

"It has been too long." François sighed.

"François you must come home. Your father and sister deserve peace of mind. If only for them, not for me or anyone else. I believe Suzanne and your father saw the Duke of Albany as well, that same day. And Raoul could easily have told them of his connection with Scotland."

François felt his skin go cold. He was angry that his family had suffered the shock of that discovery. It was never supposed to happen. Damn Rochin! He should have prevented that encounter at all costs.

"I have noticed a subtle difference in them" said Pierre. "Suzanne not so much, but your father has had more time to brood, and I see a decline in him. Neither of them have spoken of it, but I have seen the pained expressions they exchange in private. It can only be because of the torment they are in, all the doubts and the fears for you linked to that day. So, for them, for their sakes, you must put them out of their misery. You owe them that."

François sighed. His friend might know what was best, but he didn't have to agree.

"Trust me, you have to do this. You know I am right" Pierre went on.

"I – I don't know" François muttered.

The emotional blackmail was kicking in, Pierre could see it in his face and he let it simmer. He was careful not to pursue it much further, since he knew by experience that too much pressure would have the opposite effect on François. He could be so stubborn when pushed into a corner.

"Don't wait too long" he concluded softly.

They were both tired of talking. They were still comfortable with their differences, and they parted as the loyal good friends they had always been.

"You haven't asked about Marie" Pierre remarked as he left.

"Haven't you given me enough to think about as it is?"

"You might as well know she is a widow. Her husband died in an accident before she left Scotland."

"It makes no difference. It is too late to rekindle the past. Don't you dare go telling her I am here" François declared, ending the discussion.

Inside his two-roomed cottage, François set about making up the fire as it hissed and burned against the December chill. Then he looked forlornly out of the window. There were moments when like this when he truly missed the childhood comfort of home. He thought about his father and what Pierre had said, which had only confirmed Gaston's previous observation. If he went home, he would have to explain something to his father, but what? What do you say to people who love you without question, people who forgave your mistakes and demanded little in return?

That the Duke of Albany had been forced to go to Scotland, despite all the attempts to prevent it, had not surprised François. The whole plan to delay Albany's journey had been impossible from the start. But the revelation that the Duke would remain there as Regent for some years had been unexpected news to him.

All this was nothing to do with him any more. He had to consider all the implications of his own return home. What would they expect of him? He had no intention of staying to take up the reins of the farm again. That living belonged to his brother, not him. François still had his own plans, his own future to build somewhere else. If he could time his visit to coincide with his sister's annual visit on her birthday next month, then he could avoid going to Belmonde and seeing Marie. Yes, he decided, that would be the more beneficial for everyone.

François rode home as if it was the most natural thing in the world, with no diversions or evasive tactics necessary. He had no qualms, no nervous excitement, just an acceptance of the surroundings. This time there was no youthful madcap jumping of fences and racing across the top meadow in his impatience to be there. Instead he followed the road like any normal traveller, pausing at each of the various turns above the property to remind himself of what he had missed.

At the last bend he saw his father in the distance, working in the fields alone, his measured tread much slower than François remembered. This was a tired old man who bent his back to turn the soil, his eyes fixed to the ground permanently as he moved. François felt immensely sad to see that Pierre's assessment of his father's failing condition had been right. And in the main it was his fault; he was to blame. He had dragged him this low, François acknowledged to himself as he picked his way along the edge of the field. How could he put it all right?

"Father" François said softly, already close to the figure.

Jacques raised his head slowly to the sound of a voice, wondering who was bothering him. The eyes were dim and the face blank.

"Father" François repeated, putting his hand to rest on his shoulder and squeeze it gently.

Jacques looked for a while, gazing without recognition as François just stood before him. François's eyes searched his father's, misting with emotion. Then Jacques was crying, tears pouring down his face as he threw his arms around his son, unable to speak. His whole body was shuddering as he hugged and held him to his chest. Then it was François who supported his father as the man laid his head on his son's shoulder. François felt humbled at the display of affection.

Eventually François unwound himself and Jacques stood back to wonder at this miracle, to touch his face. He did not see the scar, nor the lines of age, only his son's hazel eyes and the creases of a smile on his face.

"Let us go to the house" François suggested as he took his father's arm to walk with him.

Jacques nodded, holding on to his arm for support, glad to feel the tough, hard muscles and strength of his son at his side. They walked together slowly across the fields, neither of them aware of much except the comfort of each other.

His mother reacted differently. She let out a whoop of joy the moment she saw her son and raced across the room to hold his dear face between her hands and cover it with kisses. The past, when she had been angry at his lack of consideration, was forgotten forever. As if he was a child again, she ruffled his hair and asked if he was hungry. As she began to busy herself to prepare food, she would not take her eyes off him. It gladdened her heart to have him back in the house, among the family where he belonged.

Suzanne had been escorted by her devoted husband Raoul on the journey to visit Colette and Pierre. On arrival he had kissed her and left her to the company of her friends, promising to collect her from her family home in a few days.

As she enjoyed the day and played with their children she could not help reflect upon her missing brother. They had all been so happy here, running in the fields and teasing each other just as these children did now. The married couple smiled, neither of them willing to tell her of their belief that François would soon surprise her. Sometimes Pierre knew François better than François knew himself, because he had sensed that Suzanne's birthday would be the perfect occasion for him to appear. How he would have loved to follow Suzanne home and see her reaction, but he would wait. He would let the family enjoy their moment with him, just as he had.

Suzanne had ridden back into the yard of her old home without noticing the lack of activity about the place or the unusual quiet as she unsaddled in the stable. Then as she stepped out of the barn to walk to the house, she stopped, gulped, paled and could not move another step. She did not believe who was facing her by the kitchen door. Tears swelled in her eyes and her lips trembled She shook her head. This was not real! She swallowed hard and gritted her jaw, but the tears still came, now in heartrending sobs which shook her small frame. She sank to sit on the ground, unable even to speak her brother's name.

Her hands grabbed at his coat as François picked her up, clutching his sleeve in her small hands. She would not let go of him in case he vanished. She could not stop her tears, which trickled down her face. With a lump in her throat she could only stare, soaking in those familiar features and those lovely shining eyes.

François found himself equally emotional as he held his sweet sister. His heart was beating in his ears. This was almost too much. Her reaction, her obvious anxiety and now the pure relief of finding him alive put him to shame.

"I am sorry" was all he could manage to mutter.

Suzanne did not want words or need them, she felt weak with utter happiness at this moment. He was here, alive and well, what else could she ask for? This was her best birthday present ever.

That only left his brother, Jean-Paul, who, having returning from market late, had missed the drama. His response was equally fond. His face creased with brotherly affection the moment he saw François, and he greeted his older brother with a firm hand and some sense of relief. There was no rivalry or jealousy left. Jean-Paul had matured with responsibility, and his respect and deeper insight into the person François was showed itself.

François stayed on for a few days, often wandering quietly about the house fondly touching the fabric and structure of the place, glad that he had made the decision to come. Everyone was content, and any lingering anxiety and fears seemed to have vanished. Face to face with his father and sister, there were moments when he had expected them to want the truth about his last venture, but it became evident that they would rather not know. It seemed it did not matter, now that he was safe. The bond between them had been renewed, and the evenings were spent together softly reminiscing over their memories, while François talked about his plans and the life he wanted in the warmer south.

François had been to see Pierre and Colette before leaving, and he had naturally received the warmest of welcomes, for they had missed him in their lives, despite knowing where he was. He was delighted to see how happy they were together, although he had never thought of the feisty Colette as a farmer's wife, but there she was surprising everyone and making Pierre proud. It was a good match, and it was evident that they were truly fond of each other. Their affection for their children overflowed. It restored his faith in human nature.

"Well? How did the reunion go? Not as bad as you thought?" asked Pierre.

"It was fine, but overwhelming" replied François. "Their goodwill, their kindness, their understanding and their lack of awkward questions, was…"

"Too much to take?"

François nodded.

Colette held his hand and kissed him on his departure. "You need a wife" she whispered.

"I am too set in my ways."

"And I know different. You are not too changed to ignore the sweetness of a woman's touch and the pleasure of a lingering kiss" she replied.

François smiled. He had almost forgotten those pleasures he had enjoyed with her and other women in his wild youth.

François was satisfied that everyone would be fine, even his father, who, he predicted, would soon recover his enthusiasm and zest for the land within days. Indeed he was looking better already. Jacques felt equally reassured to watch his son. Although he would miss him again once he had gone, his mild acceptance that each had his own life to live was an easy thing to acknowledge, now he knew his son was safe.

"Will you stay for a while longer?" Jacques asked, although he half knew the answer. François shook his head, and Jacques nodded. He was grateful that his son was alive, fit and looking well, that he was filled out and seemed at peace with himself, older and wiser no doubt. François faced the world straight on, unbowed and unafraid, and with his whole future ahead of him. François seemed whole again, and that pleased him immensely.

Satisfied with his morning's work, François lowered himself to the ground to rest under a tree away from the hot midday summer sun. He had moved from the coast to one of the nearer inland villages, where he hoped these few fields would supplement his earnings. He had the beginning of a new life. He leaned back and closed his eyes to sleep a little. Later when he woke, stretching out his hand for the water bottle, he noticed a cart making its way along the track leading down to the village, a reminder that he should return to attend to the chores in his little cottage.

He dragged himself up and made his way back, returning the odd nod or wave from the locals, as had become a habit. Once inside, he set about checking his stores and making a list for his next journey to market, with his front door left wide open as the villagers did in the summer. So when he heard the knock on the door, he had expected it to be a neighbour calling to pass the time of day, for that was their way. Instead, when he turned to see who it was, it was Pierre, smiling mischievously at him.

"Pierre! How wonderful. What are you doing here?" François

grabbed him and dragged him into the room and sat him down, quickly finding a glass and some wine.

"I did not come alone" Pierre began.

"Colette and the children? Bring them in!" François beamed, wondering if he had enough to feed them.

"Er, no. Someone else."

François was beginning to get suspicious. "Gaston? One of the family?"

"No."

François looked at Pierre, his eyes narrowing, hoping it would not mean what it might.

"She would not stay at Belmonde."

"What?" François shook his head. Although he had expected Marie to hear the news of his return to France, he had not expected her to come here. Their relationship had ended years before. It was too late.

"She is waiting outside. Shall I fetch her in?"

"No. She should not have come."

"Why not? She loves you."

François looked at Pierre, his enjoyment of the afternoon fading rapidly.

"That was a youthful fantasy. Reality is much more harsh."

Pierre glanced at the doorway. François followed the direction of his look and there Marie stood, bright and smiling, bursting with pleasure, so pleased to see him and eager to rush into his arms as she had done so many times before.

But François turned away abruptly. "Why are you here?" he protested. "I told you to forget me. That we had no future together!"

His eyes were wild, his fists clenched. Then his shoulders sagged and his head bent low between his arms as he buried his face to the wall.

"You came home, yet you did not come to see me" Marie stated. "How could you be that cruel?"

François did not deny it. "I had no reason to. It would not have done any good."

Marie stopped short, confused at his reaction. She had expected shock, but not rejection.

"I will not leave you again" she said. She touched his back, which quivered. His whole body trembled desperately, but he would not look round. He shrugged off her touch and shook his head, moving away.

"Why have you done this? I was satisfied knowing you were home with people who loved you, people who would take care of you."

"I do not want to live there. I pretend to be content, to make the most of my days, but it does not work."

"And I do not want you here. I have put you out of my life!" he shouted, so loudly that she backed away. Tears flowed down her face as he turned on her. She had hoped their reunion would be a special moment, full of love and happiness. It was neither. He would not comfort her or take her in his arms. He had not smiled at her once. His jaw was set and his eyes now distant and sad.

"You must go back home. This is no place for you."

"And it is for you?"

He did not want a discussion; this matter was not for debate. Why would she not see reason? His anger had died, and there was only despair left in his voice. He sat down heavily to face Pierre across the table.

"Why did you bring her here? It is hopeless."

"It is her choice."

"But not mine!" He hit the table and stood up sharply.

"You will go back!" François commanded her.

"I will not!" she replied, just as defiantly.

What could he do to make her go? What could he say?

"I will not go" she repeated, softer this time. "What is the point of being apart, merely existing, when we could be together?"

"Go back. Find someone else."

"As you have?" she countered easily.

"I am not the same person you knew before."

"None of us are."

Why did she have an answer to every reason he had for her departure?

"I have no security, nothing to offer you. I will not have you brought down to this."

Marie gave him a pitiful look and shook her head. Heavens, she had been patient, she had waited, how she had waited for news of him! But now she was here, face to face with him, so close. How she wanted to bury herself in his arms, to make him believe, to persuade him to trust her and trust his own feelings! Her own feelings were unchanged. She had seen the best and the worst of François, and loved him the more for it. He had built this barrier in order to cope, but she was determined to overcome it.

"You might be able to live without me, but do you want to?" her soft voice whispered.

"But could you live with this, Marie?" he asked indicating his face. "Would you not hate looking at me, trying to avoid the ugliness of this scar every day?"

She smiled forgivingly. This was his last resort to shock her into seeing sense and it had not worked. To prove it she reached up to kiss the mark on his face.

"We all have scars, we all grow old and we still love the person inside, regardless of their looks" she said.

How dare she torment him, reawaken his emotions! He had shut her out of his mind. He shuddered and lifted his head, his eyes to hers. Those beautiful brown eyes held him fixed, melted his very soul and the core of his resistance.

There was a long, long silence in the room. The open door swayed lightly to and fro, while everything else remained motionless and calm. There in the quiet of the afternoon they simply stood looking at each other, the atmosphere soft and timeless, a spell unable to be broken.

"Do you love me?" she asked.

His hand slowly stretched out to touch that soft skin and trace her face with his fingers. He could not deny it. Much as he tried, his heart would not deny it either. It pounded so strongly at her closeness; his breath was tight. He stroked her dark silken hair, twisting the strands between his fingers as he had done before long ago, and remembering all the emotion he had buried from his mind and he could not stop the tears from swelling in his eyes.

"I will not leave you again. I left you once by choice. I left you again because it was your choice. I will never make that mistake again" she promised.

"Never, never!" François promised her in return.

This time he was smiling in wonderment at her. He drew her into his arms, unwilling to let her go from his embrace, his lips on hers, unable to ignore the sensation it sent through him. How could he ever put her from him again?

Pierre had long slipped away to leave them to their arguments. Outside he unloaded the bails from the cart she had brought with her and stacked them by the door. The practical items they would need, hard-wearing woollens, blanket, bedding, pot and pans. He did not need to wait to know the outcome.

Marie wandered around the sparsely-furnished simple cottage, while he sat and watched her, unable to take his eyes off her. She returned to his side, and they held hands in the quiet acknowledgement that they truly belonged to each other. The matter was settled.

A little later she confessed she had been prepared to camp on his doorstep in all weathers to shame him into taking her in, if he had refused to let her stay. Instead of which he was employed at her bidding removing her goods and chattels from the doorstep and rearranging his home to accommodate her few possessions.

"This will be the scandal of the village" François warned.

"Such scruples with your past reputation!" she teased, laughing.

"It is your reputation I was thinking of" he smirked.

"Why – who is there to care?"

"No one in the world but us" he gushed, whirling her around in his arms until they were both giddy and had to sit down.

He had no doubts. They should be married, he told her.

"It is a terrible commitment, when only a few hours ago you did not even want me to stay" she reminded him.

"You are doubtful? Of marriage or my total devotion?"

"I have been married before. There is nothing to recommend it."

"Nothing?" he queried, his breath gently caressing her skin, his eyes lowered suggestively, bright again, infatuated by the moment.

She was glad to have the old François back. At last.

How often Suzanne had taken the letters and read them again. The first one was very old, but she had kept it safely folded and near at hand.

Dear Suzanne

I do not know by what miracle your brother came to Scotland or on what

287

business, but I have never been so thankful that he came to rescue me. I willingly abandoned my husband, his home and his treasonable conspiracy. Since which I am told that my husband has died, but I am not ashamed for the lack of remorse I feel. It was an unhappy marriage. François has risked so much for me and there is no way I can thank him for the help I received from others for my return to France.

How could I have been so foolish as to leave France and his affection for me in the first place? How could I have thought I could love anyone else? To see him again in Scotland was to know my mistake, but how could I expect him to feel anything for me after my previous determined rejection of him? Bound by convention, I had honoured my family's wishes for that arranged marriage. I should have been braver, I should have listened to him. I never wished to cause him so much pain and heartache.

Marie.

It was only much later, after that eventful encounter, that Suzanne felt sure her dear brother had sacrificed much to save Marie. As for Marie, like many others she would remain ignorant of the problems François had faced. And now here was a more recent letter, another she would keep through the years. One full of hope and promise.

Dear Suzanne,

I have heard that François is back in France. How cruel to learn he has left the farm already, without coming to see me. And I forgive Raoul and my parents for refusing to let me have a carriage to go after him, no doubt to prevent another mistake in their eyes, but I shall be with him.

François may think all these years in between would lessen my affection for him, that I can exist without him. I will prove him so wrong. I have been given another chance. I still love him. He is my future, my very life and I am willing to abandon everything to be with him.

He foolishly thinks I am far away, but he will soon realise differently. I do not know how hard it will be, but I will be happy. I will make him happy. That is all I want.

Please remember us fondly in your prayers.
Marie.

It made Suzanne smile every time she read it. After Pierre's disclosure of his part in taking her south, she was certain of the outcome.

The afternoon breeze gently ruffled his damp hair, stirring François to look up from his labour, his smile broadening as he heard her voice softly singing to herself inside the house. The sound beckoned him irresistibly back to the adorable woman who in these days of late summer still went barefoot about the place in her favourite plain blue dress, always wearing the silver pin Lachlan had originally given François from his bonnet. His sweet wife, who had once worn expensive pretty dresses and elegant satin slippers, never pined for past extravagances. And for someone who had known nothing of domestic skills, he marvelled at how she had revelled and excelled in them. The sight of her constantly delighted him.

Pausing on the veranda of their home overlooking the lush green farmland, he knew he had never been so happy, content and so utterly satisfied with life. Here with Marie, he was at peace with himself and the world.

What on earth had he ever done to deserve such happiness, he often wondered. It was incredible to think he had survived all that turmoil, despair and danger; that so much had happened to him. Scotland was now only a memory like the rest, so long ago and so far away. They had rarely seriously argued since that day she had joined him; the only matter they never agreed on was the gold coins she had brought with her, and his refusal to take it. The coins remained in the box, unused, never looked at and never mentioned.

Their time in that village near the coast had been short. Aware of her fretting every time he had leave to work on the docks or for a merchant to boost their savings, he had always made much fuss of reassuring her on his return. He remembered how nervous and cautious of each other's sensibilities they had been in the beginning, but their first winter spent snugly confined in the small cottage had become a wonderment of exploration, slowly removing any inhibitions. They had rebuilt their special awareness, trust and confidence in each other. They had taken to walking of an evening, watching the stars, and had made the decision to travel further across France in the coming year and find a new home.

And now here they were. After a year of extensive and exhaustive hard work, they had managed to acquire title for this plot of land. It was a good place, the land was fertile, the weather was kind and the fields were already producing enough to sell the surplus in the village and at market in the nearest town. It was a productive farm which would sustain them in the future. There were hills to ride and rivers to fish and they had the company of neighbours and villagers to socialize with. Yes, his life was full, and its pleasures overwhelmed him every day.

She heard François' step and instinctively smiled to herself. She was in the middle of baking, and she could not resist the urge to dab the flour from her hands onto his face as he entered the kitchen. Mellow, infectious laughter followed as he caught her hands before she could achieve it. She sighed as he slipped his arms about her waist. This man was her life, and whatever hardships they shared, she had barely noticed, because they were each other's strength.

They had so much more to do together, and so much still to say to each other. She had never finished telling him about her stay on the coast, of the gallant hosts who amused her with so many tales and stories, silly gossip, of long-past legends and mystic sightings of royal ghosts, of the young King James and his sweetheart Margaret Drummond. But as he held her close, she knew, as so often before, that it would wait for another time. They were unimportant matters.

Although there was one, if she guessed right, that she would have to tell him about soon. She smiled to herself, for she had no doubt that François would also enjoy being a father. It would suit him very well indeed.

ND - #0460 - 270225 - C0 - 203/127/25 - PB - 9781861512659 - Gloss Lamination